Hidden Voices

Hidden Voices
The Orphan Musicians of Venice

PAT LOWERY COLLINS

CANDLEWICK PRESS

First edition 2009

Library of Congress Cataloging-in-Publication Data

Collins, Pat Lowery
Hidden voices / Pat Lowery Collins. —1st ed.
p.   cm.
Summary: Anetta, Rosalba, and Luisa find their lives taking unexpected paths while growing up in early eighteenth-century Venice at the orphanage Ospedale della Pietà, where concerts are given to support the orphanage as well as "expose" the girls to potential suitors.
ISBN 978-0-7636-3917-4
[1. Orphans—Fiction. 2. Music—Fiction.
3. Interpersonal relations—Fiction.
4. Ospedale della Pietà (Venice, Italy)—Fiction.
5. Venice (Italy)—History—18th century—Fiction.
6. Italy—History—18th century—Fiction.] I. Title.
PZ7.C69675Vo 2009
[E]—dc22   2008018762

2   4   6   8   10   9   7   5   3   1

Printed in the United States of America

This book was typeset in Adobe Caslon.

Candlewick Press
99 Dover Street
Somerville, Massachusetts 02144

visit us at www.candlewick.com

In memory of my father, Joseph Lowery,
and those secondhand classical records

Chapter One

Anetta

You can find him by following the leaping shadows along the walls of the school corridor, for Father Vivaldi often paces there and waves his arms about. This time he's so intent on whatever he hears in his head, he doesn't notice us dancing around him or running right past. Luisa Benedetto plays tag, reaching up and tugging his sleeve, yet he flicks away her hand as if it's a pesty little bird and doesn't even look down. Almost fourteen, she is small for her age and sometimes seems younger. But her voice is as large as a room and so sweet that I carry the tones that she makes in my mind so I'll hear them when I'm feeling sad. My own voice is pleasant enough. Somewhat, they say, like my face, which is almost the very same shade as my very pale hair. When I've looked in a glass, which we're not encouraged to do, I could see there was no counterpoint between the two to make me seem pretty and overshadow the marks of the pox.

Father tells me it would be wise to spend more of my time on the viola d'amore than on my singing, that I have an ear and a touch for the instrument. I would like to explain how I have a heart for it as well. But perhaps he's already aware of this in the same way that I am aware when he loses himself to the music he's making while walking the halls.

"Ouch!" says Maria.

The distracted man has given her a good swat in the face with one of his flapping hands.

"*Scusi,* my dear," he says, snapping back to the life all around him. He rubs the slight red mark on her cheek while she looks up, her dark eyes hurt but resigned. We're becoming used to these antics again. He studies his watch. "Surely it isn't so late. Almost the middle of day."

"It's a half hour past violin ensemble for the beginners," I tell him. "Maestra dei Cori has sent me to say they've been waiting long enough."

Father has been a *maestro* here, except during the few years just past, for most of the life I remember. But I don't really feel completely at ease with this priest since his unexplained recent return. Perhaps I should not have used Maestra's own words.

Often called the Red Priest because of his startling red hair, Father shakes the cap of it in dismay. Not at me, I'm relieved to find, for he seems to look into himself as he spits out a litany of complaints. From what I can gather, his great efforts to arrive before first bell seem to be complicated by the fact that the apartment of his parents, where he and his many brothers and an unmarried sister or two still live, is always in a state of upheaval.

"How do I do it? How do I lose track of time in this way? It cannot be so many hours since dawn and my father's rap on my door. Today Guido went off with my only clean shirt, and I had to search for a worn one of Tomaso's. I came as fast as I could, can you believe it, still carrying the notes that I heard in my dream. Where does the day go?"

He is not really asking me anything. But if he were, I would tell him the way he goes out of himself when the music takes hold. Afterward, he must know it, just as I do after living inside a concerto for hours on end.

"It is your fault, you know," he says, taking small steps in a hurry to keep up with me. My feet are much longer than his but have finally ceased growing, I'm happy to say. At fifteen, I am well rounded and tall. But my body seems awkward beside his slight frame.

"It's the new concerto for your performance on

Sunday. I have some ideas for the harmonies right near the end of the second movement."

He has discovered the dissonant places that troubled me. I should have known that he would. If he did but look at me at this moment, he'd see the pleasure in my eyes, for even as I hesitated to mention it, I was certain he'd find the problem.

I step more quickly, and he increases the length of his strides.

"Why are you running?" he asks at last, almost breathless. "I cannot keep up."

I had forgotten about the asthma, how it can suddenly visit him. They say that is why he can never perform an entire mass, and why Father Luigi was engaged to do it instead. In fact, though our teacher does indeed wear the skirts of his calling, he does nothing more priestly than hear an occasional confession. Myself, I think his dereliction of sacred duty is really because he cannot focus on anything but the music for long. Quite understandable, it seems to me, for it is rumored that he promised the Board of Governors two masses and vesper settings annually, plus two motets a month and as many concertos as he can devise to display the talents of those girls deemed most eligible. It is also rumored that his music is making something of a stir in Venice and even beyond, and that he will continue to perform sporadic concerts with his father at the Teatro San Angelo. If the tales I've heard of his more ambitious designs are true, it is hard to think they can be launched from this *ospedale* for orphaned girls.

I try to slow down so he can catch up. It seems my eagerness to share my own news has quickened my step again.

"I am the one to check the *scarfetta* in the church for the babies today," I say at last. Usually the students, the *figli di commun* who study no instrument, do it. But every so often, because Signora Mandano knows how I love it, I get a turn. I sometimes wait and wait in vain for the wheel to move. It is set on its side like a flat disk that can twirl from the street and deliver an infant into the nook of the chapel, leaving the one who brought the baby completely unseen.

"A child, even swaddled, could die unobserved in such a cold place," I tell him.

"Ah, yes," he says absently. It's clear the infants are of no special interest to him until they can lift a violin or sit at the cello. But to me they are . . . not family, really, not true family . . . but something, someone to care for. Though the nurses and attendants fuss over the infants at first, only the women who came here as orphans themselves can truly know. Many of the little ones are as scrawny as runts in a litter of Santa's puppies; some live only a day or two. The fat ones, the ones with no scarring or running sores, are petted and rocked from the start. Even the wet nurses choose them if given a choice.

Only when I am certain that Father is truly headed

toward the classroom do I enter the chapel and go directly to the *scarfetta*. On my way back across the narrow Calle della Pietà, I stop to watch the gondoliers navigating in and out of the lagoon and to look at the gleaming dome and spire of the San Giorgio Maggiore across the water. For a moment, I feel the warm sun on my face and I wonder at my expectations when checking the wheel and my great disappointment when it is empty — as it is today, as it has been all week. There are plenty of babies to care for already, so why is there always a feeling like Carnival whenever a new little one is deposited there? How remarkable it has always seemed that by just a turn of the wheel by unseen hands, another small shining soul can enter the life at the Pietà.

"No baby today?" asks Luisa as she comes up behind me on her way to Father's repair shop. She gives me a poke with her broken bow. "Good. Less crying. Less laundry for Signora Mandano." She raises the bow above her head and twirls. The loose strings fly about like long spiderwebs. "I will never have babies. If I did, I would also give them away."

Luisa is different from all of the others. For reasons none of us understand, she has a real mother who visits at least three or four times every year and a real last name.

I can tell that Father has arrived inside the classroom because the beginning ensemble members have all started tuning at once, sounding like all of the tabbies together that cavort in the alley each night. Then suddenly silence, that pure space of time before touching the bow to the strings when all faces are turned to the stick and waiting to bring forth the very first notes. I can feel the anticipation from here.

"Anetta, you're dreaming again," says Signora Mandano. She hands me a stack of clean linens. "Give these to the girls in the nursery."

How I wish I were holding another new baby instead.

"Don't worry," says Rosalba, on her way from the street where she, too, must have been sent on some mission. She is also fifteen but seems wiser in so many ways. She knows how I dote on the infants. "There are more bastards in Venice than ever before. They say that the present doge celebrates excess."

Rosalba is just like her name, a blossoming rose with skin pale and soft and all shades of the pink you can find in one petal. Her features are small but so bright and expressive, her eyes as black as a man's shoe buttons. "Captivating" is how I have heard her described and "so competent," but never "beautiful." I think she might be if allowed one day to wear a patch on her cheek, one near her small nose perhaps. She plays all the wind instruments well but will not agree to be called Maestra dell'Oboe, no matter her skill at it. *Rosalba* is what she insists upon, laughing and saying, "If only I were allowed to learn the krummhorn. I would gladly be *maestra* of that." As she well knows, there is no instruction here in brass instruments and thus no possibility of such a fanciful title.

"Remember," she says, "there is rehearsal at three in the church for the program on Sunday."

I have not forgotten but am surprised that she has remembered, considering her lighthearted—some would say careless—approach to learning the music each week. The thought of the Violin Concerto in B-flat makes me feel weak, however. There are so many passages I haven't mastered. Since Father Vivaldi came back, we've had a new concerto to learn almost each week, ones in which the main instrument sometimes plays all by itself. Imagine!

Rosalba pauses, then steps down and loops one firm arm through my own.

"I can tell by your knitted brow that this concert troubles you as much as the last. How can that be so when you practice five times to my one and eventually know each note and mark in the score as if you had placed them there yourself?"

"It's the violin," I confess to her. "It isn't my first instrument."

"And if it weren't the violin, it would be the placement of the chairs and music stands, or the breeze from a window that should not have been opened, or the snuffle from a nose that needs to be blown."

I cannot control my laughter. Having been here together since babyhood, Rosalba sometimes seems to know me better than I know myself. She has been sure of her path since the moment she stepped out the nursery door. I have always watched her for cues and followed a few steps behind.

"You worry too much," she says then, squeezing my hand. "You will do well. You always do well. And besides, in the usual way, we'll be hidden behind the grille. There's nothing whatever to fear."

Nothing except the large critical ears of the dukes and the doge, the ones who hold the futures of most of the girls here in hands that we can't even see.

Luisa is petulant with me when we take our evening leisure. There is a pallor about her, and I think she may be feeling unwell. Rosalba thinks I coddle Luisa, but she appears so young and fragile at times and in more need of protection than some of the others. I myself am not truly at ease in a group, and am just waiting until all the others retire and I can go unobserved to the chapel to practice my solo for the performance on Sunday. Despite Rosalba's reassurances that I will do well, I'm always in fear that I will not be as prepared as Father Vivaldi expects.

The chapel is so silent at night and completely dark except for the flickering light from the votives that burn on the side altars. The dome is as black as a deep upside-down hole. The candle I carry gives just enough light to guide my steps up to the loft of the choir where we perform. Some instruments have been left behind since the practice session in the late afternoon. Their graceful shapes and polished wood come alive for an instant when I pass among them, then fade into darkness again. My viola d'amore sits in the shadows, near the organ, lonely and proud, as if it is waiting for me. But it is the violin that must shine in this concerto, an instrument that Father Vivaldi has restored himself. When I bend to attach the candle to the music stand, I discover the new bow Father has left for me. Yet I don't begin bowing at once. I lean back in my narrow chair and absorb all the quiet and calm. The other girls say they would never come here at nighttime alone. But though it does feel ghostly and strange at the start, if I say a quick *Ave* to Santa Maria of the Visitation, for whom the chapel is named, my fears are always quieted. The same is not true about my fear of this new music. The score before me has *L'estro armonico* written along the margin in Father Vivaldi's hand. Seeing the music for only the third time, I am still amazed at its technical difficulty. So much syncopated bowing. Such lengthy crescendos and diminuendos. The sensation I get from just looking at the score is in fact one of great extravagance and unbelievable adventure. I am pleased that he has chosen me to play the second solo part with our best violinist, Anna Maria, but am intimidated as well.

I first tune my instrument with the aid of the continuo, and then, as this is not my first time alone with my part, I work for quite a time on the burdensome measures that had confounded me in rehearsal. When at last I feel ready to tackle the whole of the piece, I begin slowly, delighting in the silvery tone of this violin and making my way as I would across the slippery stepping stones in the kitchen garden after a rain. But the challenge of the notes themselves begins to take hold, and I soon find that I must deal with Father's many arpeggios in such an unusual manner, and have to modulate so abruptly that it keeps my entire attention until, at the end of the solo, I am completely spent.

When I hesitate at the last arpeggio, I hear a noise — very faint and chirpy like a bird. Absently, I think how perhaps one flew in through a chink in the dome and is caught for the night. It has happened before. I try the difficult place where the change of bow occurs on a note off the beat, then I accelerate the tempo a little and play the *ritornello* in a different key, the way it is transcribed. I think I can master it this way. I only hope Father agrees. He will notice my sensitive playing of the difficult crescendos, I'm sure, and approve. Nothing passes his perceptive ear.

There again! I hear it. A little splash of a chirp. Or could it be whimpering. Yes. Growing louder, escalating into a cry. I drop my bow and run to the choir steps as fast as I can. I'm halfway down the dark stairway before I realize I've forgotten my candle and must go back for it. As I start down once again, I hear the thin wail rising over the clunk of my footsteps, and hurry to the nook at the back of the church. Just as I suspected, there is a baby on the wheel, red-faced and screaming. It is cold in here tonight, and the child is swaddled in nothing but a rough damp blanket. There are remnants of bloody afterbirth on her small body, and the cord looks as if it has been bitten rather than cut. Her tiny fists punch at the air as if she is already angry at this world she has so recently entered. I scoop her into my arms and press her against the warmth of my chest, sticking the end of a finger between her blue lips. She gulps little sobs between attempts at sucking the make-believe teat.

When I rush with her across the street and into the light of the nursery, I cannot help but observe that her face is unscarred and beautiful, one of the favored ones. The women gather around in surprise and delight when they see her.

"It is so late," says the night nurse. "Who would leave a newborn all night in an empty church? How fortunate that you found her, Anetta."

"Whoever left her must have heard me practicing the concerto. They must have known I would find her."

I am faint with the excitement of something so unexpected, so seemingly divine, as if Santa Maria had placed this infant there herself.

"May I name her?" I ask.

"Names," says the nurse with a sigh. "There are never enough names to go round!"

"But I have one. It's perfect."

"All right. Let us hear it."

"Concerta," I say. "Concerta Maria."

She thinks for a minute, then nods her head.

"It will do. There is no other."

From the first, I feel that her words say more than she knows.

Chapter Two

Rosalba

YESTERDAY MORNING, as I quietly made my way back from the street through the side door, there was dependable Anetta at the stairwell, already returning from wherever she'd been sent. I'm sure she assumed, in her innocent way, that I'd been sent somewhere, too. But she would have been wrong. I simply had to escape the usual caterwaul of voices and strings being tuned. And since I couldn't wait for the slim chance of being sent to the chapel by one of the *maestre* or to the laundry by Prioress, I made a small careful plan, as I often do, and slipped out when no one was looking. In the Ospedale there is never a moment of peace, except when we pray silently or in the dead of night during a rare pause between snores and dream muttering.

If you climb onto the largest footstool in the front visitor's parlor, you can get a good view of the lagoon from the window on the right, and know which gondoliers are in business that day. Some are not worth the effort. There is one, *Giuseppe* I have heard him called, who sings into the sky on his arrival as if all of Venice is listening and not the few invisible orphans who, if the windows are open wide enough, are swooning all over one another. He is a beautiful man with a robust voice and forearms that expand in sunlight when pulling the oars. My eyes feast on his body whenever they can. And why not? He feasts on mine, too, if I stand in the passageway at a distance of less than a *campo,* until for a certain his pantaloons steam. It is only a game, after all, and not the real reason I need to make my escape from time to time. In fact, there's another young man who has truly taken my eye. He is often seen running along the canal on Sundays and Holy Days, carrying a pedestal with two dressed wigs, powder flying, and returning less urgently with his carrier empty. During Carnival, he goes back and forth so many times, delivering wigs to the dukes, that I often catch sight of him more than once. Though such things are strictly forbidden, I will manage somehow to arrange a meeting.

"For what reason?" asks Silvia when I boast about

it unwisely at tea. "He is only a tradesman's apprentice. Not someone a girl from this or any other *ospedale* could marry."

"I've seen him," says Luisa with a sly smile. "He wears a smart bag wig and red-heeled shoes, just like a gentleman. His features are a little too keen but delightfully full. He has a grand nose."

"Yes, he does," I exclaim. "A nose much like the one on the bust of the last doge, don't you think?"

"Well, he's far from achieving that office," says Silvia. "Head wig-maker or some insignificant whiting or merlin is all he will ever be, no matter how handsome."

"Can't you see? It is a dalliance," Luisa declares scornfully. Then she laughs. "Our Rosalba is sure to become prioress or *maestra maggiore* and never marry at all."

Neither idea appeals to me even a bit. I'm aware, however, that it's not too soon to be forming a plan for my future. And I have one, as yet undeclared, that will necessitate my leaving here altogether. It is not unheard of for accomplished musicians from here and other *ospedales* to be in demand by touring European orchestras. Father Vivaldi, when learning of my great desire to see the musical cities of the world, has even suggested such a future for me. He did caution, "This is possible only if you but discipline yourself, Rosalba, for you have the skill truly, an amazing capability. But also"—and here he all but wagged a finger under my nose—"a singular gleeful nature often too intent on mirth-making."

As a reminder of what can be achieved, he mentioned Sabina della Pietà, who was Sabina della Pianoforte within these walls and who comes back from time to time to encourage the girls here and to tell of her adventures. I didn't confide this to Father, but while Sabina is husbandless, *I* shall choose to marry someone so handsome that the women will goggle in envy wherever we go. He will be royally cared for by me, for I cannot imagine a life under some old man's thumb or devotion to a bald-pated fat fellow admired for only his frippery, a condition that dukedom seems to encourage.

One such is leering at us across the tea table where Prioress sits. He is just at her elbow and constantly wiping his brow, which is weeping great tears of cold sweat.

It is unusual to have strangers of any kind here for tea. He sits between Prioress and Father Vivaldi, and if I lean forward, I can manage to catch snippets of their conversation, which seems to revolve around his great disappointment.

"But madam," he says with another swirl of his large embroidered handkerchief, "I had thought from their angelic voices—those voices from heaven—that every girl here would be comely beyond my belief."

"And you find them . . . ?" asks Father.

The stranger clears his throat.

"Amazingly plain and . . . worse," he says, while coughing up his sleeve. "Except for a few."

He is staring at Roma's thin face, which is mottled

by burn welts and disfigured from one droopy eye. She stares back and sticks out her tongue just as Prioress says, "But sweet-tempered, Signore."

Flustered, he darts his eyes about and they finally light on Luisa. The leer returns. His jowls become shaky, with what I am sure is desire.

"Ah, that one," he exclaims. "Does her voice match her exquisite face?"

"Surpasses," is all that Prioress says at first. "But she's much too young to be leaving us. In four years or so, perhaps, and then only if she has not chosen the career of soprano soloist, which is well within her grasp."

He sighs a long, resigned sigh, and his eyes begin traveling again. I look down so as not to attract his unwelcome gaze but sense it upon me just as Silvia gives me a nudge in the ribs.

"You're his next choice," she says, loudly enough to be heard everywhere in the room.

I sneak a look, and he's sitting—hands on belly, buttons of waistcoat popping—smirking at me.

"Too young again, Signore," Father Vivaldi tells him (thank our most blessed Savior). "Rosalba will be with us another few years."

"Perhaps, Signore, our lovely Josepha or Colletta," says Maestra Vincentia in the loud operatic tones that color her everyday speech. She comes from behind Prioress, pulling each girl by the hand until they are standing, befuddled and red-faced, before the duke. Each shoves her free hand into the pocket of her watteau and looks at her feet. I search his impassive face, where their presence is not registered, even as their terror exhibits itself in trembling limbs. I could scream! Both young women are kindly and bright with glorious mezzo-soprano voices and should never be treated with such gross indifference.

"Surely neither one would consider an oaf such as that for a husband," I say to Luisa, and hope I am heard by Maestra matchmaker and the duke himself.

"What are their alternatives?" Luisa whispers back. "I've heard that no one has come forward for either girl yet. That's the real reason this low-level duke was invited to tea."

"Then they should stay here and teach." It is always an option for those so accomplished.

"Neither one is like you," says Anetta, "so sure of themselves. They may want to be cared for."

She is right. There are many girls here who want nothing more than a home of their own. I suppose they will put up with anything—anyone—that they must.

"It's a shame those girls are not attractive enough to be courtesans," muses Luisa, as if that life were really an option.

"She means it," says Silvia. It appears that we all think at once of Luisa's mother, for I and the others are suddenly silent.

"Of course I do," says Luisa. "My mother has everything anyone needs or could wish for."

Except, it would seem, her own child.

Time. There is never enough of it. With Father Vivaldi in residence again, there are new concertos to learn almost every week. Sometimes an entire cantata as well. I sing the bass part in this latest one, an octave above what is intended. Maestra says the school will not hire a true bass for fear he will run off with one of us. Who but me, however, would take up with an impoverished singer the likes of whom would accept the single ducat Maestra can part with? Of course, chaste and dependable Rosalba is the last person anyone would expect to lose her head in this way.

I am working on my usual after-dinner headache as the girls begin to exercise their voices or practice their parts, and the halls and common rooms of the residence become filled with an oppressive mix of trills and scales. Luisa always drowns out the others, and sometimes there are ridiculous battles between sopranos determined to outsing her. So many tra-la-las and ah-hah-hahs, I could retch! The *figli di commun* play charades and backgammon above-stairs, their giggling and shrill shouts of victory carrying down the stairway to remind us that there can be something other than music to fill leisure hours. Those of us in the *figli di coro* cannot afford to engage in such games, however. It is constantly impressed upon each of us. But at times I long for a wider world in which I could go to the shops or to hear the opera or for a ride in a covered gondola with my sweetheart. When I have a sweetheart. It will be soon. Next Carnival, I think, when the doors are opened wide for a time and we mingle as much as we dare with the other masked revelers. I will know him by his unusual height, swift gait, and strong thighs. He will know me — somehow. For I am determined to wear a mantua wild with color that shows off my small waist, slim throat, and ample bosom, and not the white silk sacque in which we perform or the drab blue everyday watteau. How I will make this happen is still unclear to me.

After the usual scripture readings, talk at the tables this evening had been about the unidentifiable parcel of dark meat on each plate, covered in a tasteless watery sauce, and about the new infant left in the chapel last night. If she were scrawny and mottled, there would not have been such excitement. Anetta is certain that this one is a miracle child, protected by angels that no one can see except her.

"I am sure that I saw just the tips of their luminous wings when I picked up the baby," she claims. "They had risen, you see, when I stooped and gathered her into my arms. Now, of course, they will keep out of sight, ready to be at Concerta's side in an instant if she is in need."

The others believe her. And, I suppose, it cannot do harm. But since Prioress has often assured us of at least one guardian angel apiece, and as every girl invokes her aid before each concert, I begin to think how very crowded it must get up near the ceilings and can't help smiling.

"Go ahead and smirk, Rosalba," says Anetta. I had not meant to anger her, and it is usually not so easily done. "But you will see after a while that this baby has been singled out."

"If you ask me," says Silvia, "she has one angel too many. Who would want to be watched over all of the time?"

Luisa has been quiet until now. She gets annoyed when the talk turns to infants. She's probably hoping that God hasn't taken her own extra angel away for this new little orphan.

"It might be so," she says at last. "But I simply don't believe that you saw their wings, Anetta. I don't believe that, and you shouldn't go around saying it."

"Not saying it doesn't make it any the less true," says Anetta. I'm surprised to hear her oppose Luisa. Almost always Anetta will agree with whatever she says.

"And I suppose you think that she's bound to have a grand voice when she grows up," Luisa adds. "Just don't be upset if she takes to embroidery or some other domestic skill and lives with the *commun* girls where she'll make dresses, chemises, and kerchiefs for the *coro*."

"I can't know the future, Luisa," Anetta says, somewhat chagrined, "but the signs I have seen make me feel certain that something unusual is in store for this little one. If you don't want to believe it, then think what you will."

"As if I had need of your permission for that! Really, Anetta. You take quite a lot upon yourself."

"For a certain," says Silvia with a sly grimace. "She will be sent to live with a wet nurse for her infancy, and who knows what will happen to her after that."

"No," protests Anetta, "I have beseeched the signora in charge of the nursery, and she has assured . . . well, almost assured me . . . that Concerta will be kept at the Ospedale."

"And if she isn't?"

"I will not even consider of that possibility."

Tonight Signora Mandano has laid a small fire in the parlor to dry out the dampness that's begun to creep back into the building with the coming of cooler weather. Some of the girls arrange themselves around it on small cushions, but Anetta spreads her entire body facedown on the tile floor and rests her head on her hands. When she bends her knees and waggles her big feet in the air, it's too much for Luisa.

"You cannot laze around in that way," she states. "It is so . . . so . . . unwomanly, and not charming in the least."

As if formerly unaware of her odd comportment, Anetta turns over and sits up very straight.

"No one would mind," I say to Luisa. "Prioress has gone to bed. Why be so stiff-backed?"

"Luisa is quite correct," Anetta defends her. "I'm sorry, Luisa. I sometimes forget myself. I'm not naturally graceful like you."

"Ooh. And please do not grovel. I cannot bear it."

Anetta becomes very still and composed, as if she's a puppet with strings that Luisa can pull. It's upsetting to watch.

"When Father Vivaldi finally returns in the morning, he'll be so surprised at the progress you've made," I say to console and distract her. He lives not far from here, I'm told, but is often quite late.

"But you haven't heard me play the new solo."

"I caught the very last movement," I lie, "when I went back to the school at night for some . . . ink. It seems much improved and is certainly . . . lavish and . . . lively."

She jumps up and sits down again awkwardly in the chair next to mine with a hand on my arm, her wide brow furrowed with concern.

"And did you see anything in the street? Did you see anyone? Someone carrying a bundle perhaps?"

"No. I mean . . . I don't think so. I don't remember."

She sighs.

"You probably passed her. Concerta's mother. You must have passed her. Poor woman. I wonder what will become of her."

Luisa shakes her head and pulls on a dark lock that falls along one cheek. "Fortunate woman is more the like. Isn't it enough that the Ospedale takes in her child to feed and educate?"

"But to have to give her own baby away like that. I cannot imagine what that must be like."

Why does she think it so extraordinary? Weren't we, in fact, each like this child, given away for whatever the reason? And except for Luisa, we have no real knowledge of where we came from. We know nothing about what it's like to give birth and only a little of what must happen to make it possible. (What meager information *is* divulged seems highly improbable.) Except for the male infants who are sent to one of the *ospedali* for boys when they are six or seven, sometimes as old as ten, the only men that come into the school to teach might as well be *castrati*. It is enough to be groomed, as we are, for a life that is better and all our own. It can be that way if we let it. I know that it can be that way, for many of our teachers were once just like us. Most no longer live here, but come and go to apartments and sometimes to husbands and families. Though I am perhaps too impatient for it, isn't to be loved what we all want in the end? How I long for a suitor who will quickly be overcome by this fire that stirs me.

Chapter Three

Luisa

SINCE THIS IS NO CONVENT, the others were watching as usual during my mother's visit yesterday, and they leaned like caged monkeys into the grille that separates them from visitors. Perhaps from a distance her caresses appear warm, her kisses sincere. But as soon as she sees the girls spying on us, her eyes flit about and she poses and fawns over me. Anetta, as if she's obsessed, always pushes and shoves for a place in the front. Afterward, too, she is full of rude questions. When I simply don't answer, she grows morose. I know they think I am favored, and that Anetta has even wished at times that she could be me.

She has said as much, once wondering aloud how it must feel to be held for a moment and pressed against all the satin and silk of my mother's fancy gowns.

And I have heard the girls discussing how none of them know why I remain in this place, since it is well known that everyone here is a ward of the state, and a child with a family is unlikely to come here to stay, no matter how gifted, unless the family is royal or completely impoverished. When I tell them it is only because of the excellent musical education the Ospedale della Pietà can provide and because of my wonderful voice, it annoys them in the extreme.

Another thing that sets me apart is the fact that I have a real last name and am not called by the name of my primary instrument like some of the senior girls, as if there is truly a flesh and blood family named Violin or Bassoon or Flautino. For an instance, Maestra della Viola is what Anetta is called and will be until she takes the veil, becomes a true *maestra*, or attracts a husband. Because she is not more comely, perhaps it will not be a duke, but some gentleman, a rich merchant, perhaps, who would value a wife who can teach the children to sing and play for his guests.

I begged Mother yesterday, something I promised myself I would never do. And today I feel ashamed. It was not as though the others could hear me, for the parlor is somewhat below the grille and all the commotion behind it. And I made very sure that I stood quite still, my hands at my sides, and called her *Mother*, as she has told me to do.

"Take me with you this time, Mother," I said. She made me repeat it, and it seemed as if she would truly consider my words. For a wonderful instant there was this fragile bubble of hope, soon pricked when her dark brows curved down and her fan went up to her lips.

"None of that, Luisa," she said, touching my fingers with a cold gloved hand. "The life that I lead would never permit such a thing."

I turned my head toward the door, for I could not allow the others to see the quick tears.

The life that she leads. I often imagine the apartment she has told me about — the gilded chests and armoires, carved settees with satin cushions, silk curtains enclosing a deep feather bed surrounded by tapestries, and, think of it, even a fanciful Murano glass chandelier with fat beeswax candles. In fact, at times there are little flashes of my first few years there with her and of a shadowy nursemaid, the milky smell of her, the tuneful songs that she taught me to sing. The duke, my father, keeps my mother well — much better, she says, than his own wife and legitimate children.

"A mistress is always loved best," she said before pausing to study her long fingers. For this visit, even her stomachers were embroidered with gold and her frontage was pleated and high over honey-hued ringlets and rolls.

"And the voice," she said. "The voice will be trained as in no other place in the world. The Pietà is renowned throughout all of Europe."

As always, she spoke as if my voice is not part of myself but something I must cater to as to a perfect child who is demanding and spoiled. She never asks about my progress on the clavichord or violin. To her, they are only instruments of accompaniment.

"It is opera that must be our goal, and now that Father Vivaldi is back at the Pietà, he can help us. Already his folios are being performed in cities like Vienna. You will be more than a courtesan, child, though that is hardly a life to be spurned. You will be a famous soprano. I will be your companion." She tittered. "For no one would take us for mother and child."

She has everything planned. And she's right to believe that my voice is exceptional and will someday be heard everywhere. But how does she know? How many times has she come to our concerts to hear me sing? I have caught sight of her only once, and then she left before my recitative. I was thrilled to see her arrive, even though very late, but her seat was empty the next time I looked, and I could hear the flutter of voices and laughter and the shutting of doors. I wanted to run after her then, but of course, there was no way that I could. I think my desperate feelings went into my song, for after the concert Father remarked how I really must have more control of my emotions.

I am trying to sleep when Anetta comes into the room and flops down on her bed. There are six of us in this one space, and the beds are so close beneath the high windows that you can feel each girl turn in the night, especially she whose large feet and sharp elbows stick off at all angles.

When I keep my eyes shut and roll to my side, my stomach feels surprisingly sore and full, and I notice a strange sticky wetness between my upper thighs. I reach down and bring my hand back. In the light from the hallway, my fingers look stained and dark, and they smell of blood. *(Madre di Dio!)* I had hoped this day would not come, even though all the girls near my age and even some younger ones have begun their monthlies and must deal with the mess and the bother! Only Lucretia, who is sixteen, is fortunate enough to have nosebleeds only and doesn't bleed from her bottom. I had hoped to be such an exception, but now I will have to leave my warm bed and find those disgusting rags that the other girls wear. I will have to ask someone, Anetta, where they are kept and what exactly I must do with them. The others are sound asleep, or I'd never confide such a thing to her or ask for her help. When I'm forced to at last, she acts as if I've been given a prize.

"Luisa, just think." She claps her big hands. "You're a woman today."

A woman has bosoms and a fat posterior. I am straight up and down and as spare as a bird, and intend to remain that way. The rough rags that Anetta gives me are stiff and cold. With a great wad of them fastened in place, I can barely sleep from discomfort.

In the morning I'm roused by Silvia, who shrieks and points at two scarlet streaks on the coverlet.

"It's her first monthly," Anetta declares in a whisper that's as shrill as a shout. It causes Rosalba to fairly leap from sleep. Her feet slap the floor.

"What's the matter? What is it? Have I overslept? Not again."

"I thought," says Silvia, her small, feeble eyes growing narrow and mean, "that Luisa was bleeding to death, that she'd finally slit her own fabulous throat."

"What a terrible, vicious thing to say," gasps Anetta, clutching her own throat with both hands and then doubling over as if in pain herself, "and when she suffers the *dolori,* too." She drops down next to me and pats my hair in a gesture that makes me cringe.

Though I push her away, she continues to play my defender and coos and coddles until I could retch.

What she'd never believe is that I prefer Silvia's snarling to all of her cosseting ways. Silvia's envy is something that I understand; Anetta's constant toadying is foolish and weak.

Nonetheless, I have no choice but to listen as Anetta instructs me how to place the rags I have soiled in a crock to await washing and fasten some fresh ones into my undergarments. It is an odious ritual that I rail inwardly against. I do indeed feel changed—achy and clumsy and clammy. I'd sooner curl back into bed and sleep away whatever days it may take to expunge these secretions than disguise my condition with the customary watteau and clean apron and go about my lessons.

"You will grow used to it, Luisa," Anetta says finally.

"It's one more thing about this life that can't be helped," says Rosalba as she adjusts her own undergarments and pulls on her watteau.

"This life?" I ask.

"A girl's life. A woman's life," Rosalba calls back.

"For a certain the Creator is a man," says Silvia, "to have devised such wretchedness. There is more misery in store for our sex, no doubt, to which we are not yet privy. What little information they give us about such things is probably more wrong than right."

"Don't frighten her," Anetta says. "Father Vivaldi says God never gives anyone more than she or he can stand."

I've heard him say that, too, and hope I will not need to test such limits.

"Don't worry, Luisa," says Silvia. "Anetta here will make quite certain you never so much as stub your toe."

"And will come between you," says Rosalba, "when you attempt to stab Luisa in the back."

Rosalba means well, I am sure. Sometimes I think she is one of the few here who do not covet my fine voice and lineage. Knowing me as she does, however, she should realize that I have strength sufficient to defend myself. Silvia is not the only thorn in this garden. I have needed to learn early to ignore the snide remarks and envious asides about my mother. And sometimes, when I am chosen for a solo that others bargained for quite openly, there is a jealousy or rage released that saturates the very corridors.

That Father has chosen me to feature, a girl so far from being ready to be affianced to a nobleman, shows his esteem for my ability—and, of course, his great desire that this concert will stand out and be remembered. There is a pride in this affable priest that I recognize and understand.

Later, when we are at leisure in the large parlor and I am thinking of how Father Vivaldi's desire for perfection has often put Anetta in a state of near paralysis, I suddenly hear "Luisa!" close to my ear. Then I bump to the bare floor as Silvia, much to her amusement, gives me a push and slides behind me to appropriate the footstool by the fire.

"Ha!" she exclaims. "It was easier to dislodge the queen from her throne than I had expected."

"If you had but asked me to move, Silvia," I tell her while trying to appear unfazed as I brush off my skirts, "I would have obliged."

"And you should not frighten people like that," says a little *iniziata* I have not noticed before. I am surprised to find someone so young coming to the defense of a senior girl. They are usually too timid by half and are not often found in either parlor taking their ease.

"Be careful," I whisper to her as I pass through the room. "You do not want to make an enemy of Silvia."

"She does not frighten me," says the bold child, and plunks down upon the carpet with her embroidery. Given the rude example of Anetta earlier, I have no heart to scold her. It would be a mean reward for her defense of me as well. There are enough girls here who find me haughty and aloof. I do not need another enemy, no matter how insignificant.

Anetta

IT IS SATURDAY, and those of us who are to be in tomorrow's concert have been practicing with Maestro Gasparini all morning. The violins are beginning to sound to my tired ears like a swarm of bees and the wind instruments like the lowing cattle I once saw driven along the Riva, only heaven knows why. I sense how well Father Vivaldi has prepared us, however, by the way in which the *maestro* looks almost pleasant from time to time and makes only feeble attempts at correcting the dynamics of any phrase. Our ranks are bolstered by some of the older *maestre*, and, as I have said, Anna Maria, our most accomplished violinist and Father's obvious favorite, is playing the first violin solo. But in fairness, he has not neglected my part, but made it both wildly colorful in some passages and calm in others. In fact, the parry between my violin and hers becomes a highly charged duel that I'm beginning to think we can each win if we keep our wits.

Of the three concerti we will play tomorrow, this first is the most difficult and the most delightful. There will be a short *sinfonia* as well and a lovely cantata composed only last week. We've been told there are to be important personages from the papal city in the audience and a famous composer from Vienna named Signore Bach. Plus the usual overdressed dukes and wives or consorts. From our high perch, we always look down upon a sea of color, fur, and feathers that glints with gold and silver embroidery and flashing jewels. Here and there are the bright *berrette* of the monsignori, the elaborate frontages of the women, and very occasionally the tall hat of the doge. Rosalba claims it is a great blessing that we can't see the features of some of the dukes and merchants too clearly, and it is just as well that they can't see a number of us.

Maestro Gasparini taps the podium with his stick, the signal to put aside our instruments and assemble for the noon meal in the refectory.

"And do not return until after my nap," he instructs us. "You play like drunken street performers right after lunch. Take a nice long siesta or go for a walk."

The little *iniziate,* the young assistants, pass among us with the corrections Father Vivaldi has made that have just arrived from the copyists. We can never be certain that there will not be additions or omissions in any piece of his music, even after it is performed, and we are all anxious to discover what has been changed.

After a few minutes, Silvia moans and smacks the case of her theorbo. "He's removed the most beautiful part of the second movement in the first concerto. Poof! Just like that."

"I think it's a vast improvement," says Luisa.

"Only because it isn't your notes he's stolen. It's always my notes. He shrinks my part every time. Why does he write the notes down at all if he's just going to take them away?"

"He doesn't know he's going to take them away," says Luisa, "until he hears you play them."

"That isn't true, Silvia," I say quickly to assuage her hot temper, but it is too late. She has already reached for a handful of Luisa's black hair and pulled it hard enough to bring tears. When I get up and try to separate the short little squabblers, it occurs to me that I could easily smash their niggling heads together if I were so inclined. Instead, and only because of my new role as *maestra* and section leader, I hold them apart, one hand on each head, until they have calmed a bit and stopped squealing. The few ducats I have recently begun to earn

37

for my position are not nearly enough pay for handling this sort of business.

For all concerts, though we can barely be seen behind the grillework that surrounds the high choir balcony on which we sit to play or stand to sing, we dress in white Spitalfield silk and feel quite special. It does not rustle the way some taffetas do and thus distract from the performance.

The same cannot be said for the materials of those who mull around in the chapel below or perch on small couches and tiny brocaded chairs. They dress in all manner of noisy fabrics and swish about and call to one another as if at a fair.

"At least we can't smell them," Rosalba whispers to me when we are in our places.

It is said that one reason we perform from above is to spare us from all the perfumes and pomades and sweat—a lethal blend for a singer or asthmatic priest. Luisa wears a pomegranate blossom in her hair that Geltruda eyes suspiciously. It is a mystery where Luisa could have found such a flower, yet she always thinks of something to set herself apart. We have come to expect it, and she is so beautiful, who can object?

The first concerto is for cello, one of the instruments Father himself plays, plus strings and basso continuo. I'm told that this work was requested by the cello teacher for Maestra Georgetta del Cello, who is almost ready to leave here and desperately needs to attract a suitor. (It is especially fortunate that she cannot be seen too clearly, as the way in which she grimaces, spreads her legs, and attacks her instrument is simply indecorous.) The allegro is very bright and rhythmic and the adagio curiously languid. After the sprightly third movement there is much nose blowing and shuffling of feet below us—a very good sign that the audience is both awake and enjoying the performance.

The second concerto, one of the *concerti ripieni*, has no name and no real soloists but is carried by the strings, so I am kept busy. Maestro Gasparini himself plays the harpsichord, flinging his arms about when his fingers are not occupied on the keys, and it is completely thrilling when all the strings converge to deliver the *ritornello* and then go their separate ways for the little fugues.

The concerto in which my violin is featured—the one for two violins and basso continuo—begins the second half of the concert. Maestro Gasparini steps forward, raises his stick, counts noiselessly, then brings the stick down, and we are immediately into the difficult allegro that bounces motifs back and forth so nervously that it's no surprise to hear a loud pop right before the adagio. It echoes from the high ceiling like a hollow cannon shot, and there are many exclamations and titters from the crowd. As he always does, Father Vivaldi races off to the wings with the offending instrument and replaces the broken gut string immediately, a feat only he can accomplish in such a short space of time. He rushes back, and we resume playing at the exact place of the interruption, completing the stirring allegro and launching into the tuneful adagio, where I ultimately lose myself in the rich weave of the music. Even the final allegro seems to be played in my sleep, for I am in fact as startled as a sleepwalker might be when the last note is delivered.

The shuffling, foot stomping, and blowing of noses is even louder this time, and Father Vivaldi grins at me, extremely pleased. Maestro Gasparini wipes his glistening brow as though weary beyond belief.

Almost at once, Luisa and Geltruda step forward and the other singers take their places. Luisa appears almost unearthly, as if she has stepped out of a fresco by Tintoretto. The gasps from the audience must be caused by what little they can see of her behind the grille, for she is a vision truly, and she delivers her solo like an angel.

Afterward, we gather in a schoolroom for an assessment of our performance. On our way there, Maestro Gasparini makes excuses and turns down the Calle della Pietà. He is clearly feeling spent, his rotund backside swaying a little as he picks his way along the cobblestones, dark patches of sweat revealing themselves on his jacket when he raises his arms to steady himself. It is left to Father Vivaldi, as is often the case, to point out our difficulties and suggest how to correct them. For this, I believe we are all grateful, for he is ever considerate and not given to displays of temper.

"Well done," Rosalba suddenly states to the entire small assemblage. She gives a low bow as if she herself has been entirely responsible for our collective achievement. "A magnificent performance. The dukes will come running."

"Sit down, Rosalba," says Father, chuckling and pulling her into a chair. "You, as much as anyone, need to hear what I have to say."

As always, he has little to correct in Anna Maria's playing. To her credit, she is not smug about this, but does leave early, having heard what little pertained to her. My own performance was not without fault, yet I'm relieved when there are only a few suggestions for changes in the bowing. Even Luisa has some pleasant comment to make about it, though later I cannot recall what it was. (Were it a true compliment, you can be sure I would have treasured it and committed it to memory.)

When Father is finished, I cannot restrain my own praise of her wondrous solo, which to my ear was the pinnacle of perfection.

When I say something of the sort, she waves me away with a small gesture of her hand that suggests she would rather not dwell on her performance but remark on the concert as a whole. Such a gracious response should have been expected.

She then tarries a little and stays behind to speak with Father, and the thought occurs to me that she is actually waiting for her mother to appear. I myself make a hasty departure. I do not want to witness Luisa's great disappointment when that mysterious and ornamented woman does not come.

Chapter Five

Luisa

ARE YOU HERE TODAY, Mother, as you promised? Is that you wrapped in the scarlet *bagnolette* and wearing a satin mantilla? Or are you the woman with the dark blue cloak who has just turned to the man with the very high periwig? From here, looking through this iron grillwork, it is so hard to be sure. Did you notice how well I played the *flautino* in the little *sinfonia*? Please be here somewhere, Mother. Please be the elegant lady who has just bustled in late. Please be here now to listen to me sing, even though this cantata is not as pretty as some and to my mind relies too much on Geltruda's thin contralto.

I do realize, however, that Father must write to each of our strengths. I only wish that this time it were not at the expense of my part, which could have been much expanded and a great deal more operatic. You would have been so pleased by that. It is not an overly long little piece, however, and has a few places where I can show my ability to swell and sustain a note or sing a run with great rapidity. At any rate it is over very quickly, and did you notice how it was followed by a great deal more feet shuffling than I've heard this day? A little triumph, I must confess. Though Geltruda is red-faced and looking a bit spent, she has truly done her best.

The lady with the cloak is looking up, and I can see clearly now that she is not my mother. The woman in scarlet is already passing through the chapel doors, a red-heeled man at each elbow. Quite possibly Mama. The latecomer is holding court and obviously has not come to hear me or anyone else perform.

We do not bow, as I'm told other performers do after such a concert, but file down the stairs from the choir loft and back into the school, where we are congratulated or corrected as our professors see fit.

Anetta is beaming at me and clasps her large hands at her waist.

"You sang beautifully, Luisa, as always. We were all entranced."

I cannot return her effusive compliment, for her

playing to my ear was awkward, the solo part not mastered nearly as well as it should have been. It was Anna Maria who shone.

"We all did our best, I am sure," I say in retort, but she doesn't seem to have noticed the slight at all. Her constant good nature grates on one's nerves so. When Geltruda compliments me as well, I do manage to tell her the small improvement I've noticed of late in her tone.

Imagine—Maestra Alicia has chastised me for the pomegranate blossom, saying what poor form it is to try to stand out from the rest. She reminds me that we are all doing our best to earn a steady income for the Ospedale in order to pay for our educations. Doesn't she realize that some of the paying customers come especially to hear me or some other soloist who is unusually gifted? Is one not to be thought better than another if it is true? Should such truths be hidden?

Just in case Mother is allowed into the school after the concert, I stay behind while the others go for their tea. So many instruments have been left haphazardly around the room that it looks a good deal like Father's repair shop. It amuses me to think that my best instrument cannot be seen but resides safely within my throat and chest, where only I can tune it and protect or repair it. Only I.

"Catching some time to yourself, Luisa?" asks Father as he passes through the room on his way to his shop. He is carrying a small birdcage with a house finch inside and holds it up for me to see. "My little bird is not as gifted as you, perhaps. But such a sweet voice, like a piccolo."

I have seen Father looking up into the pear trees by the kitchen garden or chasing the gulls that gather at the water's edge and the pigeons that pester the tourists. He stands for long periods studying the birds or cocking his head at the song of the goldfinch or call of the gull.

"I will capture that sound sometime. Someday you will hear a cluster of shimmering notes fall about you as if they have come from above — perhaps you will play them yourself — and you'll say, 'That is Father Vivaldi's small finch.'" I smile to myself. I cannot believe he will ever cause an instrument to sound like a bird. It is too preposterous.

I make little chirping noises at the tiny creature and bend over to admire his shiny green feathers. "Where did you come by such a bird?" I ask.

"A street vendor was selling them, cage and all." He is quiet for a time, watching me with the little songster. "Would you like me to obtain one for you? They could both stay in the repair shop. Two birds would be company for each other."

It is such a delightful and unexpected suggestion, I don't know what to say. But I sense my expression betrays me, for he suddenly concludes, "Of course. Of course, you would love such a creature. On my way home tonight, I will seek out that vendor and obtain one especially for you."

But that is apparently not the only surprise he has in store, for he suddenly sets down the birdcage and claps his hands together like a child about to divulge a great secret. "I have obtained permission to take you and Anna Maria to see the Teatro San Angelo." He looks down in a shy manner before continuing, "It is a sublime place where I have hopes of becoming impresario one day and where, praise God, my operas will be staged." He had told us earlier about the publication of his first set of concerti, *L'estro armonico,* and his grander aspirations are no secret. When he finds the time to pursue them, however, is a great mystery.

I tent the fingers of both hands before my smile but don't utter a word while he continues his little speech. "You see, it is so important for you very serious girls, the ones most apt to make a profession of your music, to see where and how true professionals outside of the Ospedale perform."

"And Rosalba, too," I interject. "Rosalba needs to come and see the theater as well."

He pauses for such a time that I am afraid he has not heard me.

"And Rosalba, too?" I ask again.

"Not this time," says Father. He sighs, removes his performance wig, and sets it on a waiting pedestal before turning back to me. "Rosalba's thoughts are somewhere in the clouds of late. I believe it would be a great mistake to reward her for the flippant attitude and actions she consistently displays."

"But that, Signore, is simply our Rosalba. You know her nature."

"I know it well," he says firmly, "and hope by this denial of an outing she could surely profit from, to make her see the error of her ways."

On Monday, just the three of us set off by gondola, a conveyance Rosalba has desired to explore and travel by for years. I feel a measure of guilt that I am the first of the two of us to have a glimpse of what it's like inside one and how it feels to sway and bob like this upon the water. In truth, this boat is not as fine as most; the gondolier is stooped and old, and cannot sing at all. She would have been quite disappointed.

Teatro San Angelo is grander, however, than I ever could have imagined. We go up a steep stairway, then through pillars and a lavish entry to an enormous hall lined with blue-and-gold viewing boxes from floor to ceiling. Plush seating is available in the center of the room, and all—boxes and loges—face an open stage with heavy velvet drapery ensconced beneath plaster garlands and gold figures.

"When all the candles are lit," Father tells us wistfully

as he points to the lanterns on the wall and the enormous glass chandeliers, "the light is soft and wondrous."

He is disappointed that there are so few performers about and no rehearsal in progress. A few musicians, however, recognize him at once and call out to him, and it is startling to see how well he is known in this imposing space. A mezzo is practicing with her pianist, and she ignores our progression up the aisle, except for a wave of one plump hand. Anna Maria is quiet and somber as if in church, her eyes shining and focused, like mine, on the stage. For my part, I have a great desire to immediately fill this hall with the sound of my own voice, but content myself with merely imagining what it would be like up there on such a large platform with no grille to hide behind. If Father had hoped to ignite my desire for a career in such a place, I have fallen into his plan with abandon. Standing here, at the center of such immensity and grandeur and tingling with an excitement I have not felt before, it feels as if I may, indeed, have found my true and future home.

Chapter Six

Rosalba

APPARENTLY SUNDAY'S CONCERT was not exceptional enough to land a husband for anyone. At least no one has heard of any offers so far or tried to arrange a tête-à-tête. It is definitely not the way in which I will seek a mate.

It is a great gift not to have another concert for an entire two weeks. It will, however, give Luisa more time to trill and torture us, and Anetta more opportunity to worry herself into hysterics over the score.

The little escapade to the Teatro San Angelo on Monday was pointed out to me by more than one *maestra*, but I refuse to feel slighted or to become additionally inclined to spend more time on my instrument than I feel it warrants. All I can think of at the moment is that in these next weeks I will have extra chances to observe my heart's darling and plot how to meet and ensnare him. Just closely observing his muscular grace as he lightly balances the wigs and goes about his deliveries will have to content me for the moment. It does afford the necessary study of the routes he takes and the times he takes them. I've seen him hop upon a gondola more than once and head off who knows where. If I could only manage to hide aboard sometime. I have observed many a fine *signora* or *signorina* peeking from behind the curtains of the windows in the gondolas and their elegant gentlemen alighting from the closed black boats onto the dock. But what can it be like inside those lovely gliding chariots? Are there velvet cushions and little stoves or heated stones? Are there feather couches to rest upon, fur bundling rugs, and places in which to be sequestered? How surprised my little merlin would be to find me there beneath a silken coverlet, my hair and girdle loose, my arms outstretched and beckoning. It is too sweet a scene to be endured!

But I am getting much too far ahead of myself and courting disaster. A careful plan is what has always served me well in the past. That doesn't mean, however, that I will not be alert for my opportunities. Carnival will not begin until Saint Stephen's Day, but there is much I can do before then to ready myself.

"Where have you been? What are you doing here?" asks Anetta as she gallops through the front parlor, and, on finding me there, stops abruptly. She is always on her way to or from somewhere and always in a great hurry.

"Slow down," I say, pulling her with me onto a settee.

"We shouldn't even be in here at this time of day," she says, stumbling to stand up again. "You have missed solfeggio twice already this week and this third time I have been sent to fetch you. We may have been given a little more time to practice for the next concert, but it is already only a week away, and they will expect us to be that much better prepared."

"They? Who is this 'they'?"

"Father Vivaldi and Signore Gasparini. Prioress. And the others. Our teachers. The people who come to hear us."

"There is plenty of time. There is always plenty of time."

"It is difficult music, Rosalba. Even you will find places to trip you. If you ever look at it. If you ever come to a rehearsal and pick up the score. Do you even know which instrument you will be playing?"

"No. But I'm sure you will tell me."

"Not this time, Rosalba." She bites her chapped lips, which look as if they've been bitten many times before. She seems truly distressed. "For your own good."

"I will be there this afternoon. I promise."

"No. Not this afternoon. Now. I'm the one who takes

the attendance," she wails. "I'm the one who must check off your absence."

She seems so distressed that I can't help feeling a little discomfited. I knew several days had gone by, but not an entire week.

"It's all right, Anetta. You must do it in the correct way, I know. I don't blame you." I jump up and try to tussle her hair but can't reach the top of her head. Instead, I give her a soft pat on the cheek and am surprised to find it wet. "Surely, you're not crying. You're not crying over this?"

Tears are actually starting to flow from her wide-apart eyes and to splash onto either side of her knotted kerchief.

"I don't want to see you punished," she whimpers, "or removed from the *privilegiate del coro*. We have grown up here together. We have always played in the same ensembles. You belong among the *privilegiate* with me." She makes a fist of each hand and all but stamps her foot. "But you have to follow the rules."

She then begins to study the pattern in the carpet, for what else can be so interesting upon the floor? As if she does not really want to be heard, her hands go up to cover her mouth while she speaks. Her voice becomes a whisper.

"You were not there yesterday to sign the pay sheets for the *maestri*, so I, heaven help me, signed for you, making my letters as wiggly as I could to match yours."

"I suppose I should thank you, but it is a silly assignment. Which one of us should dare to keep a professor from his rightful earnings, no matter how inept we may feel him to be."

"You are changing the subject," says Anetta, "something you do so well."

She takes my arm and pulls me into the passageway. "You must come with me now. Right now."

"Yes, yes, Maestra della Viola d'Amore," I say to tease her. I let my arms go slack and allow myself to be led. "Right away, Maestra. Right away."

Chapter Seven

ℒuisa

THERE ARE SNAKES twined all through my throat with scales that slice as they slide up and down. I am tugging a snake out through my mouth, enduring intense pain just to be free of it, when my fingers will not move and I must release it back into the pit of my neck. I scream in an agony of frustration and open my eyes. Anetta is holding both my hands and keeping me pinned to my bed.

"Why did you make me let go?" I sob, desolate from the defeat of my great effort and the terrible soreness that seems to be causing my air passages to close.

"Shush. It's only a nightmare," she says as I thrash and wrench out of her grasp.

The others, awake now and up on their haunches in their beds, peer at me as if I've gone mad and say, "It's all right." "Stop screaming." "You'll wake up the entire floor."

My chemise is wet with perspiration, my hair damp and hot against my face. I can barely swallow. The dream is still so real; the snakes a writhing tangle pressing upon my chest from within. I barely feel Anetta's hand on my forehead, but I hear her.

"She's feverish," she proclaims to the others.

Even in my pain and panic, it galls me to have Anetta take charge like this. I try to sit up but am made dizzy by the effort.

"It's another bid for attention, if you ask me," says Silvia. "Isn't it enough to always drown out the other sopranos. Does she also need to accost us nightly in our sleep with her bodily infirmities?"

Silvia's bed is behind mine, and I'm grateful at least that I can't see her little wizened face and her eyes, bare of spectacles, that always look like blank thumbprints.

"She cannot help feeling sick," says Rosalba. "Anetta, please walk with her down to the infirmary so the rest of us can go back to sleep. All of us have Latin exams in the morning."

"More reason for her to feign illness," says Silvia.

"Luisa would never have need of such a dodge. She

is proficient in many languages." Though I cannot speak up for myself, I am not pleased to hear Anetta do it for me, embellishing my accomplishments.

"Come," Anetta tells me, pulling me to my feet. "The night nurse will have a comforting potion for you."

When I stand, the dizziness overtakes me so completely that I must lean upon Anetta so as not to fall over. She leads me along the unlit hall and down the stairway as if she is some nocturnal animal most alive in darkness. I myself can barely see to put one foot ahead of the other. I have no choice but to trust her; she prods and drags me along until we are at the door of the infirmary and I am tucked into a lumpy bed by the night nurse before I have a chance to complain that it's much too close to the drafty window. After I am covered with a sheet, my sopping chemise is lifted over my head and a wet flannel poultice, smelling of camphor and mustard seed, is slapped upon my bare chest and wrapped roughly in place with strips of flannel.

"Attend this candle, Anetta, while I look at her throat," says the nurse. She presses on my tongue with a cold spoon handle, and I start to gag.

"It's all right, little duchess," she says at last. "This is the third throat this week I've seen with such a grand lot of pustules and raw red flesh. And such a furry white tongue. You won't be leaving here in the morning or anytime soon."

I have heard myself referred to as "little duchess" before. It is truer than they know.

"But there's a concert on Sunday," says Anetta.

"And every Sunday," says the nurse.

"Do you know who I am?" I finally manage to squeak out.

"Who you are or who you think you are?"

Anetta defends me: "Don't you realize that Luisa is the most accomplished soprano in this or any other *ospedale*? The coming concert will be nothing without her."

"I know that she is a spoiled little singer who won't be able to sing for a while. That's what I know. Here," the nurse says to me, forcing a spoonful of liquid between my lips. It tastes like something fermented and is so bitter that I cough and try to spit it out, but the nurse's hand clamps my jaw shut.

I fall back against the pillow, too weak to do battle with her.

When Anetta begins her treacly litany of consolation, this strong nurse takes both of her shoulders and turns her around.

"Get back to your own chamber, Anetta. There is nothing you can help with here."

There is only one other girl in the school infirmary tonight, a small little thing to judge by the size of the bump she makes in the bed. Since the moment we entered the room, her raspy snores have accompanied all our words. Perhaps she was given the same draught that the nurse has given me, for I am beginning to feel a peculiar calmness, my throat seems swabbed, and my thoughts tumble over each other into darkness long, I'm sure, before the candles are extinguished.

When I open my eyes, it is morning, the little girl is fastening her dark blue sacque and pulling on her hose, and I recognize the *iniziata* who came to my defense in the parlor. She seems entirely well.

"Where are you going?" I ask in a high, bruised voice I don't recognize as my own. There is no sign of the ill-tempered nurse.

"I didn't mean to wake you up," she says. "But I am better now. I think it must be time to breakfast."

"Hunger is a very good sign," I tell her, not harboring even a little of it myself. I still feel hot and weak, and my throat is as swollen as ever. It is an effort to speak.

"Would you like me to get something for you from the kitchen, Maestra?"

"No thank you," I croak. "But, tell me, is that allowed?"

"Oh, yes, Maestra. I spend a great many nights here, you see, because of my breathing problems, my *strettezza di petto*. They say I sometimes sound just like Father Vivaldi when he is at his worst."

"And what are you called?"

"Catina. You wouldn't have heard of me," she says, as if she has forgotten our encounter. "I'm not often in class or ensemble. I'm not very strong."

Catina is fair with pale skin and corn-silk hair that falls down her back like a shawl. Her eyes are the deep green color of the lagoon just before a storm. She has a reticent smile but does not otherwise seem to be cautious of strangers.

"I have a very sore throat," I say, even though she has not asked. I don't know if I say it to garner her sympathy or simply to explain my presence here.

"Yes. That is a common complaint this week. It will not last long, I think." I can't help smiling. She sounds so much like one of the pompous physicians or like the night nurse herself.

"I am glad to hear it," I rasp. "Do you think it will leave me by Sunday?"

"The day of the next concert?"

"How did you know?"

"Oh, everyone knows. Listening to the senior per-formers is part of our education."

Of course. It had been part of mine as well. But now that I'm in the *coro privilegiato* myself, it feels as if I have always performed at this level.

"And I know who you are. The soprano, Luisa Benedetto, the one who sings just like a saint." Her eyes grow impossibly wide. "And yes, I am sure you'll be able to sing on Sunday next, perhaps even by Saturday afternoon."

She is so certain, it picks up my spirits, and when she leaves, I savor the quiet—the hollow tick of the clock and the faint faraway songs of the gondoliers. I think about how Mother may really come to hear me this time, how she is sure to. About how very proud she will be.

Chapter Eight

Anetta

IT HAS BEEN DECIDED. Luisa will not sing at the concert this Sunday. She has lately been moved to a room far away from even the infirmary. The rumor is that her fever has risen, a bright pink flush has spread over her trunk, and her throat is as red as a strawberry. Maria's throat, too, has seized up just at a time when there are plans for her to be introduced to a suitable gentleman. They say she is more aggrieved about this than about the pain she endures. She is the oldest one yet to be stricken.

It has also been reported that a few of the young-est *commun* girls are affected as well. The nurses are in a frenzy of trying to isolate the infected ones as soon as they contract this peculiar throat malady that turns them scarlet. Rosalba and Silvia have been sent to the apothecary in the Piazza San Marco for certain herbs and medicinals to reduce swollen throat membranes. (Rosalba because she can be trusted to complete the transaction; Silvia, I believe, to keep her weak eyes upon Rosalba.) It is unusual for any of us to be sent on such a mission outside the school and Ospedale. But because of so many falling ill at once, no nurse or teacher can be spared for this errand. My help has been requested in the nursery to care for the little ones, who know nothing of the current crisis and whose demands are constant. May Jesus and His Dear Mother keep them from harm. I pray frequently to Saint Blaze over their small throats and can't help wondering if Luisa's throat was blessed on his name day, as it should have been. Why wasn't she more careful of her wonderful instrument? The touch of arrogance that others detect in her is undeniably present. But I have always felt she has a right to it. She must be cautioned, however, not to take her talent for granted. I do wish that I could be allowed to comfort her, to wipe her brow and cool her fever. I am so strong that there would be nothing for me to fear, but Prioress has decreed otherwise.

Concerta is sleeping so soundly that I don't dare pick her up to enhearten myself. Her dark birth hair has already been replaced by golden fuzz, and her dark eyes, when she is awake, have many tiny blue specks that have begun to merge. Signora Mandano says we will not know their true color until she has attained six months or so. I hope they are as blue as Our Lady's mantle. To my way of thinking, there are too many dark eyes among us.

"I must tell you," says Signora, "that we had thought to send Concerta to a wet nurse in the countryside. But with this sudden throat malady afflicting so many, the doctor has decided any move of the children would be unwise."

"She will remain here, then," I say so joyfully, the lady steps back as if I had tried to embrace her. It is such welcome news, I become almost giddy.

Someone has given the toddlers some cardboard soldiers painted in bright colors, and the little boys are singing pretty tunes and making the soldiers dance. I think the girls would sooner have dolls, but there are but two of these, beautifully dressed and kept on a shelf. Their glass eyes stare straight into space as if the dolls are bored to their petticoats.

I wind up the mechanical monkey, and it stutters across the floor right into the children's game, causing giggles and squeals of delight. Again and again I wind up the toy, and the frantic tykes run around the room as if pursued by a dragon.

"What are you doing!" says Signora Mandano when she comes upon us. "The children are much too excited. Just look at all that high color in their cheeks."

She flutters around them like a distraught hen and cautions me to settle everyone down again immediately, as if that can be easily done. To make things even worse, one of the infants begins to cry. Since I don't want to be banished from the nursery on any account, I quickly make a very serious face and hide the monkey under some pillows. Francesco and Carlotta begin to cry, as I was sure they would, but I wipe their faces, blow their noses, and promise raisins with their afternoon snack.

"It is time for their nap," says Signora—more sternly than necessary, I think. "And it must be time for your afternoon classes as well."

"But who will help you? Who will bathe Concerta when she wakes up?"

"The wet nurse will do it. She's due here at any time and might as well make herself useful for once. Field cows. That is all those women are."

I think how, though they are somewhat indolent, it wouldn't be such a bad occupation, really, always dressed in a loose *chemise de couche* and putting a babe to the breast throughout the day. For the most part, they seem such contented, comforting women. Without them our orphans would surely starve.

I hate to leave before Concerta opens her eyes. I do want sometimes to be the first thing she sees, so she'll feel that she has always known me. But today I don't argue. I am already late for a history lesson I was hoping to miss with the very good excuse that I was badly needed in the nursery.

All the way down the side stairs, I can hear the sweet chatter and cries of the babies, but they cease as soon as I close the heavy door onto the narrow Calle della Pietà. I am pulling on the handle of the equally heavy door into the chapel and school when I happen to glance toward the lagoon where a woman with a black *zendaletta* over her head is flirting outrageously with one of the gondoliers, swishing an edge of black lace back and forth across her eyes with the same rhythm as she swishes her hips.

At the exact moment my vision stops at the sight of a skirt, blue as the watteaus we wear every day, Silvia bursts into the street from around the corner, her pinched face purple as a Lenten vestment.

"What is she thinking?" she mumbles to herself. Then, seeing me, her voice becomes strident. "Has she gone mad?"

"Who?" I ask, guessing the answer but not certain I want to know.

"Rosalba, of course. Who else pastes her gaze to every doublet and pair of breeches that passes along the Riva degli Schiavoni?"

"Rosalba!" I exclaim. When I look more closely I don't want to believe my eyes but am unable to pull them away. "Are you sure?"

"Of course I am sure. Who else would ask me to play

her lady's maid? 'A little fun,' she said, 'a little entertainment.' Entertainment for her, perhaps. If she continues to move her hips in that way, she will wriggle herself into the lagoon."

"You must tell her to stop," I say.

"I have. She is suddenly as deaf as the mast of a ship. Why don't you cross to the boat dock and tell her yourself?"

"You were sent to make sure she returned . . . undefiled." I'm not sure what I'm saying when using a word we've been warned with before. But I know that Rosalba must come back at once or risk being sent someplace else. I don't know where. It has happened before, but not to anyone that I have known. Or liked so much. Or trusted to be on my side and to tell me the truth of things.

Rosalba

THEY THINK I DON'T SEE them there, wringing their hands and trying to get my attention by whistles and coughs. They are bobbing their heads up and down like two pigeons over their brood.

"Yes, I have noticed you before, Signore. On my many trips to the Piazza San Marco." I hold the edges of the *zendaletta* over my face so he will not recognize the silly girl who has been posing for him by the doorway to the street. "Your singing is always the . . . loudest and most . . . entertaining." I don't dare tell the truth—that his notes are quite flat a good deal of the time.

"Ah, Signorina," he cajoles, peering closely at me. I made sure that my rosy bosom is well exposed above the sheer fichu of my bodice, and am pleased to see that it catches his eye and keeps it for quite a time. How deliciously close he seems, one hand on the oar but the other one poised to encircle my waist, I am sure — if it wasn't for all of the hisses and fuss from those two at the corner of the Ospedale.

"Rosalba," Anetta shouts at last. I turn very slowly and stare at her as if she is deranged, which I feel she must be to create such a scene.

"Do you know those two?" asks Giuseppe, who offered his name at the start, though I didn't tell mine. "And are you Rosalba? Is that what they call you?"

"Those girls are mistaken," I say. "They have me confused with somebody else."

"Rosalba," he says. "What a beautiful name."

"I suppose that it is, Signore, but it isn't my own."

He laughs. "So you tell me. And are you perhaps from the Pietà?"

"What a ridiculous conclusion," I say with abandon, still attempting to appear gay and reckless. And I would have succeeded, I'm certain, if Anetta hadn't suddenly stridden across to the dock and barrelled between us.

"*Arrivederci*, Signore," she calls to Giuseppe, waving one hand at him and pulling me away with the other.

Embarrassed in the extreme, I hide behind my veil, turn very quickly, and scurry after her like a disobedient child, hoping he will at least not know this face the next time we meet. Silvia is waiting to pull me through the door, and they both chatter away in the entry and rail at me as if I have committed some high crime.

"You spoiled everything!" I shriek. "His gondola was empty. He would have allowed me inside."

"Exactly," says Silvia. "Right before you lifted your skirts and allowed him the same."

"Ohh," I wail in an agony of frustration. "How can you believe such a thing! That was simply my best hope of finding a place for my plan to unfold."

"And for whatever else to unfold that you did not plan. It would have come to no good," says Silvia.

"As if you can even imagine the good it would come to."

"Enough of this," says Anetta. "Signora Mandano is in a state wondering what has become of the two of you. Where are the medicines?"

"Here," says Silvia, producing a fat parcel from under her cloak. "I snatched them away from Rosalba the minute I saw her sashay to the water's edge. So much for her responsible nature. Ha! I can tell by the look in her eyes that she never missed them until now."

"I knew you had them, you simpering fool," I tell her. "Of course I knew that you did."

Sweet Anetta is aghast. "Don't you realize, Rosalba, that he who calls his brother . . . or sister . . . a fool shall be 'liable to the fires of Gehenna'?"

"A very good place for such a busybody," I say, and rush up the stairs to our chamber just as Signora Mandano comes fluttering down the hallway in some sort of tizzy.

There is no one about in the sleeping quarters so late in the day, and I can open my clothes trunk and look through my things unobserved. At the foot of each cot is a large chest with plenty of space to hide my new *zendaletta* and shiny little patch box. (Silvia threw such a fit when I stopped at the milliner's to purchase them. The shop is so near the apothecary that I can't see why she objected.) I fold the *zendaletta* and place it beneath the lovely red velvet girdle I was able to purchase one day from a street merchant who sells used clothing. I simply called from the doorway, and he came running over. It is only a little ripped in one place. I take out the tiny gold serpent and chain I found in the alley, wrap it in my kerchief, and put all my clean undergarments and my quilted wool petticoat on top of my treasures. If anyone snoops, and there isn't much time around here for that, it is unlikely they'll dig all the way to the bottom. Though we are given our clothing, the dresses that are so alike, each one of us has managed to collect a few special things that we rarely wear, but bring out from time to time to simply look at and put back in place.

After what happened this afternoon, I will have to be on my best behavior for the rest of the week. When

I turn up in my place at rehearsal, Father does not scold me quite as much as I had expected, but he does say, "Rosalba," rather gravely, I think. Then he continues: "You have mentioned before your desire to play professionally after your time here with us. I think you're surely capable enough to do that."

"Oh, thank you, Father," I say. How congenial of him!

But unfortunately he isn't finished.

"Capable enough, to be sure, but not disciplined enough. You do know what I'm telling you?"

"I . . . think so, Father. But it will be different when I am out there"—I gesture at no place in particular—"on my own."

"Yes, it will be different. No one to urge you along, to provide your clothing and food. No kindly violin-maker to tell you when you need improvement or to help with a difficult passage." He smiles to himself. "To polish your instrument when you have left it bumping around in my shop like a raw piece of wood."

"And you won't be able to play in Venice. It isn't allowed for the students who leave here," says Anna Maria, as if I had asked her advice.

"That cannot be true!" I exclaim.

"Oh, yes, it is true," says Father. "And if, heaven bless you, you decide to take the veil, it will have to be in a true convent in some other part of Italy."

"Who decided this and why?"

"The Board of Governors. And only heaven knows why," says Father.

I am so overcome that I stand up and shake my finger at him before I can stop myself. As he is a priest, it is probably some kind of sacrilege. But he doesn't seem angry at all when I do it or even when I say, "Are we to be prisoners here for the rest of our lives?"

"Your prison," he says, "is a great deal more spacious than my little home, which I share with five brothers still, and our father and mother."

"But you come and go as you please."

He strokes his beardless chin. "Hmm. As I please. And so may you when the time comes. But the Ospedale will not want you to compete with the talented musicians that you leave behind."

"Or haunt our halls in a habit and wimple," says Silvia. "Just what kind of veil were you thinking of for Rosalba, Father?"

"It could happen," says Anetta. "One never knows."

"Oh, one does," says Silvia.

And for once she is right.

There is a new little *iniziata* today, very thin and frail with fine yellow hair. She begins to pass out the corrected scores, but not before Father puts out an arm to stop her for a moment and tell us her name.

"This child is Catina," he says. "We have much in common."

She laughs weakly and looks at him shyly from under long lashes. Does she play the violin, too? Many of us play the violin.

"We have a common foe," he says, "from which we must protect each other, eh, Catina?"

What can he possibly mean?

The other little *iniziate* are red-eyed and stumbling about this morning. They trip over each other and hand out violin scores to the viola section and oboe scores to the cellos. Their yawns cause a mild epidemic of slack, gaping jaws.

"If I had not tucked you in myself," says Father Vivaldi, "I would be certain you had missed a good night's sleep."

"It was Catina," says Angelina. "She kept us up with spooky stories." She whispers the rest of her tattle behind one hand as the others squeal with laughter. "Margaretta and Antonia wet their drawers. Elena got such a case of hiccups that Catina had to give her honey, which I think she stole from the kitchen, and then made her hold her breath until she almost exploded."

"You promised not to tell," wails Margaretta.

"Where did you get the honey?" I ask Catina.

"From Cook for when I have a coughing fit."

She turns to Father. "The stories were indeed very scary, Signore." She puffs up proudly. "My best tales yet, I do assure you."

"Well, there will be no such tales tonight," he cautions her with gentle brusqueness. "You need your rest as much or more than anyone, and I need helpers who are wide awake.

"Indeed," he says again, while looking deep into her oval eyes, transparent as glass, as if to find an answer for them both. "We must protect each other, you and I."

Chapter Ten

Anetta

IT HAS BEEN DAYS since Luisa was sent to the infirmary, and her absence from my life causes that same bereft feeling as when something valuable has been lost and no one will help you look for it. There is but little news about those taken sick, and certain of the younger girls, afflicted before Luisa, have not yet returned.

The older girls among the *privilegiate del coro,* except for Luisa and Maria, have remained well and are relieved to have a chance at solo parts that would in normal times not have come to them. They must, of course, know how poorly they perform if one allows comparisons. I think the audiences, too, must be quite disappointed, although when I have put forth such sentiments, Rosalba and Anna Maria have roundly disagreed with me.

"Your judgment has been colored by your great affection for Luisa," said Rosalba when I complained after the last concert about the unevenness of vocal tone.

"Truly," added Silvia, "it is a relief to be spared Luisa's ragged diction and deliberate phrasing."

"As if you'd know the remedy for either one," I countered, and with great restraint did not repeat what is very well known—that Silvia has at least one ear made of tin.

One night when sleep will not come and I am desperate for news of Luisa, I slip quietly from our chamber and creep up a flight of stairs and into the corridor leading to the hospital door, passing no one on the way. It is very late, but there will surely be a night nurse in attendance, perhaps one who is more forthcoming with information than those I have encountered during the day.

Candles burn within sconces on either side of the double doors, casting their light all the way to the stairs. Afraid to learn what is inside, I stand in front of the doors for a very long time, even reluctant to touch the knob or knock. When I do knock softly, there is no response, so I rap a little harder. At no response again, I rap harder still. The door suddenly springs open, and I lurch with ready knuckles into the same surly nurse who sent me away during the day. The stench of puke, fevered bodies, and strange medicinals makes me stagger.

"Not you again," she says, holding me from her. "Such a big oaf of a girl," she declares. "What business can you possibly have here in the dead of night?" She slaps a hand against my head. "Not sick yourself, are you?"

"I've come to find out about Luisa Benedetto. How is she faring? When will she be released? Will she be well in time for Carnival?"

"You shouldn't be in here at all," she says, grabbing my arm and shoving me back through the door until I lose my balance and must hang upon her like a giant leech.

"For heaven's sake! Get off me, girl," she says, shaking me from her.

"But I must be told something," I wail. "I am sick with worry."

"As you should be," she says, softening enough to let me regain my balance at least. "Her fever is still climbing. This peculiar malady makes the older girls much sicker than the young ones."

"What of Maria?"

"The young lady who was to be married?"

"Yes, that's the one."

She pauses such a long time, it's almost as if she wants to tell me something with the words that are unspoken. Finally, she looks directly in my eyes and says, "I have no news for you on that one. Please leave now. You shouldn't ask about these things."

My heart thumps into my stomach. But it's clear she will not divulge a bit of information about Maria, even as I feel certain I sense the truth.

"You don't understand. I must at least be told about Luisa. Luisa is my dearest friend. If you would let me, I could care for her. I'd help you with the others, too. I have proven myself very useful in the nursery."

"The best that you can do for her is stay away. Go toot upon your horn or whatever it is you are good at. You are not needed here."

In a sudden frenzy, she pushes me with all the strength in her bulbous shoulders and two rough hands and slams the door behind me.

I'm much too wide awake and worried to return to sleep, but there is nowhere else to go but to my bed, the blankets now as cold as wash upon a line in winter. The other girls sleep deeply, so tired out from last night's rehearsal that they have not heard me leave or return. Luisa's chamber pot is empty, her bed undisturbed. Just before dawn, I climb beneath her flannel coverlet, which contains her skin's sweet peppery scent. I tuck it securely around me, pull it up over my face, breathe deeply, and am able at last to doze.

Chapter Eleven

Luisa

EVERYTHING IS SNAPPING INTO VIEW after what seemed like days of fuzzy dreams and floating voices. How long have my eyes been wide open this way? There are many more beds than when I arrived, and nurses are squeezing between them to tend to moaning and feverish patients.

"You're awake at last, I see," says a large nurse, whom I've heard called Sofia, on her way to another patient with a compress of some kind. When she uncovers the girl's chest, it is bright pink. I look down at my own to see the same color spreading over my trunk and onto my arms like a cascade of tiny strawberries. Another nurse puts a hand to my forehead and smiles, exposing a number of missing and broken teeth.

"Your fever's down, praise God, *bambina*," she says, the words whistling softly over me. "You have much *buona fortuna*."

"What day is it?" I ask. My words sputter out the rough track of my throat, which is still unbelievably sore.

"Why, it's Friday at last. The end of another terrible week!" She clasps one hand with another. "Of course you wouldn't know about it. You've slept it away."

"The concert," I say, but can't finish the thought.

"No need to be thinking of that. While you've been here, more than one concert has gone on as planned with the girls who are well. Except for you and one other, it's only the youngest ones who've taken sick."

"Has my mother been told? Does she know where I am?"

She looks at me strangely, winks at another nurse, then touches my forehead again.

"The delirium should be long past. What's this talk of a mother?"

"My mother. Sabina Dolores Cincotta," I tell her as loudly and deliberately as my voice will allow. "She must be told I am sick."

"I don't know what you're saying. This is an orphanage. All the patients are orphans."

How can I convince her? I am so weak that I burst into tears.

"Signora Mandano knows my beautiful mother. She must find her and tell her," I repeat. "My mother needs to know I have been ill."

"There, there, Signorina. Don't excite yourself. Didn't we all have a mother once?"

"My father is a duke. His name is in the Golden Book."

"But of course. Every duke worth his salt leaves a bastard or two at our door."

"You must send a message. She lives near the Rialto Bridge on Calle del Carbon. It isn't very far."

"Yes, my darling," she says, pulling the blanket up to my chin. From the brusque way she does it, I can tell she has no plans at all to do as I ask and thinks that the fever has taken hold again. Though I'm too exhausted to even lift my head, when another nurse passes between the beds by the window, I call out to her.

"Please, Signora. Will someone please make sure my mother is told I have this *malattia*?"

Her smile is as vacant as that of Sofia. "Of course, *bambina. Immediatamente.*"

If only I could scream or lift my body somehow from this narrow bed. If I could just jump up and run or fly. If I could even sing, it might make them listen and be convinced that I'm not afflicted in the head.

Instead I sink back onto my cot and slip into sleep once again, waking only when I'm propped on a nurse's arm and a spoon is thrust between my teeth or when there is some commotion in the room. Once, late at night, I wakened for a time to stare blind-eyed at the greenish shadows and shapes, which, as I watched, became a child being wrapped in linen, head to toe, and taken from the room on a litter. The silent, solemn movements made me certain that she would not be returning to this life, and I lay awake for a long time afterward, terribly saddened yet very aware of my own body's juices and rhythms building again, struggling to assert themselves.

Days, I believe, pass in sleeping and waking. Finally it seems I am waking for much longer periods, eager to drink the potions and other beverages offered to me, even taking small bites of the millet porridge I would ordinarily shun. There are fewer beds in the room, and some are empty. No patient is groaning or seems to be in a crisis. My skin itches, and long strips of it are peeling from my hands and feet.

"Don't worry," says Sofia. "That is the last stage of this strange canker rash. It means you are surely on the mend."

I would like to tell her that it feels as if I am breaking into little pieces instead, but I know she will not understand.

The door opens suddenly, and a nurse I don't remember seeing before fills the opening. She cradles a small figure whose hair drapes from her limp head like a damp yellow kerchief. The child's eyes are closed, but she wheezes and gasps in her fevered sleep. As she passes my bed, I look at the troubled features and am startled to find that I know this patient, that it is Catina, the confident little girl who did her best many days ago to console me in the infirmary. How wrong she had been then about this throat disorder. How very sad that such a frail child is now its victim, for many stronger than she have succumbed to its fearful hold. That I have escaped death is perhaps a miracle. When I am no longer so terribly weak, I must study why I have been spared and what it can mean.

Chapter Twelve

Rosalba

I HAVE BEEN VERY GOOD, showing up for almost every rehearsal and trying hard not to anger Maestro Gasparini or Father Vivaldi by not being prepared. It has been most difficult without Luisa and Maria. I myself have had to sing the contralto solo on more than one occasion, and now that Father is planning a grand biblical performance of his first oratorio, *Moyses Deus Pharaonis,* I simply don't know how he will fill all the difficult roles.

Today we were told that Maria has left us, and not for a husband. She has, in truth, left this world entirely in the throes of the terrible illness that has claimed some of the younger girls. I did not know her well, so it is not a great personal loss, but there is always deep sadness on hearing that someone has died whose life had not really begun.

Apparently Luisa is improving, praise God, but they say it will be a long recuperation. There is even talk of sending her to the country in the spring to the same Tuscan farm where other students have gone to recuperate after illnesses not nearly as severe.

Anetta is pining to see her and writes long letters of consolation, never receiving any in return. Poor Anetta seems thinner and gaunt, as if she has been ill herself. I think only the sight of Luisa, restored to health, will make her well again.

There is such a pall over everything, one would hardly suspect that Carnival begins in only three days and we celebrate Christmas in two. It is rumored that the Board of Governors will want the Ospedale to ignore Carnival this year. Would such a decision apply to all of us? I wonder. I have been preparing for this grand pre-Lenten celebration since last year, when I first spied the wig-maker's assistant. In fact, I've been working secretly on a magnificent mask made out of all the dusky blue pigeon feathers I've been able to find in the street and the square. Unfortunately, I cannot seem to capture the beautiful iridescence that can be seen when massed on the bird. No matter. The mask will still be like no other.

And I am so very ready to meet my own dearest love. Another year's wait would seem endless.

Just before supper, I have sequestered myself in the little storage room outside the kitchen to work on my mask and am surprised when Anetta comes by with the porridge bowls from the nursery. She stops when she sees me, clearly upset at discovering what I am up to.

"For the love of Our Dearest Lord, Rosalba. You didn't kill that bird, did you? Father Vivaldi will have an attack!"

She is so serious, I cannot help laughing.

"What bird, Anetta? Do you see a plucked and limp little body somewhere?"

"But all those feathers?"

"Are from many wild pigeons. I have been picking up these feathers from the street for almost a year. Don't you think it a clever idea?"

"If you want to adorn yourself with all the filth to be found in the square."

"You give me no credit for my cleverness. I have washed each one with a soap made of lard and lye according to Cook's recipe, and have dried them all in the sunlight."

"I suppose . . . if it entertains you. But it does seem quite frivolous at such a time as this when even the bells from the campanile in the Piazza San Marco sound like a dirge. Haven't you noticed?"

"I have noticed that we cannot continue to exist in this saddened condition, that we must begin to see goodness in the world again, to celebrate joyfulness. Doesn't Father Vivaldi tell us this himself with his music?"

"And doesn't the Bible tell us that there is a time to mourn?"

"And a time to set it aside. Truly, Anetta, though we have lost Maria and a few of the little girls, our own Luisa has been spared, and you must begin to hope again."

She looks confused and stricken, as if offered a sweet that is in the process of being snatched away.

"You expect me to hope, when I haven't laid eyes on Luisa for weeks?"

"You've been told she is well again. Is that not enough?"

"I will only believe it is true when I see for myself, when I know that her lovely lean body has not been wasted or her sublime voice lost."

"Of course, she will not be quite herself for a while. You must expect that. We must all expect it. For a while."

"For a little while or a long while? That is the answer no one will give me."

"And cannot," I tell her. Then, changing to the only subject that might still capture her attention, I ask, "And what of Concerta? Is she happy and well?"

Anetta responds as I thought she would, a smile creeping into her words.

"And growing so fast she needs new linen shirts, larger flannel petticoats, and muslin slips. Even her caps and undercaps are becoming tight. When I have the time, I shall make her new ones with embroidery and knotted fringe."

"That will be lovely," I assure her. "She is surely the best cared for infant in the nursery."

"Oh, I do not neglect the others."

She has misunderstood me.

"Of course you don't. I only meant—"

"That is not to say that I wouldn't if I could. She has become so like my own, my very own child. Sometimes . . ." she begins, but then stops herself and says, "I am being very silly. You would not want to know."

"Sometimes what, Anetta?"

"Well . . . sometimes . . . I think of myself, Luisa, and Concerta living all together. In the country somewhere. In a little house. Living together in a little house."

"It is a fine dream."

"Yes. But I know it is only a dream."

"It is good to have one. A dream."

"Do you?"

"Yes," I tell her. But she doesn't ask what it is, and I don't offer it.

My dream is of Carnival and my handsome wig-maker's assistant. My dream must happen, and soon. I will make it happen.

Chapter Thirteen

Anetta

THE OSPEDALE ALWAYS CELEBRATES the Feast of Natale very simply. This year each girl received a packet of sweets and a new everyday pleated cap, for which we are grateful. And Father has written a small festive violin solo that he plays himself during our noon meal, which includes dishes that are far grander than usual. Cook carries out the steaming platters to a sideboard decorated with pine boughs. There is a goose stuffed with truffles, a roasted wild boar filled and basted with all manner of herbs, pasta with a hearty sauce, the usual *granturco*, or polenta, made from corn, and a very special side dish, sardines in a *saor* made of onions, vinegar, spices, pine nuts, and raisins. There are even cakes spread with apple jam and bowls of the sweet biscuits called *baicoli*. We are each given a quarter of a fruit called a *melarancia*. It is orange in color, tastes both sweet and tart at once, and causes all the little girls to wrinkle their noses with pleasure. We are told that it is a great delicacy and will not appear on our plates soon again.

I mention the food first, because it will not be easy for me to describe my greatest gift, the return of Luisa to our table if only for the noon festivities. When I see her being led into the room, walking very carefully beside the burly nurse who evicted me from the hospital more than once, leaning into her, actually, as if one small misstep would cause her to lose her footing altogether, I become both dejected and then full of a sudden energy I haven't experienced in a very long time. Immediately, I jump from my chair and run to her side, against the protests of Prioress, who clucks her tongue when I clasp Luisa to me as gently as I can. The bad-tempered nurse tries to pull us apart, but I do not budge until Luisa herself withdraws from me, breathless, it seems, with her effort at simply standing up. I then fetch her a chair near the head of the longest refectory table. It is but one of a few newly vacant places and not near my place at table, but just to have her in the room is delight enough. Dressed only in a chemise and dressing gown, she is extremely pale and thin, with violet crescents above her cheekbones.

I turn often to see if she is eating what has been put upon her plate, that is, until Rosalba pokes me and tells me to stop.

"She will eat when she is ready," says Rosalba. "It is feat enough that she has made it to Christmas dinner. Do not anger her with your constant attention."

I am not allowed to take Luisa back to her sickroom, as I request when she rises to leave the meal in a short space of time, quickly tired, it seems, from raising a few forkfuls of food to her lips. Watching her leave the refectory with the odious nurse is very difficult for me, since it is doubtful that Luisa will be joining us again soon.

"You must think only of her being restored to health," says Rosalba when I sigh overmuch at Luisa's leaving our company so soon.

"It would seem you might have enjoyed the quiet nights and extra space in our bedchamber," says Silvia. "I for one have luxuriated in such a sea change. No hysterics over normal bodily functions. No bouts of whimpering for her mother."

"Neither was ever a burden to me," I tell her, "nothing on a par with your thrashing and whistles and snorts in the night."

Silvia becomes red-faced and Rosalba smirks.

"I do nothing of the kind, and you know it," says Silvia. "I keep even my wind to myself so as not to annoy."

"The noise," says Rosalba, "but not the odor."

"As if you could separate mine from all of the rest."

"It would not be a task I would care to undertake," says Rosalba.

I delight in the way she rises rather grandly and goes off to return her plate to the kitchen, while Silvia scrunches up her tiny features until her mouth and eyes are but slits.

"The only way she can have the last word with me," she says, "is for her to leave like that. She will not be so high and mighty when she discovers what I have found out about this year's Carnival."

I cannot resist asking. "What is it? What do you know?"

"The moment I tell you, you'll run right away to tell her."

"There are other ways — more reliable ways — to find out," I say, still dying for her to divulge what she knows.

"No one knows but me. I overheard Prioress scheming with Signora Mandano and Maestro Gasparini how to keep the lot of us indoors until Shrove Tuesday."

"There. You see? You've told me yourself."

She presses her lips together, sticking the upper lip over the bottom one until she resembles a jackanapes.

"That's not the whole of it," she says at last. "When we're all told, you will be astonished."

"Or you. For being misinformed again. Your gossip can never be trusted. And, think of it, how often are we allowed out of this place during Carnival or at any other time?"

"Judging from her actions of late, Rosalba has been counting on the loosening of some rules, I am certain. She'll be livid to discover that we're all being held by a tightly woven net with no possible holes. Beginning tomorrow."

"Tomorrow?"

"The first day of Carnival."

Saint Stephen's Day dawns gray and dismal, a heavy dark sky hanging low over the lagoon, the islands obscured by fog. Already, however, there are decorated *peote*, smaller gondolas, and other small craft plying the canals, songs and shouts leaping so high into the air we can hear them through slightly open windows. And there are already revelers dancing along the cobblestone streets and suitors throwing perfumed eggs at women in stark white *bautta* masks, which cover their forehead and eyes and nose and accentuate the elaborate layers of black clothing beneath. As intended, there is no way to tell the lower classes from the upper. Except with the wheelbarrow parade, where the pushers of barrows wear no masks at all and are clearly all manner of farmers come to town.

At the risk of letting in damp, frigid air, many of the girls are already hanging out windows to view the festivities in the street. We are so close to the Piazza San Marco, where most of the performances will be, as to get the overflow of musicians and jugglers, the grotesque *gnaghe*, dressed as women, and a few harlequins on stilts.

We all know that the Parade of the Doge is to begin in the afternoon and still nothing has been said to indicate that we may not attend in chaperoned groups, as we have in the past. We are just finishing the noon meal when Prioress rises from her chair and clears her throat, as she does habitually before any announcement. Silvia looks meaningfully at me, but I pretend not to notice her.

"Signorine," says Prioress, tapping her glass with a spoon for better attention. The room becomes suddenly quiet, for we are all expecting something by now.

"As you know, this has been a very sad time for the Ospedale, a sad time indeed." She clears her throat again, but has no need to tap on the glass. She clasps her hands together and loses them within the folds of her large sleeves. "We have had to consider a change in our usual lenient attitude toward the celebration of Carnival, one in keeping with the period of mourning that has been forced upon us."

There are small gasps of disappointment, but still no one speaks. Silvia tries desperately again to catch my eye.

"In the past we have, as you know, allowed you to join the throngs of revelers for short periods when properly chaperoned. We have even encouraged a few chaperoned trips to the performances in the Piazza San Marco."

There are murmurs as girls agree and as they evidently remember some happy times.

"The Board of Governors has thought long and hard about what to do during these days before the penitent ones of Lent, and has decided that, though you may all watch the revelers as much as you please from windows on the lagoon or even from the street of the Pietà if you stay in the shadows of the chapel, mixing with the crowd in any way will not be allowed."

There are a few audible objections, Rosalba's low moan among them, but many of the girls remain silent.

"However," declares Prioress at length, "there will be one exception, a light in the darkness, so to speak, for, as you must understand, this is no punishment, and it has long been the Ospedale's policy, in music as in everything else, to encourage the joy of living." With great effort, she composes her stern features into something approaching pleasantness and continues, a tilt to her expression, almost a smile: "So, children, we have made another decision. And one that you will find quite delightful as the weeks of celebration continue."

"Let me tell them," Father Vivaldi interrupts.

"It was Father's idea," says Prioress, sitting down abruptly as he stands up. "So, yes, I will let him tell you himself."

Father Vivaldi seems a trifle more breathless than usual, but it is clearly not from ill health but because of his excitement at unfolding his little plan, which appears very little indeed when he has finished telling it. All it amounts to, in fact, is a trip to Saint Mark's Basilica to hear him and his father perform together, followed by a puppet show in the square and a treat of *frittelle*—the small round fritters made from goat's milk, rose water, and saffron, and sprinkled with sugar. *Frittelle* can be found only during Carnival, and we would be utterly despondent if we had to miss out on them.

"It is like throwing a hungry dog a very small bone," says Silvia.

I myself am so encouraged at having seen Luisa yesterday and by knowing that she is getting well, that any restrictions during Carnival seem unimportant. Yet looking across at Rosalba, I see that she is crestfallen and this troubles me because of her unpredictable nature. Surely, I tell myself, she is planning to observe the rules. She must. And I must do everything I can to see that she does.

Chapter Fourteen

Luisa

I DID NOT WISH to go down to supper yesterday. I felt much too unsteady on my feet and in such an ill humor it was all I could do to be led downstairs by Sofia and into the clutches of Anetta. Such a scene was inevitable, for I had been told of her repeated attempts to enter the sickroom. Afterward, I was too upset to converse with anyone at table or force more than a few mouthfuls of food down my throat. In just moments I was also too light-headed to sit comfortably and had to beg Sofia to take me back.

"The little excursion did you good," she kept saying on our way upstairs. "You must begin to build up your strength again."

What I can't understand is how one can build upon something that is missing. I all but threw myself onto my bed as soon as we made our way into the hospital room. I clung to it as if it were a raft, and soon fell fast asleep, not waking again until the candles were being lit and their soft light flickered and fell over empty beds and those few occupied by the girls who were mending and those still with fever.

Little Catina has coughed and wheezed mercilessly since she first arrived, even as she seems to slip in and out of sleep. She cannot sleep soundly this way, however, and that is what the nurses say she absolutely must do if she is to recover. In just the light from the candles, I can see that her face is quite red now and am certain the rash must be covering her chest and arms, and that her tongue has turned as spongy and white as mine had been.

Pails of water have been brought into the room to put moisture into the air, which is constantly dried by steady fires in the grate to keep the room warm. A warm wet cloth, wrung out and placed repeatedly upon Catina's chest, causes her breathing to become more even for a little while. But then the hard hacking coughs begin to wrack her small fragile chest once more, and it is as painful to me as if my own breastbones heaved up and down in consort with hers. One nurse prays under her breath continually whenever Catina launches into one of these terrible sessions, and I find myself desperately repeating every prayer I have ever known or thinking that if I keep my eyes closed to the count of ten or stay absolutely still without moving a muscle or hold my own breath through perhaps three of her violent gasps, then she will magically stop. When she doesn't, I can't help feeling betrayed, as if I have held up my part of the bargain, however foolish it was.

Afterward, I sleep quite heavily again, barely waking off and on in the night when Catina's attacks are at their worst, then exhausting myself again in prayer and useless bargaining, promising all manner of things to the saints, things that I cannot remember in the light of morning.

This morning I have awakened from a very deep sleep, which came upon me only as the windows were beginning to change from midnight blue to gray streaked with pink and yellow. My first thought is of Catina and how she has fared after another troubled night. But when I glance at her bed, it is untidy and slightly soiled and entirely empty.

She has left us, too, I tell myself, and the thought is so unbelievably sad that I curl into a ball and make a shrill wild sound that I have never made before or heard uttered by a single soul.

"What is this keening?" asks Sofia. "Are you in pain?"

"Catina has left us," I cry into my chest. "Little Catina, good little Catina, is gone."

When Sofia laughs, I find it cruel beyond belief.

"Only to another room," she assures me, "so that you and the others can get some rest."

"Is it true?" I ask, uncoiling slowly from my ball of misery. Can it possibly be true?

"Of course it is," says Sofia. "And we are watching her even more carefully. And," she adds, "seeing some slight improvement. Nothing is easy for that child, but she has a center of hard gold that cannot be cracked. You will see."

Catina has been so terribly sick and she is so young, it is difficult to believe that she has not lost her fight. But remembering our conversation in the infirmary that night that seems so long ago, I realize what Sofia has said about Catina's hard center is right, and that I should have suspected her amazing will may actually be able to transcend things that would take the life of someone physically stronger.

I continue to ask about her, however, even as my own strength does indeed begin to eke back into my limbs and mind. My throat cannot be trusted just yet, however. I can speak well enough but am afraid to test my singing voice, stricken by panic at times when I think how it might have simply disappeared.

When Sofia tells me that I may move back into the chamber shared with other girls from the *coro*, it seems like a huge step for which I am unprepared.

"You cannot stay in the infirmary forever," she tells me. "You are one of the last to leave."

"It is only this one bed I occupy. There are many ones empty now."

"Because some of the girls who were in them have returned to their lives in the Ospedale. As you should. As you must."

She begins packing up the few things I have accumulated here — a small bone-handled brush for my teeth, a comb for my hair, and an extra chemise — and she hands me the nightdress I wore to the infirmary that first awful night. She has fetched my everyday clothing and lays it upon the rumpled bed. When she gently pulls me to my feet, the room spins less than in the past and soon rights itself. Still, it takes a great effort to dress myself. With the apron, it is all I can manage to tie it properly behind my back. What good fortune that the cap covers this head of hair matted with body oil and sweat, for until one is entirely well, we are told not to wash overmuch for fear of a chill.

Our chamber is empty when I return there — not surprising since it is the middle of morning and classes are in session. My bed has been made neatly by someone, probably Anetta. The things in my trunk seem undisturbed. I was, of course, certain they would be, for the students here are taught honesty above any other virtue. My guitar, an instrument that I rarely play, stands invitingly in the corner, and soon I am sitting by the window, strumming it, my fingers stiff and shaky but warming to the vibrations of the strings and the indescribable feeling of making music again. It is the first time since I was very little and, as Mother has told me, I would sing for her amusement, that I have played or sung with no others to join in. Just melding the notes into a chord, their exact harmonies always the same even when repeated again and again, seems such a perfect thing. It is a thought that expands my weakened spirit and causes me to consider this moment only and not all the days stretching before me that I must somehow rejoin.

"You are here!"

It is Rosalba who proclaims this and not Anetta, thank heaven, who I am forced to admit has been most kind in her constant concern for me these many weeks. Of course it is Rosalba, for who else would manage to leave her lessons before the appointed hour for them to end?

She rushes to me with a quick embrace that, thankfully, does not suffocate like Anetta's.

"How grand it is to have you return to us in good health, Luisa. Many prayers have been answered."

"Including my own, for I was not yet prepared to hand over every solo rightfully mine to Geltruda."

"*Buono!* You return lighthearted as well."

She appears not to know why she came here, for though she opens her trunk, she takes nothing from it and walks back and forth, back and forth, from window to door.

"It is Carnival," she says suddenly. "The doge's parade

should begin soon. We may be able to see the end of it from our own window, though it will not be easy."

"And not from the street?"

"Not this year. This year we will only be treated to a dull-witted puppet show."

She is so obviously disappointed that it's clear Carnival must matter overmuch to her, and I cannot help wondering why. For my part, I feel scarcely able to walk to the parlor downstairs, let alone to the square, and do not wish to celebrate anything.

She quickly takes something from the pocket of her apron and turns her head away and then back, a blue-feathered mask now placed over her piercing black eyes. It is quite beautiful and not at all like anything I have ever seen on a reveler's face before.

I must have gasped my approval, for she seems pleased.

"Would you know me in this?" she asks.

"I would know you anywhere, Rosalba."

"You, yes, for we are like sisters. But what of a casual acquaintance? A passing gondolier, a shopkeeper's assistant?"

"To them, I believe, you would be quite a mystery in such a splendid disguise. Quite a mystery indeed."

Her smile is catlike under the mask.

"But what can you be thinking?" I ask. "Surely you will have little contact with such people at a puppet show."

"Don't worry yourself, Luisa. It was a frivolous question. Nothing more."

"And the mask? How did you come by it and why?"

"It is my own invention, made when I had reason to believe we would be allowed the same freedom of Carnival this year as we have known in the past."

I am relieved to see her put the mask inside her trunk. It must have been the real reason she came up here before Latin instruction was over. Yet I feel I must warn her, as she is sometimes so willful, and I try hard to think of something that will make her listen.

"One Carnival is like another," I say.

"Oh, no," she quickly corrects me. "Each one is as different as . . . as one springtime to another. One year the trees bud beautifully and burst with color at the proper time; another, they are frozen in their sleep and drop blossoms before they bloom."

"You describe a natural event, not a fanciful celebration devised by men and attended by all manner of riffraff."

"And kings and dukes and mysterious strangers. Therein is the beauty of it. The mystery, the chance meeting, the possibility of a great romance."

"Or great disaster."

At this remark of mine, she sticks her lip out petulantly and thrusts her mask into her pocket.

"The long days of your illness and seclusion have infected your good humor and level judgment more than

I realized at first. Last year at this same time, you were quite ready to join in the fun and revelry."

"Last year I was a different girl entirely. And so were you."

"What do you mean?"

"Only that, for myself, I am more somber and much older than just months ago, so woven through with mourning and with God's bewildering will that I can scarcely recognize myself. As for you, the Rosalba I've so often turned to for advice, the one whom I have always considered sage enough to see things as they truly are"—I pause to look at her and make quite certain that I have her full attention—"that Rosalba seems right now to be replaced by someone foolish, bold, and disobedient."

She laughs, grabs the top of my cap, and gently shakes it.

"And you are fast becoming a depressing scold." She bows and sweeps one arm across herself from shoulder to toes as if to introduce an actor. "There is but one Rosalba," she declares, "and she is here before you."

"Be careful, dear Rosalba," is all that I can muster after that.

Chapter Fifteen

Rosalba

I WAS SO OVERJOYED to see Luisa back in our chamber that I almost forgot why I came there in the first place in the middle of the morning. It is not easy to slip out during Latin, for Maestra Duval has enormous eyes that take in everything but the very corners of the room. Even with her back to the class, one must be directly behind her and not even a little to the side to be clear of the broad sweep of her sight. I waited most of the hour for just such an alignment and was quite certain that Silvia would tell on me, but at the time of my escape, her little head was almost down to the paper on her desk because of her need to squint so.

Luisa is much changed in ways I probably cannot describe properly. She is thinner, true enough, but also less fidgety, and I detect a new, uncommonly deep place within her dark eyes in which both sadness and calm seem to reside together. Her lovely auburn hair is completely covered by a cap, which makes her look even younger than she is.

In truth, it is a great gift to see her without the others present. She is idly strumming her guitar and not singing along, which of itself is unusual. I do not ask about her throat for fear there might in fact be some small problem with her voice after so long an illness. Befuddled at first and forgetting what I had come for, I roam about the room for quite a while before taking my mask from my pocket and putting it over my eyes to surprise her.

Her reaction is just as I had hoped, for the mask is surely as unique and beautiful as she declares it to be. Still angered by the decision of the Board of Governors concerning Carnival, and even though they may feel they are giving us a great treat under the circumstances, I cannot help making a bitter pronouncement about the puppet show.

Of course Luisa is untroubled by the Carnival ban, for I suspect she will not be allowed out-of-doors for quite a while. Few of the celebrations ever really appealed to her anyway. She seems, however, overly concerned for my welfare when she says, "Be careful, dear Rosalba."

I have to tell her, "When was Rosalba anything but careful!"

She does not, of course, know about the little incident with Giuseppe, which seems very long ago now, or about my increasingly careless attitude toward some of the concerts, which, to my mind, are entirely too frequent of late. In this rather confidential and unexpected meeting, I must remind myself that it is right to think she will not understand and that it is enough to already have more than one watchdog at my back.

And no one, thank the heavens, was privy to my little encounter with Father Vivaldi yesterday at noon when he chided me for my sudden emergence of great mirth whenever it is time for work or concentration.

"I had thought," said he, "that the little rapscallion who could never observe the rules might have grown wise, punctual, and obedient in my absence."

"Me? Rapscallion?" I countered. "Have you not noticed that I am a *maestra* this year. Think of that! Surely the board would not reward me for bad behavior."

"Perhaps," he said, more somberly it seemed to me. "But be that as it may, I am frankly astounded at the improvement in your playing. It has given me a wonderful idea for a concerto for you."

I was so taken aback by this unexpected praise and

his offer of a new piece especially for my instrument, that I played the fool again and said, "You can't already be trying to make me the bait of some duke. Surely it is too soon."

He smiled. "Too soon, indeed, little renegade. I am simply planning ahead. Always planning ahead."

More grateful for his kind words than he could know, I stood on tiptoe to kiss his cheek, but he blushed so furiously that I quickly rushed away from him and right out the door.

"Come down with me," I tell Luisa now. I am already late for the class in solfeggio, in which we tediously learn strange sol-fa syllables that note the tones of the scale. I must not miss it again, even though it is sure to bore me to my undergarments. But she shakes her head and doesn't rise from her cot, while I say something about languishing up here that makes her laugh.

"You go. I'm not ready yet."

"You'll have to make a start sometime."

"And I will. But not just yet. And don't tell Anetta I am here."

Luisa will not be teased about Anetta's great attachment to her, and so I offer her something in the way of consolation.

"I will tell her that when you do get back from hospital, she must not crowd or pester you. Does that please you?"

"If only she would listen!"

"Her heart is as soft as a pillow and can be shaped, truly, if one takes the trouble. Believe me, I will make certain she doesn't oppress you. I will."

As I start down the steps, Anetta is on her way up. At first I think she must have been told about Luisa and am relieved to discover that she is only looking for me.

"You are lucky that you were not caught slipping out from Latin this time," she scolds me.

"It was not luck. It is never luck. I always know just what I'm about."

"I should have said both cocky and lucky."

I take her hand and turn her around. "Come with me to solfeggio. If we run all the way, we will be there before Maestra bolts the door."

She locks step with mine, and we start off at a fast trot.

"She only does it to teach you a lesson."

It amuses me when Anetta becomes so solemn. How she manages it at such a pace is confounding. Just as we approach the door in question and try the knob, I ask, "Is there no end to the lessons I must learn?" Then *"Madre di Dio!"* I exclaim as the door opens and swings wide. "What luck!"

I'm happy to see that there are quite a few who are missing, the ones I noticed on our way here who were hanging out windows to watch a spindly parade of street musicians. There will be much better things to take our attention later in the week. According to my plan, I will bide my time for a bit until the running of the bulls begins. I feel such a kinship with those animals when they are set free. It is all I can do not to follow after them.

Chapter Sixteen

Anetta

AT FIRST I WAS OFFENDED at the way in which Rosalba spoke to me after solfeggio. I could not believe she was faulting me for my care and concern for Luisa or that she was privy first to the information that Luisa would soon be returning to us. But after a few moments of a little jealousy at Rosalba's new role as Luisa's confidant (yes, I do admit it) and no little anger, my relief at knowing my dearest girl will soon be in good health eased the unworthy feelings aside. They had come upon me like a flash fire and seemed out of my control at first. As I was slowly restored to my better self, however, I could not help thinking how impossible it would be to harbor such resentment of my own true friend, Rosalba, for very long. I will not feel at peace until I confess this to Father Luigi.

"Luisa will no doubt be very fragile for a while, considering her weakened condition," says Rosalba, "and so we must all try not to intrude upon her as she recuperates."

I am confounded. "Intrude? Have I ever intruded?"

"At times. In your zeal for her welfare. But no one would fault you for it."

"Intruded how?"

"In . . . affectionate, small ways. Enthusiastic hugs. Too much touching of her hair and brow. Some small exaggerations of her many accomplishments."

"I don't understand. These are all good things."

"And . . . a good deal of . . . hovering."

"Hovering?

"Being always about," Rosalba continues with a small sigh. "Going wherever she goes. Placing your chair nearest hers. Attending to even her unspoken needs." She pauses for quite a time. "Sleeping in her bed."

I feel my cheeks burn.

"How will she know that?"

"I will not mention it, but you can be sure that Silvia will."

"Oh."

"So it's best, don't you see, if you simply stand off for a bit to let her get used to the life here again."

"Yes, I see," I tell her, though the idea of restraining my deepest feelings seems pointless to me. If by some mere chance it will make Luisa feel better, however, I am determined to try.

"And," says Rosalba, "there is one other thing. Do not gaze at her overlong with such calf's eyes. She does find that oppressive, I'm told."

"By whom are you told?"

"By Luisa."

"Calf's eyes?"

"I believe that's what she called it."

My veins run cold at this affront by Luisa herself, and at the thought that I have done this oppressive thing, apparently time and again, without my even knowing.

"What kind of monster am I then?" I ask in words so soft Rosalba has to lean her head toward me to hear them.

Ever kind to me, she has a ready antidote.

"No monster at all, dear sweet Anetta. Just overzealous in your deep love for her."

"Can love be such a bad thing?"

"Never bad," says Rosalba. "But it should be tempered if it is not returned in the same measure that it's given."

Tempered is a word I do understand. It is so like a diminuendo, when the music gradually decreases in intensity until the pure harmonies can barely be heard. It is difficult to do this well on the viola d'amore. It will be even more difficult to tame my feelings for Luisa.

My attention to these hurts, however, is taken away completely when Signora Mandano bustles into our conversation and pulls me aside.

"Come to the nursery when you can, Anetta."

"I have some free time now," I tell her. "Is something wrong?"

My thoughts go to Concerta and all the possibilities and unforeseen events that can occur with infants.

"Do not alarm yourself. It is a small thing really, but Concerta runs a fever, and I thought you'd want to know."

From my work in the nursery, I've learned that fevers can indeed be little things or they can be swift messengers of death. Hardly bothering to bid good-bye, I gallop up the back stairs and arrive breathless by Concerta's little crib, where she is motionless with sleep, her golden head damp and glistening, her tiny thumb resting against a small blister on puckered lips that have stopped sucking. She's so still and tranquil that I wonder if indeed Signora Mandano can be right. When I touch her brow, however, heat rises through my fingertips.

"Do not wake her," says the wet nurse, who had evidently come to suckle Concerta but is busy now with another infant. "I couldn't rouse her long enough to feed. Such heavy sleep may bring her round."

Or take her from us, I think, and cannot help searching the space above for a hint of wings. I long to lift her little form and hold it close, but resist when thinking of the better good. I cannot leave her, though, and so I pull a chair beside the small bed, implore Our Blessed Lady with a litany of prayer, and rest my own head against the little fence around her cot until I feel a hand upon my shoulder.

"Have you been here all this time?" asks Signora Mandano. "Why, it's the middle of the afternoon."

I rise up in some kind of trance with Rosalba's earlier words to me and Concerta's fitful breathing all entwined in something like a dream. The wet nurse is no longer in the room.

"You can't continue sleeping here beside Concerta, Anetta."

My mind begins to stumble back to life.

"If it is truly so late, I've missed the sectional for contraltos. Maestro Scarpari must have wondered what became of me."

"I'm certain he'll understand. You're usually such a punctual girl. But there's nothing you can do for this child right now. We'll watch her carefully and tell you if there's any change."

"Are you certain there's nothing?"

"Very certain."

Nothing I can do. There is nothing I can do, it seems, for anyone I love.

Chapter Seventeen

Luisa

ROSALBA TELLS ME there is a sectional for sopranos this afternoon. She says it will not be taxing and that I must begin somewhere to enter back into the life here.

"You can't just sit up here and rot," is how I believe she put it.

So I won't have to converse with anyone, I make my way there late. Maestra Loretta is at the continuo and looks up when I enter, delight upon her face and such surprise that her single eyeglass slips from her eye and bounces, still on its ribbon, upon her ample bosom. When the students all turn to look at me, I realize there is no possible way I could have come in unobserved. Two of the *iniziate* scurry over with fistfuls of musical scores, and I quickly sit down on an empty stool near the back of the room while Maestra shushes the commotion I have created.

The singers are in the middle of their scales. And though they are disturbed for a moment by my entrance, Maestra quickly regains order and they resume their exercises, mouthing the vowels while keeping their jaws slack and forming the notes with their tongues against their teeth. She motions to me to join in, and when I don't, she looks over with concern but does not badger me, I'm happy to say. Opening my mouth to sing and drawing breath into my lungs even for such an exercise seems quite out of the question at present. Just arriving here, without having fainted at some point in my trip down the stairs and across to the school, is feat enough for one afternoon. I will tell Maestra this if she presses me. When she doesn't, I am much relieved.

It is a great temptation, however, to try to join in when the score itself—another new cantata from Father Vivaldi—is being sung. I wonder whom it is intended for this week, whose voice it will put on display, and am certain it cannot be mine, as Father could not have known I would be returning and as it is fully within the range of most of the other sopranos. It is such a lovely lyrical piece, so full of light trills and pastoral refrains, that I find myself transported during the singing of it to a place where small birds fill the trees. Of all the things that I have sorely missed, it is the making of music, or the absorbing of it as it is played or sung by others, that I have missed the most. At times during the rehearsal, I feel the new melodies rise into my throat and earnestly desire to simply open my mouth and let out what is building there. My fear at attempting this is so enormous, however, that I listen ever more intently during the entire sectional—listen to Geltruda softly attempting the notes I would have been able to sing with ease, to Loretta trilling so unevenly, to Marietta warbling like a giant thrush with no thought to the careful modulation that her part requires. Since Father very rarely makes notations for dynamics in his texts, she can be excused. A more sensitive singer, however, even in the absence of indicated slurs, ornaments, and other markings, would be aware of his preferences and distinctive style.

Afterward, when Maestra asks when I will be well enough to be assigned a solo, I find myself telling her that I'm not quite sure.

"Certainly not for another few weeks," I say.

She is so encouraged that I wonder if I have misspoken. I should have told her I am not strong as yet and may not be for quite a time. I should not have given her false hope.

After the sectional, the girls are very dear and welcome me as if I've been abroad and not just in another wing of the Ospedale for weeks. Up close, they seem too rosy and plump, too animated. Their continual chirping is overloud and discomfiting, their eyes too bright. When Lucretia links arms with me, I gently pull away. Is this truly the world I left behind?

Just as I am turning from the group emptying into the hallway, I spy Anetta coming toward me, and I freeze in my footsteps. To my great surprise, she also stops stock-still, an uncertain hint of a smile upon her lips. The smile grows when I return it as best I can. She gives a slight wave of one hand, enters another schoolroom, and shuts the door behind her. This new demeanor is more shocking to me than her usual smothering behavior. I can only think that Rosalba has done as she said she would and that Anetta has listened to her. I am not an ungrateful person, however, and, remembering Anetta's great care and regard for me, I am a little ashamed that I behave toward her in this way.

Father Vivaldi and I pass in the Calle della Pietà, and he seems overjoyed to see me. Although he is never given to embracing or other touches of endearment, I can discern his delight from how his eyes glint and the lids briefly flutter, how his voice rises in a joyful greeting, and from his earnest words.

"Luisa! We have missed you indeed." He holds up the beads that he always carries, his fingers continuing to move upon them. "You have been in my *Ave*s for weeks. How happy I am to see for myself that my prayers have been answered. And," he adds, "you'll find your little finch in great good health and voice as well. She puts my own sweet bird to shame."

That he has been praying especially for me is a humbling thought, even as I realize I am not known for such a virtue. And that he did indeed procure a little bird for me, some living creature of my very own, is most touching and kind.

"I have been reining in my notes to accommodate the others," he tells me then. "Next week I'll begin a *seranata* that makes full use of your range."

Not yet, I long to tell him. *Not yet.*

But he disappears into the school before I can utter a single word and just as Rosalba swings the door to the Ospedale wide and almost knocks me over in her great haste.

Chapter Eighteen

Rosalba

I NEARLY TOPPLE poor Luisa as I rush into the Calle on
my way to tell the news of how the senior girls, the ones
so newly turned Maestra, will not be going to the puppet
show and have to suffer through those silly wooden fetes
or listen to the drones who try to sell all manner of strange
potions on the side. Indeed, our treat is something that
I never dared to hope that I would see: the Commedia
dell'Arte, true theater with men and women acting out
their love upon the stage, I'm told, and even kidnappings
and tragedies, while performing tricks and such.

I hold on to Luisa with both hands and jump up and down.

"Can you believe such good fortune?"

She stands as still as a high-backed chair and seems about as overjoyed.

"I'm happy for you," she says at last. "And for the others. I'm sure it will be great fun for all of you."

"And for you. Surely you will come with us?"

She hesitates, and I believe she is considering it, but then she says, "Not this year. I simply cannot tax myself by doing anything but what I must."

"Even something so enjoyable? Something so transporting? Really, Luisa, it is a most unusual chance. Next year the fickle Board of Governors might well decide a puppet show is just the thing for all of us."

"Truly. I cannot."

"Don't say that yet. The play isn't until Wednesday afternoon. By then you may feel differently."

"Oh, Rosalba. You're always hoping for things to change. For people to be who you want them to be."

"Not always," I tell her. "For an instance, I have completely given up on Silvia."

She laughs. I have made her laugh.

"As well you should. What is upsetting is the fact that she doesn't even care."

"Nor must we. Enough of her. I do implore you to attend the comedy. It will be such great fun. All you'll have to do is sit and watch."

"And walk for quite a way until we reach the theater."

"It isn't far. I passed it on my way to get your medicine, so many weeks ago now, and saw the posters by the door and could have wept for my desire to attend. Oh, Luisa, there are fine ladies and harlequins and even devils pictured. It is a whole entire world up there upon the wall."

She is about to resist again when I think of something that will surely make her want to come.

"Perhaps your mother will be there?"

Just then a little troupe of acrobats goes tumbling by on the Riva in white leggings and tight jerkins that show each muscle of their sinewy bodies. We are so stunned to see them just appear like that, that we're speechless until they're out of sight and on their way.

I deliver news about the Commedia to the junior *maestre,* who are all chattering at once like a covey of baboons, and I am just about to go back across the Calle when I see him, the wig-maker's assistant. He is carrying only one dressed wig today and walks languidly as if in no particular hurry, gazing at the boats in the lagoon and humming a pretty tune I've heard sung in the street before. It is the time of day when shadows fall upon the chapel side of the street all the way to the wheel, and I shrink into them and simply watch him as he strolls by. If I had only thought to bring my feathered mask, so I could flirt with him. But even if I had, the dresses that we all must wear would be an obvious clue to the Ospedale, and if he was amused by his first sight of me, I couldn't bear it. So I stay hidden. This close, he is even more handsome than I had thought, taller, more finely turned out, as if he could put the wig he carries on himself and fool almost anyone into thinking that he's a young duke. His breeches cling to rounded calves and thighs, and he wears a jaunty jacket of carmine-colored wool with ribbon trim.

How I long to call to him and say, "Here. Over here. Here in the shadows of Our Lady of the Ascension is your own true heart's desire."

I awake on Wednesday so distracted by my thoughts of the afternoon performance of the Commedia dell'Arte, that I cannot keep my mind on anything. Father Vivaldi himself has cautioned us not to attract attention, as the musicians from the Pietà have a remarkable reputation to uphold, and Prioress would not like any individual performer to be identified. In fact, we're given *bautta* masks with veils beneath before we leave, and it must be quite comical to watch as we help each other put them on.

At two o'clock there are some fifteen of us gathered in the parlor for our trip, Luisa not among us. Since my last question to her did not make her want to join us, I'm considering if running back and hounding her would help, when her slight figure almost plummets down the stairs, her lovely hair set free to fly about. Thank heaven she has washed it and removed that cap! A long sigh of relief comes from Anetta and makes the others laugh but Luisa wince . . .

We are such birds of a feather as we start out with Maestra Loretta and Signora Mandano—masked blue martinets in step behind them like an infantry. Anetta, near the front, takes longer strides than either of the women and soon is in the lead, causing all the rest of us to scamper like so many mice.

"I hope she knows the way," remarks the breathless Silvia. "I will not tramp like this through the Piazza San Marco."

"There is a shortcut I have told her of," I say. "Remember when we searched for the apothecary?"

"The memory of it is engraved upon my behind," she answers scornfully. "Where it belongs. It's not a day I want to think about ever again. Why, you nearly came to ruin, and I would have been blamed!"

"I did no such thing. And think of it. If I had, you would, right now, be rid of me. A prayer answered, I should think."

"I never wish ill upon anyone," is her retort.

Just as I'd told Luisa, it isn't very long before we're there. The large red doors of the theater are ajar, and noisy revelers are entering in droves. She scans the crowd, as I knew she would, resting her eyes upon one lady with a mask called a *moretta*, which makes the face appear to be a black, featureless hole, and is kept in place, I'm told, by a button held between the front teeth. The body of the lady is all covered, too, the sleeves voluminous and long, the hands within a muff. As Luisa can have no way of knowing if this scary-looking woman is her mother, except for the fact that there is only one man at her elbow and he is decrepit and quite stooped, she soon turns back to the group and comes with us to find our seats.

"They think that we are nuns," she whispers as we sit in regimented rows upon hard benches.

"We should have stopped for the *frittelle*," moans Maestra Loretta, "before there are none to be had."

"We should have gone by way of the Piazza San Marco then," says Signora Mandano. "That's where all the bakers are today."

The thought of the sweet delicious bread makes my mouth water so, I want to spit, but I restrain myself, as I would not if I weren't in such company. But soon the thought of food is driven from my mind as the players begin to strut out on the stage — first the Lover, Flavio, a dapper, dreamy-looking fellow, and next the flamboyant Captain, who wears an ugly mask with an enormous nose and swaggers about in a scarlet doublet and brightly striped breeches. He is the bigger talker of the two and brags and dictates to the Lover, with his hand upon the scabbard of his wooden sword as if he plans to draw it out at any turn. The Lover is such a comely, courteous fellow that he has my sympathy right from the start, and that of others, too, who swear at the braggart Captain and throw eggs. It isn't long before the Beautiful Lady makes her appearance and things calm down a bit, however.

"'She' is really a 'he,'" whispers Silvia, so everyone but Beatrice can hear.

I've heard that this is true, but it is difficult to believe when looking at such a lovely face and trim bodice. And Flavio's declarations of love are so delightfully sincere, so full of compliments, that she swoons a little as another "lady" plays the mandolin against a painted backdrop of a country house with olive trees and potted palms. It is all so beautiful I want to cry, but bridle such an inclination until it seems the lovers will be separated by the odious Harlequin, who leaps into the air and forces the Lady to dance with him, the oafish clown.

"Unhand her!" cries the crowd, and I am on my feet with all the rest begging for the lovers to escape, to run away.

Luisa pulls me down beside her and thrusts a handkerchief at me to dry my tears.

"It's only make-believe," she says. "It's not your life up there, you know."

Oh, how I wish it were!

Anetta

I WANTED SO TO WALK ALONG beside Luisa on our outing and make sure that she was safe. But because of how
Rosalba cautioned me, I fought against my truest feelings
and tramped ahead of everyone to lead the way. It wasn't
far to the theater by the shortcut, but Signora Mandano
complained bitterly throughout the play that we had not
come near enough to the vendors selling sweets. We went
the long way going back so as to pass through the Piazza
San Marco and buy the *frittelle* we'd all been promised.
Signora would not let us eat them in the street, however,

and we were made to carry the delicious treats back with us to share with all the younger girls.

"Who will eat our share and then buy more to eat when *they* go to the puppet show," says Silvia. "It's most unfair."

I notice that Luisa doesn't even sneak a nibble. Any food at all would surely do her good, and I would love to have seen her show a spark of happiness while in the theater. Whenever I looked over, her eyes were roaming around the audience, barely glancing at the play upon the stage in front of her. In contrast, Rosalba seemed about to fly up with the actors, as if the life up there were more real than the one she leads. How well reasoned she can be sometimes, but the side of her on view today has often been apparent recently and troubles me. "Just a few years," I've told her many times, "and you can leave this place and do just as you please."

I pray that she listens to me as closely as I do when she counsels *me*. What is it about Carnival that makes a person court the risks she wouldn't at another time? What evil spells are in the air right before Lent? Why, yesterday, I caught the old cook lifting up her skirts to bare her backside to the butcher, who thrust himself between her heavy buttocks and grunted just like one of his own pigs. She went about the kitchen business after that, unruffled, as if she'd never ceased to stir the pots.

All the way back, I have such uneasy feelings about Rosalba, I plot to walk beside her, and even though Luisa holds her other hand, I do not try to meet Luisa's gaze. She is still glum, but Rosalba is in a wistful state much like the Lover in the little play, smiling at nothing and at complete strangers, masked or not. She wants to know if I was as overcome as she was by the Commedia, had I ever imagined anything so fine, were not the actors beautiful, the scenery a work of art?

I tell her that I did enjoy it, yes, particularly the tricks, the *lazzi* and other comic business. Several of us laugh to remember the somersaults of the Harlequin while carrying a full glass of water that doesn't even spill, and how the Captain boxed the ears of his servant so many times, the man grew cross-eyed.

"It is the lovers I'll remember," says Rosalba.

"That simpering Flavio? He is too soft by half to be a man," declares Silvia.

Rosalba is quick in her retort.

"And who do you know to compare him with? The priests in their black skirts? The *castrati*? The lustful errand boys who lurk below stairs for a glimpse of one of us in a chemise? The overfed dukes who sometimes come to tea?"

"Not to mention your mysterious merlin and your bold and leering gondolier," adds Silvia.

The girls who've heard Silvia stare at Rosalba as if shocked and mystified.

"Who are these men you've named?" asks Geltruda. "What have they to do with Rosalba?"

"They have nothing to do with Rosalba," says Silvia. Her little smirk grows into a self-righteous grimace. "That's her complaint."

I have never known Rosalba to turn red in the face before or to become so absolutely quiet.

She doesn't speak again until we've crossed over the Rio di Palazzo where we can see the Bridge of Sighs and are almost to the Calle della Pietà. Just as some girls begin to enter the chapel and others go off to the Ospedale, Rosalba pulls Silvia aside and tells her very quietly so that few of us can hear, "You know nothing of true love between a man and woman, Silvia, so do not scoff at others who do."

"Don't tell me of true love," declares Silvia. "You have been as cloistered here as any of us."

"Think what you will. It doesn't matter a wit!"

"As if I needed your permission to do that. But if you don't want my opinion, just keep your silly lovesick pantomimes to yourself. Don't involve me in them again."

What does Rosalba know of love? What secrets does she keep? Is the kind of love of which she speaks what I witnessed between the butcher and the cook? There was no more tenderness to it than such an act between two mongrel dogs.

"Anetta," says Luisa suddenly, and I cannot believe that my own name is upon her lips.

I look at Rosalba, and she isn't giving me a look of warning as she has so often done before.

"What is it, Luisa?" I ask.

"I merely want to thank you for the care you showed me when I was so very ill. You were most kind."

What can I say that will not turn her away from me again? That I would do anything in the world for her, that I did not leave her side of my own accord, that I would watch over her forever if she would let me?

"I am glad that I could help you," I say at last. And then I turn and head inside and to the nursery, where Concerta is just waking from her nap, her forehead as cool as my own. I pick her up and clasp her to me with such gratitude to Our Blessed Savior and to His Mother. With this same gratitude, I hold Luisa's words within my mind, words I didn't think that I would ever hear.

Chapter Twenty

Rosalba

PRIORESS HAS ASKED THAT I GO with Signora Mandano to accompany the youngest girls when they attend the puppet show. She is sending small groups with two chaperones each, and so, no matter what, I'll have the silly entertainment stuffed right down my throat. It is one way to miss solfeggio, however, and I have not been given any choice. I must confess, it will be good to be among the crowd again, the musicians and the acrobats, those crazy people balancing on stilts, even the ugly men in women's clothes. The Piazza San Marco will bustle with excitement every day until Shrove Tuesday. It is a shame we get to see only small bits of Carnival this year. The balls and parties in the nighttime must be too marvelous to be believed.

As we start out, the little *iniziate* are so full of excitement that they don't appear to feel the cold. Even without masks, their rosy cheeks beneath their hoods seem painted there. Right away Signora points out an uncommon spectacle in the lagoon, a man with long wooden shoes who slides upon the ice with brisk and lengthy strides. We watch, certain that he'll break the crust and fall into the water, but when he stays on top, passes swiftly into the canal, and disappears from sight, the children squeal with pleasure.

"Have you ever seen anything like it?" asks Signora, and I must admit that I have not. There are so many wonders that I haven't seen in my short regimented life, however, that it does not surprise me to have missed such a one as this. It makes me think how unimagined wonders must be everywhere within the wider world.

"Now hold one another's hands," Signora tells the group. "And don't let go. Keep your distance from the tumblers and revelers. I suggest you whistle like a bird, the way Father Vivaldi has taught you, if any stranger comes too close."

The shrill little whistles begin at once and continue until the knot of *bambine* sounds like a frantic aviary into which a hawk has swooped.

"Not now! Not now!" Signora cries, and insists on

silence before we start our journey, which will take us only over three short bridges that we can see from here. How far that seemed to me when I was very young.

Just as we are about to set out, Catina appears in the doorway, wrapped in her own cloak and cap and looking so wan I feel she may faint into the street. She is definitely not strong enough yet to come with us, but the other *iniziate* are clearly delighted with this brief send-off, and I'm amused to see her smile and pull the skin down at the center of one eye the way Signora often does when she signals us to be careful or alert. The gesture is duly noted by these children, who, I'm told, often look to her for guidance and who, after this send-off, hold ever more tightly to one another.

The girls, like a dark blue daisy chain with bright flower faces, wind single file and are so excited that the chain appears to throb. Most have never seen the Palace of the Doge before and are struck dumb as we pass in front of it, gazing up at its many arches and the ornate entrance with tiny gaping mouths. The church itself, of course, with its three golden domes and many spires, overshadows everything near the square, and the children wind their chain around the base of its steps as if in a dream. It is only mid-afternoon, and the square is filled to brimming with people of every kind—tourists from the continent, hawkers of every ilk, street musicians, harlequins and acrobats, both masked and unmasked. The noise is indeed deafening but so filled with merriment that I revel in the way it washes over us, and I collect the sounds and colors, the madcap roistering, so deep inside myself that I am quite drunk with all of it by the time we reach our destination.

Father's little concert for our benefit within the cathedral is the first event. How I would resist the sudden quiet forced upon us by this church if I could. The girls, however, seem enthralled with the still and massive interior and beautiful paintings and speak only in whispers as we lead them to a side altar, where Father and his own *padre* are waiting for us, both tuning violins.

"Ah," says Father as we assemble on the chairs in front of them. "You're just in time." He winks at me. "Quite an achievement with such a guide."

His father is a trifle stooped, but robust for a slight, older man, and even somewhat dapper in a bob wig. Already, a small crowd has formed outside the communion rail, made up of people who obviously recognize the elder Vivaldi from his frequent performances around Vienna. The Red Priest seems to be known as well, perhaps for his operatic pieces, which, we've been told, have taken some notice of late. It is somewhat confounding that his compositions reach out into the wider world and we must share him.

"Look. The father and the son," murmurs an old woman behind her hand as if commenting on the first two persons of the Trinity. "The Vivaldis," can be heard whispered by many other spectators, and Father, wearing a stylish wig himself, looks up.

The older man smiles and nods when his son tells him who we are, but doesn't leave his chair or take his violin from underneath his chin. It is so cold in here that we do not have the girls remove their cloaks, and one wonders how the fingers of the men can stay flexible enough to play the notes.

Very shortly, however, they launch into a wonderful duet that seems, in places, to imitate the sounds of animals, for I can clearly hear a thrush and then a bleating lamb and once the barking of a dog and the coo of turtle doves. The girls seem quite aware of this and sit up in their chairs, alert for any new surprises. It is a clever ploy to keep them fastened to the music, and Father beams throughout the quick performance. This whimsical invention of his own has clearly been designed to please such small children, and they are indeed completely delighted, clapping hands as children do instead of blowing their noses in appreciation as their elders might. They actually seem loath to leave this most majestic place and their dear friend from the Ospedale. But Father himself remarks upon the puppet show in store and cautions them to hurry in order to find places up close enough to see the entertainment clearly.

The puppet theater is set up on a platform near the center of the Piazza San Marco, very near the campanile.

The children gape at the tall spire, their small heads tilted back in an attempt to see the top. As all of Italy loves its *bambini,* the little girls are soon ushered to the front, right by the hangman's noose painted on the front curtain. The star of the show, Puncinello, has already, it would seem, killed his own baby, and is beating his ugly wife with a stick amid shouts and catcalls. There is no love at all to this story. Why it seems to please the crowd is quite a mystery to me.

Throughout the gruesome play, I am distracted by a roving group of street musicians who perform quite proficiently on somewhat shabby instruments and draw a large crowd. One man is bearded and blows competently on a cornet, while the younger of the two plays the recorder. The lady among the two gentlemen is not young and is clothed in the sort of muslin that a shopkeeper might wear. Her hands are strong and sensitive upon the strings and bow of her violin, but her face beneath the small eye mask is as ordinary as a peasant's, and a trifle pocked. They play such sprightly, cheerful tunes that many people start to dance to them right in the open, with men holding ladies in both graceful and indecorous ways. How I'd love to be among the dancers, for I can easily imagine my handsome merlin's helper clasping me around the waist and whirling me about until I faint into his arms.

"Rosalba," says Signora right into my ear, "have you become as deaf as Beatrice? I've called your name three times."

"I was distracted, Signora, as anyone would be," I add, "with so many entertainments all around."

"The little girls can be excused, but you must have your head about you and keep a count of all these bobbing noggins entrusted to our care."

I tighten my hold on Isabel and Paulina, who cannot tear their gaze from the puppet clown, who is now cavorting wildly with a dog. There are no strings, just someone's fists beneath the garish outfits and molded puppet heads, and yet the audience shouts out to these strange dolls as if they're real. "Take that, you numbskull!" "Hit him again!" "Run for your life!" The street performers who had taken my attention have packed up and gone, but I still feel their melodies within my loins and almost can't resist the need to dance along the cobblestones.

"The *frittelle*," Signora Mandano reminds me. "That vendor over there! Hurry, Rosalba, before the baker folds up his tent."

I pull the line of little girls with me as I hurry, and Signora is whipped along almost faster than her chunky boots can manage.

This time our charges are allowed to eat their treats right on the spot.

"They're much too young to wait," declares Signora, and it's probably true, though all the hands are so sticky on our walk back to the Ospedale that each child seems glued to the next. For the trip here I was in the lead. This time I dawdle behind and, as the light begins to fade, cast a fond eye over all that we are leaving. In the distance, heading toward the Grand Canal, I see the little troupe of traveling musicians I had watched earlier. What a carefree existence they have, playing right from their hearts and not having to endure, I'm sure, hours of practice and instruction. How close they are to their audiences. How loved by everyone who hears them. I noticed there were many gold coins in their basket, too. Quite enough, I'm sure, for all the things they need to live in this free and happy way.

"Rosalba," calls Signora Mandano, and many high little voices begin to call my name as well. "You're slowing down the line. I promised we'd be back in time for vespers. Pick up your feet!"

It is unnatural, this being set free among all the festivities, then thrust back immediately into the staid and regulated life we lead within two cold, damp buildings.

Chapter Twenty-one

Luisa

THE BEST THING THAT HAS HAPPENED since I've returned is that I've taken up my violin again and begun rehearsals with the others for next Sunday's concert in the organ gallery, where a somewhat smaller audience than usual is to be entertained. When Father Vivaldi suggested it, it seemed a good first step, and though I felt quite tentative and unsure, I found that the music did indeed restore me. By the end of the first three-hour session I was more energetic than when it began. We will be playing a concerto in D minor for violin, organ, oboe, strings, and basso continuo. It is as vigorous as most of Father's inventions and as rich in harmony and lovely melodies. Anetta will play the solo violin part, and Rosalba was to have played oboe. When she didn't attend the first rehearsal, however, Father assigned her part to Constancia's cello.

After rehearsal, walking beside me on the way to the refectory, Father broaches a subject that I suspect has been on his mind for quite some time. He dances round it, complimenting my playing, noticing that my cheeks are pinking up a bit, and asking how I'm feeling after so long a practice session.

"I'm feeling much better than I had expected," I tell him. And, in truth, the pores of my entire body seem to breathe again.

"You are like a tree in springtime," he suggests, "stretching up to catch the light after a long dismal winter."

Not unless it is a tree that has felt death lodged in its throat, I want to tell him, but I cannot speak of that to anyone and am uncertain why it haunts me still. And then he begins to talk about the oratorio he is planning to stage and how he is already assigning parts to it in his thoughts and how there is a wonderful soprano part for me. He goes on to say that he cannot imagine anyone else being able to sing this part that he intends to feature in what he is calling *Moyses Deus Pharaonis*.

"And I suspect," he continues, "that your voice will spring right back in the same way as your skills upon the violin. With such a voice, all that it will take is a few extra sessions with Maestro Scarpari to put you in top form again. I'm certain of it."

"*Scusi,*" says Prioress, coming upon us before I've had a chance to reply. "Is Rosalba still within the practice room?"

"She hasn't made an appearance there at all today," says Father. Well aware that she and I are friends, he asks, "Do you know where she is, Luisa?"

"No," I can say truthfully, for she was simply . . . playing with the things she keeps within her trunk when I saw her last. There is no other word for how she takes her treasures out and gazes at them. She cannot be there still. "Perhaps she'll be at the noon meal."

"Well, she wasn't at breakfast," continues Prioress, "and it seems that no one's seen her since she returned yesterday after the puppet show."

Prioress has not asked me if I've seen Rosalba. And Father has only asked if I can say where she is right now. I want to reassure them that she's still within these walls, but why would they suspect otherwise, and how can I be sure, and what exactly do I tell them?

Rosalba does not join us for the meal in the refectory, which is especially disappointing when I see there is polenta with red sauce, her favorite dish, and a plate of the small herring she loves, prepared with herbs and wine. Anetta sits across from me and also asks about her.

"Perhaps she isn't well," I say, although I know this isn't true. Then Anetta turns to Geltruda, and I am pleased to see that she talks more to her throughout the meal than she does to me. If she continues to behave in this way and does not hang upon my every word and gesture, perhaps I won't need to avoid her in the future.

Immediately after saying the grace at the end of the meal, I hurry back to our bedchamber to see if Rosalba, has, in fact, sequestered herself there all morning. The mystery is solved, however, before I even climb the stairs, for I decide to go first down a narrow hallway to the small front parlor, which has many windows onto the lagoon. There I spy the top of her head at once. She is curled into a chair and facing away. If she is trying not to be seen, she is under a delusion, for no one could mistake the deep red flashes all through her thick dark curls, so visible against the yellow brocade of the chair back.

When I creep up upon her and suddenly appear, she cries out.

"Luisa! You have given me a fright. I was prepared for Prioress and have been listening for the loud clap of her hard, wide heels."

"And she is looking for you, to be sure. She can't imagine where you've disappeared to." I will not miss a chance to tease her. "And when I tell her where you are, she will be so indebted to me. Perhaps I'll merit a second dish of prunes at tea."

"You must not say a word," says Rosalba, rising and trying to clap her hand over my mouth. "It will spoil everything."

I push her away.

"What is it that I can so easily spoil?"

"The running of the bulls! You know how every day of Carnival they charge through a different neighborhood. Well, today, I learned from Cook, they will be let loose on the Riva. I've been here all morning long and will stay until I hear them gallop past our door."

"You've seen it all before," I tell her.

"And will see it every year until I die."

"They're just bulls. They're just big black frightened bulls."

"Oh, Luisa. They are much more than that. They are . . ."

"What are they, Rosalba?"

"They are animals set free and running for their lives."

"They will be caught."

"But not before they've thundered down the street and chased away whatever—people, dogs, cats—is in their path, before they've felt their own dark blood run wild, run absolutely free.

"Listen," she says, and hurries to the window. "Don't you feel it? Can't you feel their hoofbeats through the very floor?"

There is something—a resonance I can't identify at first, something reverberating through the floorboards, that, as it begins to grow, discharges such a rumble that it rises into the air and makes it feel as if the room itself will crumble and collapse.

"Come look, Luisa! Watch them tear along the Calle!"

She is standing on a footstool and has flung the window wide. The scent of field and dung and hot bull breath envelops everything, until I also climb upon the stool and stretch to see what she sees and hold tightly to her so that neither one of us will fall.

Chapter Twenty-two

Anetta

THE NURSES WHO HAVE BEEN so occupied ministering to the sick with canker rash are now back in the nursery for part of every day, so I am not as needed there. It has been good to be so near Concerta for so many days, and the need to care for her has helped to keep my mind and attentions from Luisa. I am behind in all my lessons, however, and must endeavor to make up the things I've missed, including practice sessions for the concerts, which, during Carnival, attract a great many tourists and must be better prepared than ever.

This Sunday I will be playing the violin solo again, and Father, knowing I am disappointed, has promised me for the second time a new concerto for viola d'amore. I will believe him when I see it. Why is my instrument such a sticking point for him?

Luisa is also upon the violin for this performance, which is some consolation. We are five seats apart and do not speak, however. If we could, I would commiserate with her. What would Rosalba have to say to that? I wonder. Cannot I be Luisa's true friend in any way?

The session is so long that I can't help but be troubled for her, as she is still not strong. She does appear revived, however, at the end of it and not as sallow as she looked at first when she sat down and lifted up her bow.

At the conclusion, when we pass each other on our way to put aside our instruments, our skirts swish together for an instant, and she does acknowledge me long enough to say something about my propensity to worry and to encourage me.

"It is not such a difficult part this time, Anetta. You play it very well already."

What does she mean by "very well"? Does she mean just good enough, or does she mean competently? Has she really been able to hear my part while concentrating on her own? Father immediately begins to ask about her health and other things, and there is no opportunity for me to say more than "Thank you."

At lunch I sit across from her and exchange pleasantries as if we barely know each other and ask about
Rosalba. Though it pains me more than I can say, I make
myself turn away then and speak with Geltruda throughout the meal. From the corner of my eye, however, I can
see how Luisa picks at her food, and it disturbs me a
great deal. I am also concerned about Rosalba's where-
abouts but would never discuss such things, or anything
important for that matter, with Geltruda.

I'm certain that Luisa knows where Rosalba is. But I
do not intend to ask her anything more, for I would not
want Silvia to be privy to whatever Luisa might confide.
Perhaps Rosalba is simply studying, as I must do, in order
to catch up on the things she's missed of late—solfeggio,
a language quiz, the rehearsal just past.

When Luisa rises to leave the room, it occurs to me
that if I wish to know where Rosalba is, I should follow
her. I must do it without attracting attention, however,
and must move rather more slowly than Luisa does, not
entering the hallway until some minutes after she has
disappeared into it herself. As it happens, just as I pass
under the lintel of the doorway, she is at the end of one
corridor and turning down another that is rarely entered.
I trace Luisa's steps as quietly as possible and am much
surprised to find, at the end of the second corridor, both
girls together in the smallest of the parlors. In making
certain not to be observed, I cannot, in fact, hear all of

what they say, and their talk, though agitated, is in low tones.

When I do finally infer from a few intelligible words that they're talking about the running of the bulls, that thunderous event is already causing the very walls to shake and Luisa and Rosalba to embrace each other in fear or joy or both. I am much distressed to see this, for it is a surety that Luisa would never cling to me in such a way. Even their being cosseted together in this remote room makes me sick to the core of my being and causes me to wonder if Rosalba's cautions to me about my behavior haven't been for my own good, as she has always insisted, but for hers.

I am not used to this new sentiment, which I am horrified to think may be the capital sin of envy, and don't know what to do with it or how I should proceed henceforth with either of the two people I have for so long considered my closest friends.

After vespers, Rosalba does appear at dinner and seems ravenous, wolfing the roasted fowl and root vegetables in an unseemly manner. She is not as talkative as usual, which is not surprising, as her mouth is always occupied. Her serving of *panna cotta* with dried berries lives only seconds upon her plate, after which she scurries into the kitchen to wheedle second helpings from Cook. If I did such a thing, I'd be considered gluttonous; Rosalba, on the other hand, is merely thought of as resourceful, something even the *maestri* and *maestre* eating with us look upon with amusement and good humor. I, too, have often excused her carefree attitude toward any of the rules, but wonder now how she survives her escapades. It seems as if Signora looks away on purpose and rarely chastises her for absences. Is it from habit, or from some disposition toward her, coaxed from all of us over the years by the jolly flippant temperament we've learned to coddle?

"I will not join you in the drawing room tonight or attend the small rehearsal Father has *just* announced," she says at length.

When I don't ask her what she does intend to do, she continues.

"I need some extra sleep, you see. Silvia's snoring keeps me up most half the night."

Silvia, who has been listening from across the table, snorts with indignation and rolls her eyes.

"It doesn't bother me," I say. "I am so tired when I finally do retire, that even cannon shot would not disturb me."

"Yes. You do sleep peacefully. It is the gift of a good conscience."

If she but knew of my new penchant to be envious and of my great lack of patience. I cannot help but try to warn her nonetheless, but I do it in a whisper.

"Rosalba," I tell her. "You cannot shirk your duties

as you do and not get found out eventually or have your tasks as *maestra* taken from you along with the small stipend they afford."

"I am careful," she confides. "You worry more for me than for yourself. A very noble thing, to be sure, but quite unnecessary. What troubles me the most is that you blame yourself when I don't listen."

"Perhaps I should solicit the help of Luisa. Perhaps you would listen to her."

"There seems to be some meaning in those words that I don't understand."

"I merely wonder if another voice would encounter your deaf ear so often."

"I do hear you, Anetta. I do. But if I make mistakes, they are my own. You cannot, you must not, blame yourself. Ever."

Those are the words I think of when entering the bedchamber myself at the proper time and finding Rosalba's bed as tightly made as in the morning, with her crucifix upon the pillow in the prescribed way. There is a shadow across the coverlet from her watteau and apron hanging lifeless from a wall peg.

Looking for answers, I pull open the cover of Rosalba's trunk and find a great empty space and then nothing but two woolen petticoats, some extra undergarments, and a paper advertisement for the next play at the Commedia dell'Arte.

Chapter Twenty-three

Rosalba

THE STREET STILL SMELLS of bull, and there are splat-
ted bull turds all along the Riva. Lanterns for Carnival
along the lagoon cast enough light to keep me from
stepping in the great clots of manure. I keep to the shadows and pull my cloak about me and watch as, in the
lantern glow, perfect strangers, it would seem, embrace
one another, flirt and kiss and go off together. There is
laughter close by and bursts of it carried on the air from
a distance. Costumed figures dart between gondolas at
the pier; songs float across the water from boats on their

way to parties and palaces, magnificent places that I can only imagine.

Earlier today, when I saw the wig-maker's assistant going by the Ospedale for the second time, I mustered my courage and tossed a note from the window. He looked up immediately to see from whence the little paper had drifted, and I, of course, stooped down where I couldn't be seen. *Soon enough,* I thought at the time, *soon enough I will make myself known to him.* The note had said: *Meet me tonight at first dark across from the Calle della Pietà, near the gondola of one Guissepe.*

I wanted to say more, to let him know what I would be wearing and to declare my love, but on the other hand, it seems to me that there is always some suggestion of mystery in any great romance. It took me most of the morning to decide what the note would include, and then, when he came by again, as I had dared to hope, it was necessary to compose it in great haste. "The Blue Dove," I decided at the last, would be my nom de plume.

When the *gondolieri* begin to light their lamps, I have my feathered mask in place and have slipped my cloak down from my shoulders to reveal the velvet girdle and the golden snake that rests just at the place where my breasts begin to swell. I stand this way for many minutes, no doubt turning pigeon blue in the raw weather. To dispel the cold, I tap my feet up and down and rub my hands together. I search the Riva with my eyes from one bridge to the next. And just as I tell myself that he is not coming and turn to leave, hoping the Ospedale door has not yet been locked, I see him, dodging bull turds the way I did as he runs toward me. He wears no mask at all but is as well turned out as I have seen him on his missions to the dukes, with velvet breeches and a silken coat. I let my cloak drop down so he can see my small waist and rounded bosom and the lovely colors in my gypsy skirt purchased from a vendor only yesterday. Perhaps he thinks I am a gypsy. What does he think? Who does he imagine that I am? When he comes close, I know only that he is pleased at what he sees. He hands the note to me and bows a little.

"Signorina. Does this belong to you?"

"Of course, Signore," I say.

In the dampness of the night, I know my heavy hair is curled and massed about my face, that my cheeks are quite a match for the red velvet of my girdle. But he appears enchanted, just the way I dreamed he would be oh, so many, many times.

His hands, when I've observed him, have always held a pedestal for wigs. Now they do not hesitate to draw me to him as he reaches down to kiss my neck and shoulders and as he presses me roughly against the rail. The first attentions are delicious, but the second is so indelicate it makes me feel quite breathless. I must wrest my own hands free to push him from me.

"Flirt," he accuses me in an angry fashion, and uses

some coarse words that I don't fully understand but have heard used in the street.

"Signore," I say, "you sweep me off my feet. I wish to savor your attentions slowly."

"*D'accordo*," he says. "We'll play this little game your way. But I must warn you, at Carnival I have no more patience than a hungry child."

He then proceeds a bit more slowly with his caresses, causing such delightful and unexpected sensations that I begin to feel quite giddy. It's not until he clasps my bottom with both hands to draw me to him, leans in and thrusts his tongue almost to my throat that I resist again, and with all my might, for surely these are not the gentle attentions of a true lover. Flavio did not comport himself in such a way upon the stage.

"Signore," I say, wrenching from his grasp and backing away, "I do not understand your intentions."

"Nor I, yours, it would appear."

"I thought that we might talk. Might dance."

He laughs, and I must admit it is a charming, lilting sound, and that his smile is whitely brilliant in the dim light. What have I done to ruin things?

"Might dance? You are a schoolgirl."

"No, Signore, a true *maestra*."

"A schoolgirl, nonetheless. I can't be bothered with such things. I am apprenticed to a busy man. I do not have the time for this."

His face is still as handsome as when first I saw him, his form and figure just as dashing. Can he not be, eventually, the gentle lover of my dreams?

"You are disappointed?" I ask.

"I am surprised. *You* sent for *me*. Remember?"

Why should my invitation put some rough claim upon me that is altogether unclear? Yet I have thought of no one else but him these many months. I do not want to believe that we have failed each other.

"I will be here tomorrow at this time," I tell him. "Perhaps we can begin again to come to know each other."

He laughs once more and gives me a sweet, charming cuff across the chin.

"Perhaps," he says, and spreads his hands, palms up, as if confounded, and turns and makes his way back down the darkened Riva toward the Piazza San Marco.

I cross immediately to the Calle della Pietà, bumping into revelers as if I'm blind, and lean against the wall beside the Ospedale door to compose myself, for I am strangely shaken. Light from a gibbous moon glistens on the cobblestones all the way to the lagoon, and I think how this is such a perfect night for love. So perfect, and yet so disappointing. His disappointment, too, was clear. But I had not counted on such an impetuous nature, such unbridled passion. I'm certain that given another chance, he will not behave in those same bold ways that troubled me tonight. He must be, even now, composing himself and thinking of a way to make amends. And he will come again. I know he will.

I turn the knob upon the Ospedale door. It's still unlocked, and inside is a silence as deep as those beautiful few seconds at the very end of a concerto when not a single bow or baton moves. It envelops me like a warm cloak a mother might provide. But then someone's nose begins to whistle loud enough in sleep to be heard clearly all the way downstairs, and there's the clatter of an upset pot followed by a shriek. The candles along the hallway have already been extinguished, and I must trail my fingers along the wall to find my way.

Chapter Twenty-four

Luisa

AT FIRST LIGHT, I look across at Rosalba's bed and find her sleeping there, one hand beneath her head, the coverlet pulled to her chin. The other girls are stirring about the room, pulling their dresses down over their heads, arranging their caps, smoothing out the bedclothes. I close my eyes quickly so they'll think I'm still asleep, something I will be excused for because of my recent illness. But Rosalba will be brought to task this time, I'm certain. There have been too many lapses in attendance of late, too many late arrivals.

As soon as the nosy dawdler, Silvia, heads down to breakfast, I leave my warm bed and shake Rosalba awake.

She mumbles something I can't understand and turns upon her stomach, one hand hanging limply to the floor. With a great effort, I grasp that hand and the arm and shoulder attached to it and turn her over, causing her to open her eyes wide with a start.

"What . . . what in the world are you doing, Luisa?"

"I'm trying to save your neck," I tell her. "You must rise at once and breakfast with the others. The second bell has sounded. It's almost too late already."

"*You're* still here."

"And have been excused. But you're courting a punishment this time, I'm sure. All of us saw that you were not in your bed at the proper time last night. One of us will undoubtedly tell if given the chance. Silvia was quicker than usual to be on her way and will certainly tattle if you don't soon follow."

Rosalba sits up and rubs the small of her back.

"Why is everyone so concerned for me all of a sudden? You and Anetta, you've begun counseling me at every turn as if I possess no reason of my own."

"Of late it does appear to be the truth."

She grins. "Aha! You do acknowledge it."

"Only that you suddenly have no reason of your own."

"Oh, Luisa. Stop frowning as you do. It will make tracks upon your face not easily erased. You'll begin to look just like Signora around the eyes and display those irritating tiny lines that cross each other."

"It is not my face we are speaking about. It is your predicament, which grows more perilous with every day."

She swings her legs across the bed and puts her feet upon the floor, grabbing her watteau as she does this and slipping out of her chemise. In only seconds she is standing naked in the middle of the room and pulling on her undergarments, woolen petticoat, and dress.

"Tie this," she instructs, backing up and handing me her apron lappets. "And make a proper bow this time."

Then she quickly runs a brush over her wild hair to tame it from heading in the countless directions it has chosen. She splashes cold water from the basin onto her face.

"See?" she says at last. "I'm listening to you. I'm going to be punctual from now on. You'll see."

As she starts for the door, I grab her hand.

"What of last night?" I ask. "Where did you go? Why did you leave?"

She looks at me as if at a very small child.

"You would not understand," she says. "Don't worry so. You will be just like Anetta if you keep it up. Believe in me, Luisa. I know what I'm about."

She bends down quickly and pats my cheek, then turns back to straighten out her bedclothes. "And I will return soon to take my chamber pot down to the slop closet for the maids to empty," she tells me. "Am I not being obedient and good?"

"As if anyone would be concerned about a trifle such as that," I mutter, but in her quick departure she hasn't heard me. I already hear her footsteps on the stairs.

True to her assurances to me, Rosalba is most punctual all day, attends solfeggio (the whole of it), and plays continuo, in place of the indisposed Anna Maria, for the entire rehearsal. Father is not in a humor to reassign the oboe part to Rosalba, fretting understandably and quite audibly that the new Rosalba may not last till Sunday next. "Of late, my dear," he says, "you are as changeable as the weather. And just as undependable."

Surprisingly, she does not seem offended in the least and counters with, "As is the case with most natural phenomena, Signore."

"Natural disasters, more the like," says Silvia in a *sotto* voice that can be heard throughout the room.

Father scowls uncharacteristically, quickly taps his stick for order, and moves his complete concentration to the music. For an instant, I see a surprised response to this rebuff in Rosalba's eyes.

Afterward, wanting to be certain that she truly sees the consequences of her former careless attitude, I ask if she will not miss playing this delightful new concerto in performance.

"They are all delightful," she says, "and one performance is no different from another to my mind."

I am astounded. "How can you say that! Each work is so distinct, so intricate and amazing. Oh, how I missed hearing all the instruments playing together the entire time I was trying to get well."

"There's music everywhere in Venice," she says. "Musicians play up and down every street. One sounds quite as good as another to me, and they're a great deal more carefree about it."

"You say that because you've had much more than the noise of the street musicians in your ears since birth. If the Red Priest's compositions did not appear with regularity, you'd see how much they mean to you. Don't you recall those few years he was not, in fact, in attendance here and how the music procured for us at that time was so inferior? When something beautiful absents itself after having been so long a part of you, there is a terrible void."

"Luisa, you are being much too glum and spend too much time ruminating on unimportant things."

I could have said that the void exists even when one is not certain of the absence. But she would not have known what I meant. Nor do I, at times. I only know that calling up my singing voice into my throat is as impossible right now as trying to coax a wild bird out of a tree. I cannot bear attempting it, and in the end, having it fly from me.

I am starting up the stairs for my obligatory after-noon rest (a new rule for which I am most grateful, as I still do not feel strong enough to move about all day without interruption) when I feel a hand upon my arm and see a sheaf of papers held before my face. I twist about to find myself almost level with a rim of short red hair, those telltale flaming tufts that appear, when not concealed beneath his performance wig, to extend from a brain always on fire.

"Luisa," says Father. "I got right down to work after our little talk about the oratorio. These pages are prelimi-nary, but I was sure you'd want to see exactly what I have in mind. Look at the part of Sapens Primur . . . when you have the time. You'll see I have designed it especially for your unique vocal qualities. Your timbre. Your sonorities."

I take the scores from him. What else can I do?

"Thank you, Father," I say. "I'll look them over. When I have the time."

"Show them to Maestro Scarpari if you wish. Have him work with you."

"Yes. Of course."

"You do not seem excited by this project."

"It's just . . . it's only that I'm still so weak."

At first he seems to sympathize.

"And I am rushing you. There really is no hurry, Luisa. It is a long oratorio. Very difficult. It will take many months to write. I'm always like this when I first begin a piece. You've seen the way I'm apt to carry on."

"My finch, Father," I ask to change the subject and because I truly want to know, "does she still sing as much as ever?"

"Yes, yes. She is a happy little twitterer. I sometimes need to put a cover on her cage to make her stop. You must come by more frequently to hear her sing yourself."

My true opposite right now, I think, but the very expression of my soul.

But his sympathy is short-lived. "Go have your nap," he adds. "We'll speak of my oratorio again when you have read the score."

Chapter Twenty-five

Rosalba

IT WILL BE DIFFICULT to get away this night, as all eyes will be watching me. I should have named a time next week or some days hence, when the suspicions will have died down. Even Prioress suspects something, for she has had me sit beside her at each meal and quizzes me unmercifully about my lessons. It is my good fortune that she doesn't know exactly what we're taught but only the bare bones of it, and I can easily impress her with the little more I know than she.

"You speak well, Rosalba," she says at last, "but I cannot help wondering at the substance behind the words.

If rumors and records are to be believed, you've slacked off in attendance at almost every class for quite some time. It is an abuse of the privileges that we provide you with and a poor example for the younger girls."

She is right, I know, and I do feel contrite. At least I think that is the name for what I feel, besides rancor, when she scolds me. However, whatever it is doesn't last much past my mostly sincere expression of sorrow and the length of time it takes to consume the meal that we are sharing.

Tonight I retire with the others, but undress in the shadows so that I may conceal my Carnival clothing under my chemise. Only when I'm certain that the others are soundly asleep do I make a move to slip from underneath the covers and creep quietly down the hallway and stairs to the door.

As soon as I have shut it behind me, I see him standing there across the Riva, a muted figure in the lantern light, but clear enough in form and stature to be unmistakably the object of my heart.

On coming closer, I can see he's holding a bouquet of roses out to me and grinning that bright smile. Of course. It is a peace offering, and when we are quite near each other, he takes my hand and kisses it. A peace offering indeed and courtly beyond words. How glad I am that I have given him a second chance and did not rush to judgment, as Signora's nightly readings from the Bible often tell us we should never do.

After a few caresses, as gentle as I've always dreamed that they would be, he asks in whispers close against my ear, "Where can we go, Signorina, to be entirely alone?"

"A gondola," I say at once, thinking to make that dream come true as well.

"It is beyond my means."

"I have a few florins," I tell him, and hold them out to him.

"No," he says, which makes me note again that he, in truth, has gentlemanly virtues. "Perhaps a garden."

"There is the kitchen garden where they grow the herbs and spices. There are some grassy places underneath the pear trees."

"It sounds just right," he says, and takes my hand and runs with me back across the Riva and into the Calle, where the kitchen garden gate is fastened with nothing more than rope and latch. We are like children, running wild and playing hide-and-seek. I am delirious with joy.

The windows of the Ospedale are all dark by now, and there is nothing but the calm light from a waning moon, so what looks ragged and unkempt by day is softened into shapes that could be bowers or imagined topiaries. The grassy places shine.

He leads me to the one beneath the tallest pear tree and helps me down until we both are sitting on the cold ground. He pulls my cloak around us both as well and rests my head upon his arm as he reclines. It is a lovely lover's pose, though somewhat awkward to maintain.

"There is a bench against the wall," I tell him, "where we can sit in much more comfort."

When I begin to rise, he pulls me down beside him in such a way as to suggest that he doesn't know his own strength.

"This will do very well," he tells me, and then he, all of a great sudden, removes the arm that was supporting me and fastens my own arms above my head. Laid flat upon the ground, I am alarmed and writhe and try to pull out of his grasp. But it is of no use, nor am I able to resist in any way as he lowers his whole body onto mine, then feigns a kiss upon my lips but bites them both instead, a bite so searing that it causes me to cry out from the fierce and burning pain of it.

"Stupid, conniving wench," he says against my face, my own blood upon his chin. "I'll teach you how to play at love." He reaches down between us then to raise my skirt and rip my drawers, and pins me with such a sharp stab in the soft and private place between my legs that, if I could but move, I'd double up in agony. It's just as if I have been torn in two, and my own scream appears to come from someplace far away, muffled as it is by his one shoulder pressed against my bleeding mouth. Under his continued thrusts, pain sears and radiates all through me till I think that I have not the strength to take another breath or keep a conscious thought. When after one last lunge he finally arises, velvet breeches now around his ankles, I stare, amazed, at what, in the foggy dark, I can discern of the limp organ that has caused such torture to me.

He doesn't look at me again until he turns to leave, and then he spits on me when I begin to cry and laughs that same lighthearted way, and grabs my roses, throwing them into the air.

I don't even try to stand until I'm certain he is gone, and when I do, a sticky fluid runs along the inside of my legs. I have nothing but my petticoat to staunch it with and suspect that there is blood mixed with the odious juices my cruel ravisher has left behind.

Where can I go? In what waters can I wash myself? My lips are swollen and inflamed, my entire body's stiff from cold, and there's a soreness and a deep and growing wound within me that may never mend. If he thought to teach a lesson to a schoolgirl, I have learned it very well. But what's the remedy? I cannot stay within these garden walls. Come morning, they'll be emptying the slops out here and hanging clothes to dry. Even if the doors weren't locked by now, I can't go back inside like this. I need to find another place to rest, to hide. If only I could die.

Chapter Twenty-six

Anetta

HER BED IS EMPTY. It has not been slept in. It is morning, and her bed is empty.

Luisa sits up and looks immediately across at where
Rosalba sleeps. Luisa doesn't look at me, nor I at her.
We do not say anything. Even Silvia and Margaretta and
Anabella look at Rosalba's bed and are silent, and that
silence is much louder than the things we are all thinking
to say, to ask. Can it be true? Has Rosalba actually stayed
away all night? When will Signora and the others begin

to miss her? Will they let her come back? In what way will she be punished if they do? What would we ever do without her?

We dress in silence. It is as if we've made a pact of it, though nothing of the sort has passed between us.

Luisa breakfasts this day with the rest of us. As she sits down across from me, I notice that she isn't looking really well as yet. Her narrow face seems bleached of color and of shadows. She doesn't often smile. The place Rosalba usually claims as hers has been left empty. The girls all walk around it as if someone's sitting there. We are halfway through our porridge when Silvia nudges me with an elbow as sharp as her tongue.

"They're going to start asking questions. They're going to find out that Rosalba's gone," she whispers.

"Rosalba's clever. She's sure to sneak back before they notice."

"Not clever enough by half. I told her she'd be sorry."

We all told her. It's clear why she wouldn't listen to Silvia, but why didn't she listen to me?

Silvia presses on: "Why aren't you saying anything?"

"What is there to say?"

"Well, there'll be plenty to say when Signora finds out. Just wait and see."

"Silvia," I tell her, making sure I stare directly into those little pinprick eyes, "if you should say a word, if you should tell anyone," and my voice grows dark and low, surprising even me, "I think that I will murder you."

She is as shocked as I am at what I've just said, and shrinks a little in her chair, and looks at me as if I already hold a dagger in my hand.

"You wouldn't!" she squeaks.

"It's hard to know for a certain," I tell her truthfully. "Right now, I think it would be easy."

The morning is uneventful, except for the mysterious appearance of stray roses strewn about the kitchen garden. Cook claims it is a sure sign of Our Lady's favor — whether because of the good care given the orphans here or because of her skillful preparation of our victuals, she isn't sure. I myself believe it is a miracle of sorts, as do a number of the other girls, even though we can't imagine what it means. We have decided that, as with most miracles, the meaning will be made known to us in time. And they are such beautiful roses. Such a lovely shade of red. They dot the dismal yard with their deep color. For days the petals blow about.

Those of us preparing for the concert on Sunday work until noon on it. Father Vivaldi himself accompanies us on the continuo, and Maestro Gasparini conducts us. Neither man asks about Rosalba, nor do any of the other girls, accustomed as they have become to her recent absences. At first I cannot concentrate, but the intricate rhythms of the andante soon capture my complete attention, and it isn't until we break before the next movement that I am conscious of this new source of worry that has quickly superseded all others. When I glance over at Luisa, she doesn't look away, as has become her pattern, but transmits something of her own concern and her baffled ignorance of where to turn for answers to Rosalba's absence. Each time a little *iniziata* rustles about the room during our rest, Luisa and I both turn to the door, half expecting Rosalba's jaunty entrance, her broad smile and dancing eyes.

It isn't until almost noon that Prioress appears and asks to have me step into the hall. As I rise to join her, I glance again at Luisa, and her look this time is full of warning and something very near panic. Alert to what my countenance may also be revealing, I try to keep my own expression bland, greeting Prioress with the usual "Good day."

"I think you know what this is all about, Anetta," she begins.

"No, madam."

She studies my face, and I struggle to present her with a blank slate.

"Hmm. Well—I feel the fool giving you information that you and all the ones who share your chamber must be privy to already." She pauses for a time. "But I will go along with your somewhat understandable collusion."

How long, I wonder, *does she intend to drag out her pronouncement?* I make myself look eager for the news she bears, the while she searches my expectant stare.

"Rosalba is not here," she states at last. "We think she left quite late in the night, and she has not returned."

"Oh, my," I say. "I did not know."

"Of course you did. As did all the other girls who bed with her. But only one of you came forward. What a shame."

"A shame?"

"It means that four of you will be severely punished. For you, as the one *maestra* who is left in your chamber, a docket in your wages; for all of you, some service to the *commun* girls, a diminishment of free time in the evening hours. Some extra mandatory prayers."

It seems that she concocts these disparate penalties as she continues speaking. She even adds a few when there is no reaction from me, consumed as I am with wondering just what Rosalba's fate may be and too afraid to ask.

But she goes on. "It's not too late to help us with the knowledge you undoubtedly have. Not too late to reduce the penalties I've outlined. I would not want to take away your hours in the nursery."

My reaction to this possibility is too quick and slips instantly beneath my guard. It's clear I must convince her that I do not know a useful thing, or I'll be separated from Concerta.

"Madam, it's true we noticed, just this morning, that Rosalba wasn't in her bed. But she prepared her toilette last night in the usual way and seemed asleep when I dropped off."

"And she did not divulge her plan to anyone?"

"Not to me. Nor to the others, I am certain."

"Or give you hints along the way of where she might intend to go?"

"Only that she wanted desperately to see much more of Carnival than we're allowed this year."

I hope to cover everything with this short explanation—the merlin's assistant, the gondolier, the feathered mask and fancy dress. Prioress does not need to know the details or that this was not the first time Rosalba has escaped into the night. I can only hope that the tattler has not mentioned this. If it is Silvia, I just may do her in as I have promised. I do not see another way to vent this awful rage.

"I wish that I could know that what you're telling me is true," says Prioress. "You girls do lie so to protect one another."

"I have bespoke the truth, madam," I say.

"While still, no doubt, concealing all that we should really know."

What they should really know. Could any secrets that I harbor be of help to Rosalba?

"I'll have to ask the other girls who share your chamber," she tells me.

"Madam," I interrupt, "what will happen to Rosalba when she does return?"

"Oh, she will not return," says Prioress. "However much I, myself, would wish it otherwise, the Board of Governors makes no distinctions. Though they must be informed of anything we know, Rosalba will not be allowed to come back here."

Chapter Twenty-seven

Luisa

WITH ROSALBA ABSENT, the Lenten season is a true time of penitence, somber weeks when the morning and nightly readings remind us of our great sins. Mine are clearly sins of omission, for I did not do all that I could have to restrain Rosalba from her foolish plan, the details of which, I assure myself time after time, I did not know. But how does one confess such a sin? I have refrained for weeks from receiving the Eucharist, knowing that the stain upon my soul cannot be expunged unless I do confess my offenses. Even at Easter, which we're told should be a joyous time when we are, like Christ, restored to life, I cannot shake my guilt or lift this heaviest of hearts, which seems to plummet further with each day of Rosalba's absence.

In the darkest, most empty hours of the night, I think about her — about where she can be, if she is cold or hungry, if she has a warm place to sleep, even the most terrible thought that her swollen, lifeless body may wash up on the shore somewhere or be tangled in wharf pilings. Anetta tosses at night as well, and, although neither of us voice them, I know she has the same fears for our friend. During the daylight hours, there is so much to occupy us that for blessed minutes I am free of worry. It is when lying on my cot that the troubling thoughts occur and will not leave until, exhausted, I sleep fitfully.

Come springtime and still no word of her, I wonder if Prioress does know something but has kept it secret. Why did she and others ask for my knowledge of Rosalba's disappearance if there is no recourse? And why insert her name into our nightly prayers, as Signora has done right from the start of her disappearance? I console myself with the knowledge that the days and nights are growing warmer, that even the street urchins can now find places to curl their ragged lives inside. Surely someone from the Ospedale must be looking for her.

I was excused from singing all the somber Lenten music and Father Vivaldi's glorious new Easter Mass, but since completing that, he has been working hard on *Moyses Deus Pharaonis* and is again eager to hear me sing the part he is writing for me. I can't much longer claim exemption due to an illness of many months ago. Prioress has questioned me about the condition of my throat a number of times lately. Both physicians usually employed by the Ospedale and one—sent by my mother, I suspect—have examined me and said there does not seem to be anything really wrong. One noticed some slight inflammation, one a tiny polyp. Fear, however, is invisible.

I regularly attend solfeggio, as I am required to do, but when there, I only listen and do the written work. At the vocal rehearsals, Maestro Scarpari has stopped urging me to join in and rarely even glances over at me anymore. The other students ignore me also, as if I am a fixture in the room, a music stand, the potted fig tree. When one day I am called out of class by Prioress, it is just as if a useless paper drifted out into the hall. No eyes look up.

"We have been very disturbed about you," she begins, "about how frail you still seem, about your pallor. It isn't like you not to even want to sing."

"Oh, I *do* want to," I say. How I would love to sing again, to solo as I used to, to feel the power of the notes within my throat. My throat. It has betrayed me once before. I cannot trust my throat. But Prioress will never understand this.

"That is what you've said before. And the doctors. They have found nothing really wrong. Except, of course, this apparent weakness in your constitution, which has lasted much too long."

I'm not sure what she wants of me, what she desires me to say. Do I apologize for such a lengthy recuperation?

"And so," she continues, "the board has met, and we've decided that you need to have a rest in the country for a while. There is a little farm near Verona where we've sent our girls before who needed sunshine and some fattening up."

"A farm?" I can't imagine such a place. I've never been outside of Venice.

"We will be sending two of you this year—yourself and a younger girl named Catina. Because of chronic breathing difficulties, she is never really well. The canker rash has taken quite a toll on her."

"I know the child of whom you speak. She will profit from the fresh air, I am sure."

"And so shall you. The students we have sent into the country in the past have all come back renewed."

"Perhaps my mother could have me to live with her awhile. I would be good company for her. I know that her apartment's small, but I don't need much room."

"Out of the question," says Prioress. "Your mother will not have you, I am told."

"Has she been asked to take me back? Has she refused? Perhaps she didn't understand about my illness. Perhaps she'll change her mind."

"Luisa, you must give up all these fantasies about your mother, about her coming for you."

"When I am older. Less of a burden. She will. I know she will."

"Well—right now we must do something to make you well. A farm will be the perfect wholesome place for you to take a small vacation."

I don't know what to think. A farm. I've never even seen a farm. Will there be any music there at all? Without at least a little of it, I will be bereft.

But Prioress has read my thoughts.

"Be sure to take your mandolin or a guitar, something to keep you occupied. There's nothing of importance you will miss. Father Vivaldi wants you for his oratorio, but that won't be for upward of another year or more. I've convinced him that you'll be in better form for it if you are sent away to rest awhile."

That at least is something to be thankful for. Such an excuse from Prioress will have more weight than if it came from me.

I have been sworn to secrecy until the actual time for me to leave, so others won't feel slighted. My own feelings about the rest cure are quite mixed. Should I leave now, not knowing anything about Rosalba's fate? Would staying here help her in any way? The only one I could share such questions with is Anetta, and to do this, I would have to break my promise to be silent.

I wait until the free time after dinner, when the din of scales and trills throughout the rooms is deafening.

How Rosalba did abhor the noise! Anetta is surprised to have me take her hand and lead her to the back parlor. There is, in fact, a look of shock upon her face. Her head is twisted quizzically upon her sturdy neck. "I need to tell you something," I begin when we are seated face-to-face. She has good reason for surprise. Only rarely has a conversation between us begun at my instigation. "But you cannot tell a soul."

"Who would I tell?" she asks immediately. "My one confidant has disappeared."

"And mine."

There is such disappointment in her pale, defensive eyes.

"All the more reason we should rely upon each other," she says. "At least we could have each other to tell things to."

"Well, that can't be for long," I say. "It's why I've asked you here."

"I don't understand," she says in sudden agitation. "Are you more ill than I know?"

"It isn't that. Or not exactly. The fact is, Prioress is sending me into the country. To recuperate. To regain my voice."

She blanches visibly and raises folded hands up to her lips as if in prayer.

"For how long a time?"

"Until I'm well," I say, and then try to make light of it. "Until I'm fattened up, she says."

She smiles a little. "That could take forever!"

"Not in the fresh air, she says."

I look down at her two hands now in her lap, at how the fingers are entwined and twist about. For some reason, I'm uncommonly nervous as well.

"The real reason that I've told you this is that if I go so far away . . . if I leave here . . . that will mean there will be no one left but you to wait for her return . . . no one close to her . . . waiting for Rosalba to come back. I mean . . . you will be waiting all alone."

She laughs darkly. "There's always Silvia." Then she says, "You could stay here forever, and it wouldn't make a difference."

"What . . . do you mean?"

"You cannot bargain with impossibility. The very day after the night she did not return, Prioress informed me that she couldn't, that they wouldn't ever let her back. I thought you knew."

"Never let her back! But it's Rosalba!"

"It doesn't matter who it is. It could be the perfect Anna Maria or even the amazing Agrippina. If someone runs away, they can't come back. There isn't any question of it."

"But what if she's been hurt . . . or . . . or kidnapped? Haven't they been looking for her?"

"Looking for her! Prioress says they wiped her name right off the Ospedale register the day she left. She claims that's the ruling of the board. That it has always been the rule. If someone runs away, they can't return." Then she says bitterly, "To them, she might as well be dead."

I am astounded at such cruelty. It seems so unlike all the kindness we have known here.

"As well she could be after all this time. Even if what Prioress says is true, isn't there something we can do?"

"Don't you think I've tried to think of a remedy every night and every day? And you. I know you don't sleep well because of this, that you are deeply troubled, too. I hear you thrashing in the night. And your weeping. It pains me more than you can know. But even if we could sneak away to look for Rosalba, we do not know the city or where to look, and we have no one to turn to for help outside these walls."

I cannot think of one more thing to say. After a time of sitting together in a miserable silence, Anetta comes to my aid.

"You should go to the farm, Luisa. You cannot help Rosalba by remaining here. She'd want you to be returned to health." And then she adds, "As do I. Yes, you must take this opportunity to have some time away from here."

The last words seem to take all her energy, as if they say the very opposite of what she means.

Chapter Twenty-eight

Anetta

LUISA HAS ALLOWED ME to help her ready herself for her journey, and I am both amazed and grateful. There are two new frocks made by the *commun* girls for her days in the country, two petticoats of dimity, a light chemise, a lighter *tabarrino* cloak of camlet, and a new pair of leather shoes, for though she is not filling out, her slender feet are still growing. At times, in fact, she appears to inhabit the body of a much younger child—spare and thin and a trifle potbellied.

Imagine! She will travel by gondola to Santa Lucia, where a wagon will take her to a farm and vineyard in the country. I am truly excited for her, but dread the empty time when the two people I care most for in the world will both be invisible to me.

"We can write letters," she says, and the surprising thought does manage to cheer me a great deal. I will cherish possessing something in Luisa's own hand.

"Would you . . . would you do that?" I ask in disbelief.

"Of course. How else will I know which girls have attracted suitors, the ones no longer on speaking terms, who is being given the best parts to sing. I will expect you to keep me well informed."

Her sudden profession that she will look for an answer back from me to her missives is more than I could have hoped for.

Signora Mandano even allows me to engage the gondola and to settle its two occupants inside. Catina, wrapped too tightly in scarves and capes for such a warm day, squeals when she sees the plush interior, and in her exhilaration, she begins to cough. Luisa seems no longer an orphan but a fine young lady on her way to court. We have arranged her hair with small horns above the temple and even teased ringlets onto the forehead before putting on a gathered cap with lappets hanging down the back. I am pleased to see that there is some excitement in eyes that have been dim and often red-rimmed for many weeks. I'd like to clasp her in my arms the way I've seen her mother do, but such fond expressions have no place within the Ospedale, except, of course, with the infants, and even then we're cautioned not to coddle them. And so I merely watch as she steps through the little doorway of the covered gondola, goes to a window, and shyly pulls the curtain back to wave at me. I am, truly, so happy for them both.

Yet the emptiness I feel while watching their craft make its graceful way up the Grand Canal seems bottomless, a ballooning of the constant ache I have carried with me since Rosalba's disappearance. Going back into the school building with all its noise and confusion is like taking a small potion of forgetfulness that only dulls a little of the pain. I must remind myself again and again that Luisa will be away only a short time, that she will be sending letters to me, that she will be, at long last, completely well.

"Has the little invalid been sent on her way, then?" asks Silvia while tuning her violin. We have been waiting so long for Father to appear that the room is restless. Some girls practice their new parts oblivious to other sections being played. Unlike so many of the others, I must have silence in which to contemplate my own mistakes, and so I remain apparently idle, though studying the score all the while.

"She has left, yes," I tell her, and turn my back to her to try to look over my music in what peace I can make for myself.

"You will need me for a friend," she says behind me, "now that the two you've doted on have disappeared."

"Not disappeared," I tell her with annoyance. "It's true that my two dearest friends are temporarily away. It's not true I can replace them, especially not with someone as ill-tempered as you always seem to be."

She feigns dismay. "Me? Bad-tempered? I only point out things to people for their own good that they may have missed."

"Well, point them out to someone else. I do not need to don the same cloudy lenses that you seem to look through at all times."

Before she can come back at me with her riposte, Father Vivaldi swings the door wide and rustles through it like a sudden wind. Almost always rather neat, today he is disheveled and quite red of face. He slaps a score upon the music stand and coughs into a handkerchief.

"Sorry about the wait," he says at once, "but this tightening of the chest has been plaguing me of late. Father Gasparini is not well himself, but I am here to run you through the piece we started yesterday as best I can." He delivers this entire string of words in a halting, breathless manner.

"Our instruments have already been tuned," Anna Maria, the first violinist, tells him.

"Fine then," he says. "We will start right in."

We enter into the first movement's vigorous contained rhythm without hesitation. Perhaps because of my own sadness, the score for the second movement seems more tender than it did even yesterday, and the repetition of its melodies is about to break my heart. There are tears streaking my face before the end of it. Father himself seems affected by his own notes, for he takes two short intakes of air after putting down his baton, then coughs and wheezes into a large rumpled handkerchief.

"If you are not feeling well," I overhear Anna Maria whisper to him, "I can rehearse the group for you." She has done it before, and rather competently, I must confess.

He thanks her, but instead of accepting the offer, he struggles through the next few hours, wheezing unmercifully. It is most discomfiting, and we are all relieved when the last of this earnest but unsettling rehearsal comes to an end. I, however, am not to be dismissed as yet, for Father motions me to the front and holds some pages in the air above his head.

"The concerto for your viola d'amore," he declares, waving the score about in triumph. "I stayed up all night to finish it."

His effort to make this announcement causes another breathing crisis, and he goes quite purple in the face.

"What can I do, Father?" I say, distressed. "How can I help you?"

He calms a little, but his words are rough and breathy when he speaks again.

"The only thing that you need do for me is play my

music well. I think you'll find that this piece accents your skills. I think I've made a marriage here."

If he only knew the irony he speaks. Me and my instrument. United in a love match like no other. Still, the music is a wondrous gift and far more welcome than any duke it might attract. It is, perhaps, the best match I will ever make.

I am not feeling hungry for the midday meal, so I go up to the nursery instead to help feed the babies. Concerta stands now if placed beside a little chair and thumps her bottom up and down if I sing to her.

"She is musical," I tell Sofia.

"She had better be," says the nurse, "if she wants any kind of life here. It's the ones who play and sing who have a chance at something better than the life I lead."

I do not tell my thoughts to her, that a life entirely within the Ospedale would not be so bad, that tending the babies, watching them grow, loving them, continuing to love even when there's no love in return. It is not so very bad.

Chapter Twenty-nine

Luisa

OUR GONDOLIER IS OLD and does not sing at all, but Signora says he can be trusted, that they have engaged him many times before. He simply guides his boat, and after seating us inside, doesn't pay any attention to his passengers.

I had not thought it would be so hard to leave the Ospedale behind, or Anetta. Especially not Anetta. But watching from the window of the gondola as they both fade from view, my eyes sting and a thin stream of tears runs down to my chin.

When I try to wipe away the dampness with the back of my hand, wise little Catina notices and counsels me. "We will not be away for long, Luisa. In just a few months, this same sight we now leave behind will greet us."

Her attempt at consoling me would be amusing if I weren't feeling so bereft and timid about this journey. I am, after all, the one who is supposed to be in charge. At other times she seems easily as young as her years, too excited to sit still, even though all the jouncing about makes her cough and wheeze the more. She rises repeatedly to point out the sights she has seen before when on a trip with Signora to a see a specialist in breathing disorders.

"Look, Luisa, the Doge's Palace! Look, Luisa, Cá Foscari! Look, Luisa, the Rialto Bridge!"

I search fruitlessly for Calle del Carbon as we approach the area of my mother's apartment and for anything that looks familiar—a building, a marketplace. I remember a small *campo*, some steep steps, the dark interior of what must have been a church, someone helping me to light a candle with a long wick. I remember how brightly it burned.

After a while, I can't help exclaiming over the beautiful houses along the water, with their own gondolas tied onto pilings at entrances from the canal, and over the filigreed gates and small gardens. We make up stories about who could be living in one or another, how the children in such places pass the time, what they wear on ordinary days.

When passing other gondolas, we try to see inside or wave to the gondolier. It is such great sport that I almost forget my sadness, and we are at Santa Lucia in what seems to be no time at all.

There is a market here with many stalls filled with colorful fruit and vegetables, all manner of freshly caught fish, their eyes staring dumbly, killed chickens tied together and hung by their legs. And there are many wagons. I had thought to be on the lookout for one wagon only. How will I know which one has been sent from the Ricci farm? Most are now empty but still fastened to a donkey or horse snuffling a feed bag and pawing the ground.

I try not to alarm Catina, but I see no way to make an identification among them. The gondolier puts our small valises and my guitar and mandolin upon the dock and begins his little speech to entice another passenger aboard. I can't help thinking how Rosalba would have flirted and cajoled until he'd found our wagon for us. Left to my own devices, I have no idea where to turn, and for the first time since departing, I wish Signora had at least come with us this far.

We have been given a few florins, so I take Catina's hand and we pass over the road to a bakery tent. We buy a small sugar cake apiece, which manages to make us so thirsty that we must then bargain for two cups of cider.

"You keep looking all around," says Catina at last. "As if you don't know what we're to do next."

I should have realized that I couldn't pretend with this child.

"I know what I was told to do. But . . . " I begin.

"You can't find the wagon," she says.

"Yes, that's right. I can't find the wagon."

"It should not be so difficult," she continues, "if you look in the right place."

"I should think that would go without saying."

"But we aren't in the right place. We're in the market now. The wagons are out by the trees."

"I was buying some time."

"If we stay here too long, Luisa, the man from the farm will think we have never arrived."

I had not thought of that possibility, so we quickly head back to the dock. Remaining clearly visible proves to be the best solution, because soon a large conveyance, more cart than wagon, pulls up in front of us, and a ruddy man dressed in the dark and shabby clothes of a farmer doffs a battered hat.

"*Ciao*," he calls in greeting, and uses one side of his open toothless mouth to make a clicking sound with his cheek and halt the small horse.

"You are the *signorine* from the Ospedale, *capisci*?"

"*Sì*," we both say at once.

He jumps down and swings our small trunks and my instruments into the back with great agility for one so old.

"One of you can sit up here with me," he says, "but the other will need to sit in the back."

"We will both sit in the back," says Catina, and I'm glad she's made that decision for us, as I would not have desired to sit next to such a man, smelling of earth and sweat and garlic and heaven knows what, or to travel all alone with the bounty of odd things that he transports.

"Bene," he says, and spreads a tattered blanket over rags and baskets of every sort. It is a lumpy place on which to sit, and the entire cart is raised in the front and tips toward the ground in the rear. To keep from sliding off, we must scoot up and put our backs against the driver's seat—downwind of him, I fear. Otherwise there is a great freshness to the air, and I notice that Catina has not coughed during all the activity of getting settled. When we pull away from the marketplace and onto country roads, we both breathe deeply, and it is like filling our lungs with sky.

Such an expanse of it overhead, such fresh green plots of land dotted with olive and eucalyptus trees. Here and there are peaceful milk cows grazing close to the road, their calves nearby. Sometimes a few bulls in separate fields, well muscled and brawny, laze off by themselves in the sun.

For all the tranquil beauty of the countryside, it is an uncomfortable trip, bumpy and rough from start to finish. When we finally pull onto a muddy narrow lane and in front of the whitewashed farmhouse we had seen from a distance, I am filled with relief. We climb down as fast as we can and both head for the little privy we have noticed in the yard.

After this necessary duty, we return to the entrance, where a round and rosy woman stands with arms crossed over her ample stomach. The set of her lips is stern until she sees us scurrying back over the weeds and grass. Then her mouth widens slowly and reassuringly into a warm smile that seems to shimmer; she laughs and claps her plump little hands together and all but jumps up and down with excitement.

"*Benvenuto,*" she exclaims over and over, opening her arms and gathering us into them as if we're her very own children. Neither of us hesitates. It is as if we had known she would be waiting for us, as if we had always known it.

Rosalba

I OPEN MY EYES to an unfamiliar room, spare of everything but a rim of dust motes along the walls, a small old table and basin, one broken chair, and the cot on which I am lying, covered by a coarsely woven blanket with the unpleasant smell of someone else's sweat. From a yellow cast to the pale light slanting through two high windows, I suspect it may be morning. Right away I raise a finger to my lips. They are still swollen and scabs have developed where the teeth pierced me. My clothing is torn and bloodied and damp just as I remember. And I remember everything, even wandering through the streets for hours and finally collapsing in a cluttered doorway that smelled of cat piss. The odor of it, and that of my attacker, linger on my clothing. It was not a dream. None of it was a dream.

But I have no idea how I came to this place, to this plain and dirty little room, and have no desire to arise and discover where the one door leads. A new heavy sensation—shame—keeps me prone and fills my entire body like hot lead. Am I still in Venice, somewhere in Venice? How near am I to the Ospedale? Have they sent someone to look for me? What streets do I travel to go back?

Unfamiliar voices come from somewhere in the distance, as if swaddled in gauze, and quick footsteps sound on a bare wooden stairway. I have just begun to fear what may lie beyond that door when it opens and a woman sidles in as if she hesitates to wake me. When she sees my eyes are open, she brings up the one chair and sits beside me. Her face is creased by time and weather and some merriment, I think, for at the edges of her eyes, there are these scratchy lines from laughing. But she isn't even smiling now.

She puts a hand upon my arm that holds the blanket to me and leans in closely till she's speaking right into my face. Her breath is strangely acrid and sweet all at one time. There is still no smile upon her thin lips.

"How are you feeling now?" she asks. "We didn't dare to clean you up last night because, for a certain, you would have been awakened from your deep sleep. Pasquale carried you just like a little babe. You didn't stir."

I don't know what to say. She must know what has happened to me then. The smell of it is about me still. Pasquale, whoever he is, must know as well. I wait for some harsh words, but they don't come.

"Whoever did this to you is an evil man. A devil."

The wig-maker's assistant? Truly evil? And yet what else am I to think? I can no longer hide from the brutal truth of it or continue to court love as I did, the way it had appeared to me within the plays and all my beautiful fantasies with such smug abandon.

"I will get water and some cloths for you to clean yourself. For now, you can wear my other dress. It will not fit too well, but I can wash and mend the things you're wearing and perhaps borrow something for a while from another musician we know who is about your size."

"You are a musician?" I ask before I realize that I have seen her face before. A violin had been beneath the chin. The eyes, more tired than I remember, had looked out from a small mask. Up so close, the same strong hands that had fingered the strings and held the bow have crooked fingers and swollen joints.

"We play at Carnival and other festivals. My sons and I. We play to earn our bread and keep a roof—this roof—above our heads."

"This is your house?"

"Half a narrow house, really, and we are temporary lodgers only. Three rooms, one above the other, and a stairway. Nothing more. You and I can share this bedroom."

It is her room. And there is only one bed. Why does she speak as if I plan to stay?

"I will be leaving when I get cleaned up," I say, getting to my feet. The room whirls a bit, but soon settles. I'm not sick, just battered and unbelievably tired, and as dirty as a lard, one of those thieves who work the streets.

"Where will you go?" she asks.

"Back to the Ospedale della Pietà, on the Riva. You must know it."

"I thought as much. You are too refined to be from the neighborhood around here, yet you're not dressed in the manner of royal folk. A runaway, I told Pasquale, and Salvatore, he thought so, too. Carnival, it is a time for such things."

"It was a foolish thing to do," I tell her.

"More foolish than you know."

"What do you mean?"

She sighs and takes my hand. Hers is thin and knobby and not warm to the touch.

"Only that it isn't the first time I've seen the likes of what happened to you. Oh, not the ravishment. But other girls have run away, thinking to find . . . whatever romantic dream they have in their foolish heads."

Knowing that others have done the same is some comfort.

"What happened to them?'

"I don't know for a certain. Except for one who kept hanging around our *campo*. She began to sell herself, you know, sold her favors on the street, until she took quite sick and died."

"Did none of them go back?"

"They may have tried. The Ospedale doesn't take back runaways."

My heart drops, and I need to sit again to think. What does a street musician know? She hasn't met Signora or Prioress. She doesn't realize how fond they are of all of us. I'm sure she must be misinformed.

I tell her this, and she just shakes her head. Some tufts of hair about the ears suggest that she will soon be as gray as all the ladies who wear shawls to Mass. Will she still play her violin, I wonder, when she is stooped and really old?

"What is the instrument you play?" she asks.

"Chiefly the oboe," I tell her, "but sometimes the continuo when it is needed, and often the mandolin and lute."

"And do you sing?"

"Yes, of course. We all sing."

What is she thinking?

"You can sing with us awhile until you earn enough to buy an instrument, a used but playable one, in the Piazza

San Marco. It won't take long. We can use a new and pretty face to draw the crowd and to give me a vacation."

"How can you tell that I am pretty?" I ask, searching my swollen lips again to see if there has been some change.

"I'll admit, you are a sight. But it came to me a little while ago that you're the one we saw at the Piazza last Tuesday week. The one with the Signora from the Pietà and all the little girls. You watched us from your spot by the Campanile while all the others watched the puppets."

"Yes, that was me," I tell her. "I thought you played quite well. I thought you seemed to be having such a grand time."

"When we don't work hungry," she said. "But you'll see. We'll make a place for you."

"Oh, no," I say. She still misunderstands me. "As soon as I look more presentable, I'm going back to the Ospedale. I've learned my lesson, don't you see?"

"My girl," she says, quite kindly on the one hand but rather too briskly on the other, "what more is there to say? You don't believe me yet, but you will never be allowed to go back there."

A rap upon the door saves me from yet another protest, as one of the young men whom I'd seen play in the Piazza, the plainer and the shorter of the two, comes into the room.

"This is Pasquale," says the woman, "And my name

is Lydia. I don't think that I told you that before."

"How are you feeling?" asks Pasquale in a much larger voice than I would have thought belonged to someone of his size.

My face must be as scarlet as my vest, for he has seen me in my complete disgrace, even carried me and my soiled clothing in his arms. I cannot look at him.

"I came to tell you that Salvatore is heating up the goat stew for midday meal. It's very good."

Lydia turns to me. "You'll feel much better when you've eaten," she says. And then she adds, "What is your name?"

I do not tell her at once. It is the only thing I have to give away, and I'm not ready to do it.

"It's all right," Pasquale intervenes. "A woman should have secrets."

A woman. I am still a child. What happened to me makes me feel this even more. I will go back to the Ospedale and throw myself against the skirts of Prioress, beg for her mercy, never leave her side. But first I must use the water this lady, this Lydia, has just poured into the basin. I must become presentable.

Salvatore's goat stew is flavorful and builds little fires at the edge of my exhaustion. He is as handsome as his brother is plain, but he does not even look at me after my entry into the small room used as a kitchen, nor I at him, and Pasquale is the one to do most of the talking. He jokes at the way I fill out his mother's dress. He takes a brush himself to my tangled hair, which must be bushing out as it does on most mornings and could not be properly cleaned with a few cloths. His strokes are as firm and sure as a woman's. He then fills my bowl a second time and pats my head and tells me to eat more. But I cannot. I am so mute in this company that they must think me very slow of mind or a true idiot, the likes of which there are a goodly number in Venice.

"She should rest," Pasquale says to his mother as if I am not in the room.

"If she's to stay here for a time, she needs to be of help at something. What can she do for us?" asks Salvatore.

His mother tells him, "Hush. There is time for that. I have already told her she must make herself useful."

She had only talked about what I would do as a member of their little musical troupe. Doesn't she know that at the Pietà, the *privilegiate* do not do common chores?

"I am not of the *figli di commun*," I say.

"Ah. She speaks," says Pasquale.

"You might as well be," says Salvatore. "Each person does their share in this group. We will not coddle a Vivaldi brat or keep a girl such as yourself from plying her loose trade."

I am mortified to think that he believes me to be one of those women of whom he speaks.

"This girl is not your common whore. I'd swear it. She's hardly old enough to leave the house unchaperoned," says Lydia.

"I'm sixteen years," I tell them.

"Old enough to earn her keep," says Salvatore.

They continue to talk above me, and I have so little will or energy to join the conversation, that I sit there like a bruised stone.

"Come," Lydia says at length. She takes my arm and pulls me up from the hard chair they had given me to sit upon. "You may as well get more rest for now. I'll fix your clothes while you're asleep, and we'll take you with us in a day or two."

"Or three or four or five," says Salvatore. "That mouth has to heal before she shows herself on the street with any of us. And sew a wider fichu into her bodice if you don't want the same thing as last night to happen to her again."

I try to imagine a time when the pain and soreness all through me will be gone, but cannot wrap my mind around the thought. It feels right now as if the mending will need to go on without end, as if I will always feel just as I do today.

"*Chiudi la bocca,* Salvatore," says Pasquale. "You will frighten her." He turns to me and lifts my chin until he looks — no, not *looks* — *sees* into my eyes. "Do not worry, Signorina. No one will harm you again. I will be there."

Chapter Thirty-one

Luisa

THERE IS WARM GOAT'S MILK on my breakfast millet and a dish of pale pink berries of a kind that I have never seen before. Catina has had a bad night, and so I do not awaken her. Though we must share a room, it is a blessing we don't have to share a bed, for I am at least spared her tossing about. Under the circumstances, I myself didn't sleep well, in spite of the background quiet of the country. When a rooster crowed and the light began to mingle with the dark, I went to the window and looked out, amazed, as a round red sun lifted above the low hills and made the fields blush crimson. After such a display,

I could not return to bed and was happy to find Signora Ricci already bustling in the large kitchen and my breakfast ready for me.

"Lazybones," she chides me as if it is closer to noon than dawn. "The men are already in the fields." She gives me a quick hug, and it is very pleasant to be so welcomed from sleep. She herself is fully dressed in her shift and bodice, and I am in my *robe de chambre*. When I mention this with a bit of chagrin, she reminds me that I am the patient, that I am here to regain my health.

"I will prepare a picnic for you and Catina to take out into the countryside," she says as I eat. "It will be good for you in the warm sun. You should both nap in it after your meal."

Catina doesn't awaken until almost midday, but she is quick at her toilette, and we head off with our basket while the sun is at its pinnacle. Our new shifts have shorter sleeves, and the sun bathes our faces and part of our arms. It is intoxicating to discover that the sound of instruments being tuned and the constant chatter of the Ospedale have been replaced by singing birds, an insect's hum, the bleating of a lamb. Every little while we both twirl in circles with delight just to feel a great rush of the warm dry air. And Catina's breathing is less labored; she does not cough at all. My own throat seems more open.

Not having a true destination, we pass many possible spots in which to linger, but are enticed by a small apple orchard along the path that's in full bloom and bursting with fragrant white flowers. There is a low stone fence at its border, on which we can sit and watch the grandeur of it. Signora has also given us a blanket on which to recline for the naps she is sure we'll need. But we are invigorated by all the new sights and sounds and smells, and for once, I do not feel the terrible weakness that has been my constant companion of late. Catina all but dances as she darts in among the trees, oblivious to the many bees that buzz through the branches and hover over the *fiori*. Soon she has tired herself sufficiently to seek rest on the blanket I have placed where sunlight through the branches casts a lacy pattern on the ground. Signora Ricci has warned us not to allow the sun to burn our delicate skin, which has only been exposed to it on infrequent trips to a nearby *campo*, or, once, on a boat ride to the island of Murano. She has remarked at how you can almost see through our skin right to the veins, that it is both *bianca* and *blu*.

"Shall we play a game?" asks Catina after catching her breath, which has begun to sound somewhat wheezy and rough again.

"I don't know any."

"We can make one up."

She turns on one elbow and coughs into her hand. "Let me think."

"Father Vivaldi watches the birds," I tell her.

"That's not a game. And, anyway, we don't know all their names and markings and special calls, as he does."

"I know a thrush when I see it. And a goldfinch. Everyone knows a goldfinch."

"What if we just count them?" she says. "Like that bird over there. Let's count all the others just like it that we see."

"That's not much of a game either."

"Well, I'll count those nameless ones over there and you count the thrushes. The one who counts the most birds wins."

I am reminded that the *commun* girls know all about games, but the *privilegiate* never have time for them. The game that Catina suggests is too simple and dull, and I tell her so.

"Not if we also take note of their markings and color and each distinct call. Father keeps a notebook with just these same things. I've seen it when clearing his desk."

"That's not a game. It's an . . . endeavor. I'm much too tired to compose such a list, and we haven't a paper or pen."

"Then I'll tell you a story," she says, unperturbed by her own labored breathing. "Sit back. It will be long. I can sometimes go on and on and on."

"You have done this before?"

"Oh, yes. Many times. The little girls, the ones even younger than me, they beg for them when I'm about, which has not been so often of late."

But I am too hungry to want stories just yet. This kind of hunger, it is a sensation I had almost forgotten.

"Let's eat our picnic first, and then have a story," I suggest, and she is quick to agree, as she has been pestering since we set out to pull back the napkin from the basket and uncover the mysterious contents. Inside are lovely red grapes, an *arancia* for each of us, a *focaccia* with caramelized onions and goat cheese on top, a small jar of tea, and a pastiche filled with sweetened raspberries and custard. It is all so delicious that I eat every bit of my share, but Catina has a very small appetite and just nibbles a little of each thing the Signora has packed.

Afterward, I am terribly sleepy and curl on my side on the blanket while Catina sits up and begins her story. At first she describes a beautiful kingdom, much like what we have seen today, with a very young and powerful queen. It isn't long before her breathy words begin to weave themselves into a kind of song filled with castles and unicorns and magicians that spill unevenly into and over one another until they become a little whirlwind that carries me off into my own dreams. When I wake up, the air is cooler, and Catina is asleep and snoring raggedly. The sun has more pink to it and is much lower in the sky. A chalky moon hangs just over the trees.

I pull my shawl from the basket and stand up to stretch and drape it over my shoulders. I tuck Catina's around her, and wonder if I should wake her and if we should be going back. The beautiful silence is too intoxicating, however, and my curiosity invites me to roam a little while. There is an outbuilding nearby that I had noticed before. It is a crude little shack, really, and when I climb over the wall and amble up to it, my intention is to take a quick look and go right back to Catina.

The undeniable smell of livestock gets stronger the nearer I come to the building. And as I step over dried cow patties, my nose burns and my eyes water and sting. But just as I decide to turn back, the swish of a tail near the opening of the little broken-down building catches my eye. Coming closer, I hear a strange hiss and muted thud and what I can only describe as mumbling cow sounds, a sustained grunt, a deep occasional moo. When, with some difficulty, I pull back the wide door left ajar, the mystery is solved, and a sight I had never imagined to see is before me in all its rude splendor.

I have startled a young man sitting upon a milk stool who is massaging the teats of a rather large and patient cow. Embarrassed, my hand goes to cover my mouth, but the boy keeps up his steady pull and squirt of milk and doesn't look up. It is clear that the little thuds are made when the milk hits the side of a wooden pail.

"Do not frighten Evangelina," he says. "It is best if you just back away."

"May I watch?" I ask.

"From a distance only. From way over there," and he nods with his head at the hay-filled corner of this odd little barn.

The cow moos most plaintively even though I am out of her sight.

"She knows you are there. She does not like strangers. Her milk may shut down if you stay. Please. Just go away."

He has still not looked over at me. When I don't move immediately he says, "You spoiled little orphans. You think you can go wherever you like."

"Spoiled we may be," I reply. "But at least we are not taught to be bad-mannered. And how do you know who we are?"

"I saw you arrive yesterday. You're not the first to be taken in by Signora Ricci. She needs the extra ducats badly."

Of course I knew that she was being paid for our keep, but I don't like it being pointed out in this way or to think that there have been a stream of others before us from the Ospedale.

Evangelina moos with annoyance, and the boy takes his hands from the udders and strokes her side, speaking more softly. His message to me, however, is still the same but delivered almost in a whisper.

"Please. Go away. Some other time you can look at the animals. Not while they're being milked."

He says this as if there is more than one animal about and not just this single sensitive cow. But I do as he says, not wishing to cause her any more consternation.

As I make my way quietly from the odorous corner

out into the field, I can hear him crooning gently, "There, there, *mio amore*" and the rhythm of the little wet thuds against the pail again.

A quick wind, warm and swift, lifts my skirt when I climb back over the wall. It riffles through the apple blossoms and sends them swirling all through the air. When I look down at the sleeping figure of Catina, there is a smile of contentment on her lips and a thin cover of white flowers, as fragile and lucent as glass, over her small body. She is not coughing or wheezing. She is at perfect peace.

Rosalba

I HAVE TOLD THEM over and over, but they still choose not to understand.

"I am not allowed to play an instrument in Venice. No one from the Ospedale may play in Venice once they have left. The rules are very clear."

"Child," says Lydia, "if you think that anyone from the Pietà will hunt you down, you are sadly mistaken. As far as they are concerned, you no longer exist. What music you make in the streets is of no concern at all to them."

"How else do you intend to earn your keep?" asks Salvatore. "It is the only reason we have for allowing you to stay."

"I think it will be all right if I sing," I agree at last. Father Vivaldi made no mention of singing when he said I could not play my oboe in the city. It has been some time since my face healed, and no instrument has yet been procured for me. I will decide what to do about that when the time comes to buy one.

"And I'm certain you will do it well," says Pasquale.

He is always so agreeable that I do not have to try to please him and, unfairly perhaps, find myself expending my energies in attempts to make Salvatore like me better. His face is as beautiful as a painting by Tiepolo, though I have yet to see him smile. Often his mother plays the coquette with this particular son and bristles when I do anything that might change his original impression of me. Pasquale notices my efforts and cautions me not to try so hard to endear myself to either mother or son.

"Salvatore is the favored one," he says without malice. "I am tolerated. As you will be if you are of any use to them. It is not such a bad thing."

"Why does this not cause you to be resentful?" I ask, for his constant cheerfulness and eagerness to please all of us confounds me.

"What is the point? Things will only change for ill if I become petulant. Life is too much of a gift to despoil it with petty wrangling."

I have no retort to such unselfishness, but I am myself determined not to become the doormat that he willingly makes of himself. *Doormat* is perhaps not the best description of Pasquale, for both Lydia and Salvatore seem to have a great deal of respect for him even as they allow him to do most of the unpleasant tasks. When I mention something of the sort, he says, "People are imperfect. Why do battle with such an indisputable fact day after day?"

"You are a philosopher, then," I tell him.

"What do you know of philosophers?"

"Not very much. But I think they are quite high-minded. As you seem to be."

"Perhaps," he says, and looks at me with those searching, clear eyes. "And an ordinary man. Very much a man."

If he is courting my favor, I cannot tell. What is clear is that he intends to protect me in both large and small ways, and for that I am grateful. Nothing of my earlier disgrace has passed his lips, and as weeks pass, I am certain that nothing ever will.

"She cannot wear those clothes," declares Salvatore as I run down the stairs to join the others with the intention of going along to the Piazza San Marco and trying a few of the songs they have taught me. My clothing has been washed and mended, but he looks at me as if I have just rolled in the mud.

"It is all I have," I tell him. Lydia had spoken of

sewing a new dress for me, but has never even begun it. We were not taught to sew in the Ospedale.

"It will have to do," says Lydia. "If she looks like a tart . . . well . . . it may draw the crowd."

To think I am being used in such a way is utterly demeaning.

"I will stay here then," I say, and sit down hard on a stair, folding my arms across my waist like a barrier.

"You will do no such thing," says Lydia. She grabs my arms and jerks me up again to a standing position.

"Here," says Pasquale, handing me his mother's short *bagnolette*, which she rarely wears on these warm nights. "There is an easy solution." He places the little satin cape across my shoulders and ties it under my chin as if I am a child on my way to school.

"Thank you, Pasquale," I say. I will wear it because of his kindness, even if I should swelter. It does seem a shame to hide my red velvet bodice, but the short cape hides my bosom as well, and I suppose that is really what bothers Salvatore.

"There," says Lydia. "She could well be a nun."

"Not with such a face," says Salvatore. He does not mean to compliment me, but I am pleased, nonetheless, that he has noticed and does not plan to relegate me to a convent just yet.

"Indeed," adds Pasquale, but this brother says it quite tenderly as if he appreciates fully not just the face but the person I am. It is not clear to me how I know this. It is instinctual and deep.

The square is, as usual, full to bursting with the oddments of Venice—well-dressed dukes dripping lace and gold embroidery, grimy little street urchins, a dwarf juggling three melons, a crippled woman sitting on the cobblestones in a stream of her own urine and stretching one crooked hand to the crowd. It has not taken as long to walk here as I had supposed, but since we have come from a direction opposite to the one taken from the Ospedale, we did not pass anything familiar to me.

Salvatore claims a spot for us at the foot of the Campanile, and after the others have taken out their instruments and played a few rollicking instrumental pieces, Pasquale motions for me to come forward. A small crowd has already gathered, and as I come to the front, it is a shock to suddenly realize that I can be seen. There is no grille to disguise me or to hide behind. The realization makes me fall silent at first, and causes Salvatore to make some excuse before replaying the introduction to my song. I am feeling lightheaded, and the queasiness that has been visiting me of late is revived.

"*Scusi,*" I say in a weak little voice that can't be my own.

Salvatore's dark look does not encourage me. But I have come this far with these people. I must try to go on.

The words and notes to the song "*Alma del Core*"

come softly from my lips at first, but then I notice the expectant and approving countenances of the small crowd, and little by little my voice becomes warmer and fuller until it has all the timbre of the *castrati* part I often sang at the Pietà. It suits this ardent music well.

With the second song, *"Amarilli, mia bella,"* I am fully in control again, lacing the music with my most heartfelt and sincere emotion and losing myself to the simple melody. At its end, I am truly disappointed not to have another song to sing, for these two are the only ones that I have mastered. And I am also pleased to observe many ducats being added to the ones already in the basket. Salvatore is bound to see my worth to the group.

"Brava," Pasquale says to me as we are packing up to leave, but Salvatore hasn't uttered a single word.

"You have a lusty voice," says Lydia, as if this is a drawback. "You must rein it in the next time."

"I agree heartily," says Salvatore. "Your singing must not eclipse the playing of our instruments."

"That makes no sense at all," Pasquale defends me. "The people loved the way she sang. Our expanded coffers tell that story."

His quick and resolute defense of me is welcome, and I'm happy to see once more that Pasquale doesn't bow to these most insensible decrees of his family.

"Truly?" asks Lydia. "There is more in that basket tonight than is usual?"

"A good deal more."

"It does not mean that she should not take heed of what we say and try to improve," says Salvatore. "I for one am not convinced yet of her worth to us. It could be just a fluke."

"A fluke," Pasquale repeats, rolling his eyes in consternation. "We can call it that if you like. We can call it anything, and it will still be good to have the extra income."

"Please," I say at last. "I can do better. I will do better."

"All right, then," says Lydia. "The matter is closed. We'll come back here again tomorrow night. We'll try our luck a second time at this same place."

It has been good to perform again, even these frivolous songs of love that every street musician knows, to smile at an audience and—imagine—to have them smile in return.

Walking back through the winding streets, some lit only by the moon, I feel a little bit of hope, some excitable quivering within my stomach. But by the time the half house is in view, I cannot hold back the nausea that has been rising in my chest. I grip the rail of a small connecting bridge and retch over the side until I can bring up nothing but bitter mucous.

Pasquale is the only one to stay behind with me. He wipes my face with his own sleeve, and we sit upon the stones awhile.

"There's no hurry," he says. "We'll move on when you're feeling better."

"I don't know what came over me."

"Perhaps," he says cautiously, "it is not an illness of any sort."

"What do you mean?"

"Only that it's been many weeks now since you came to us."

"Since you found me," I correct him.

He becomes flustered and puts his head into his hands. After which he looks at me with eyes that have become accustomed to the dim light and contain some cast of awe or reverence that I don't understand.

"It's time enough, at any rate," he says, and smiles as at some shared secret.

"What do you mean to say?"

"Only that it has been a few months' time. Time enough to see some signs."

"Signs of what?"

He takes my hand when he sees my confusion. He stares at his feet, suddenly shy.

"Signs of new life," he says at last.

$\mathcal{A}$netta

LUISA HAS FINALLY SENT a letter. Signora Mandano
brought it to me after the noon meal. Everyone saw
her do it, and I immediately slid it, unopened, into the
pocket of my apron to take it into the kitchen garden,
where I can read it privately. It is a very rare thing for
one of us to receive a letter. I can't even remember when
it has happened before.

I am a little surprised to find her words are more for-
mal than if we were speaking face-to-face, but her hand-
writing is as lacy and fine as her lyrical speaking voice
that I hear in my dreams.

Dear Anetta,

I hope this finds you well and that little Concerta has been cured of the nursery fever that plagued her for a time. The country is exactly like the picture in the small parlor that depicts a shepherd and his flock. Perhaps the green here is of an even purer hue. There are such fresh smells all about and a feeling of great peace.

Though I often play my guitar for Signora Ricci, I do miss the music-making at the Ospedale, and many other things.

Catina seemed much better for a day or so, but then her breathing difficulties became severe, and a doctor hereabouts was called upon. He says it is the grasses or perhaps the cattle droppings, maybe even the profusion of a tiny flower that is very golden. She will, no doubt, be returning in a few days' time.

Has Rosalba returned as of yet? I sent a letter asking this of Prioress, but she has not replied.

Your friend, Luisa

It is a lovely letter, but she did not sign it *Dearest friend,* as I would have done, as I hoped she would do. And she doesn't name me among the things she misses most. No matter. She is well. It is a great pity that the country does not seem to be a place where Catina can find some surcease from her malady.

I must reply to Luisa at once, so she will know how

much she is missed. I must apprise her also of the fact that our Rosalba has not yet returned. The worry of it keeps my eyes wide open well into the deepest hours of the night. (For a certain I will not write that if what Prioress has said is true, Rosalba would be turned away and none of us would even know.)

Dearest friend, I will tell her.

Things are not the same here without you. I am glad the country agrees with you so and am hopeful that rest and fresh air will soon restore you to perfect health. Many of us left behind envy you the villeggiatura *you have been given. No, Rosalba has not returned, and I feel desperate sometimes for news of what has become of her. It is awful to know that prayer is all I have to offer at this time, even though Father Vivaldi assures me that prayer can move entire mountains. It has certainly been responsible for a great change in the health of Concerta. She grows chubbier and more ruddy-cheeked with each day and raises up her little arms to me whenever I am by.*

Someone—a duke, I think—has spoken for the hand of Beatrice, not knowing she is very deaf. Signora Mandano hopes to keep this knowledge from the suitor until they are joined as one. Silvia has been tormenting Beatrice in your absence, and it's rumored she is ready to accept any proposal at all. They say she had never expected to receive one.

Father Vivaldi has at last written a concerto for my viola d'amore that is very beautiful and unbelievably inventive, and I performed it this past Sunday. Prioress says it was a triumph, but I have no way of knowing for a certain. There were, however, a good deal of noses blown and much random coughing.

Father also asks about you from time to time and if your voice has been restored. He applies himself quite feverishly to the writing of Moyses Deus Pharaonis *in between work on the new concertos and cantatas due each week, and he says your part will be ready for study when you return. Today we practiced a* pasticcio *pieced together by the copyists. It worked quite well and almost seemed to be a whole new composition.*

You will be returning very soon, won't you? I know it's not been such a long time, but it has seemed so to me. I have no confidant at all these days, so I whisper my complaints into Concerta's little ears, which have no notion of what I truly say. She thinks it all a part of our frequent game of peekaboo and waves her hands about and laughs at me.

On the day of Sensa, Sofia let me carry Concerta outside to see the annual celebration of the wedding of the doge with the sea. Remember how you and I and Rosalba loved to watch the large golden ship, il bucintoro, *with the doge standing in the prow in his purple horn hat, white gown, and gold cloak faced* with ermine? You would always squeal when he cast his ring and all manner of flowers into the waters of the lagoon, and Rosalba would sigh. If only you both could have been with me and Concerta. As usual, the naval vessel was surrounded by decorated gondolas, and all the singing from every craft washed over us in great waves that seemed to stun my tiny companion into silence. She pointed at whatever came into view—the great ship, a running child, a tattered old man, a wiry little dog that nipped at her bare heels—and I had to remind myself that everything, any sight I take for granted, is completely new to her. She is more curious and brighter than any child I've ever seen, the way I think you must have been when her age.

Prioress just today has brought the news that some nobleman or other would like to have a closer look at me at tea, that he was "overcome" by the emotion displayed in my recent viola d'amore solo. I am reminded of how Rosalba used to say that many of these fellows wish only to employ a passionate musician and not procure a wife. I wish she were here to tell me how to behave in such a situation. I am not eager to be scrutinized by him, nor do I like the thought of leaving here. But I must go through the usual motions while keeping my divided heart in all the places that it already resides. A large part of it is still with you.

I will sign my letter, Your dearest friend, Anetta.

Chapter Thirty-four

Luisa

CATINA'S BREATHING PROBLEMS have been getting worse, and word of her difficulties has been sent to the Ospedale. I take the opportunity to include a letter to Anetta with the wagon driver as well. When I put pen to paper, however, I find it impossible to describe the magic of this place. But I had promised her a letter and am eager for news from her, so I do the best I can.

It was pleasant having a little companion to wander with through the orchards and fields. Now when I go out alone, I think of that first day and how like a dream it felt, the masses of apple blossoms, the vineyards, the endless fields, everything suspended, glittering, and green. Here there is no water anywhere but in the well. It is as if I have slipped from the watery thoroughfares of Venice into a drier, more golden world. Everything smells of rich dark earth and is anchored to it. Any moisture must come from the sky, which it does at intervals regular enough to make the fruit grow plump and juicy and deliver ripe grapes that can be pressed into wine. Signora Ricci says that it is not always so, that this is a very good year when God's blessings are abundant.

"Go," she tells me on this exceedingly warm morning when the sun is more fiery furnace than soft comforter. "Catina can help me bake bread. She'll have plenty to keep her amused."

"Oh, may I?" begs Catina. "Cook never lets us help knead, even when she's so worn out the sweat pours down her face and drips into the dough."

"How revolting!" I say, wishing she had not disclosed this unpleasant fact. Bread will now be one more thing at the Pietà that I will exclude from my diet.

"God's mercy, you never can tell it in the eating," she continues.

"It was not the kneading I had in mind for you, Catina," says Signora. "Perhaps you can add the salt and the water. It would not do to have you cough into the mixture."

"Just another thing that I may only watch," says

Catina, slumping in her chair and sticking out her lower lip, which makes her seem very young indeed.

I do not wish to leave her so dejected, but there is little for me to do if I stay, and so I take the basket of food Signora hands me and smile at her when she winks at me, hoping Catina doesn't see this interchange.

"They are harvesting the grapes on the north slope," she tells me. "You may enjoy watching, but do not get in the way."

The peculiar little barn with its single cow is in another direction entirely. There is something about it, however, that draws me back. Perhaps the cow is in the field. Perhaps I will not be so much a hindrance as I was before. I will approach quietly and leave if the boy is milking her again.

The dew has already dried upon the grasses, and there are none of the fine webs woven through the blades that glisten in early light. Far to the south, I can see workers clinging to another slope. From here they look like tiny dark bugs; I can't distinguish head from hat.

Approaching the barn from the back, I see the cow already in the field and grazing. The boy, no doubt, is off doing chores somewhere. Without the caution I had planned earlier, I sneak a look into the small out-building and am confronted by a sight that I had not expected. The boy is sound asleep upon the straw, his wide-brimmed hat perched on a post, his rake lying just beyond his reach. He has the dark bouncing curls of a child, but the more angled features of a young man. He is most beautiful in repose, even though the black eyes I had noticed before are shut tight. His hands support his head; his bare feet stick up straight, displaying calluses and dirt and straw between the toes. A small black lamb is curled into one corner. It may have been here before, but I didn't notice it in all the upset over the cow.

I have a sudden, unexplainable urge to wake the boy with a kiss upon his full, unsmiling lips and am glad no one can see the hot blush this thought produces. Instead, I back away very quietly and climb over the wall to the same spot beneath the apple trees where Catina and I had eaten our picnic. It is much different when there is no one to share the transporting sight of all those clusters of white blossoms abuzz with honeybees. The flowers give off a mystical light even in full sun. And I think how I will try to describe this in my next letter to Anetta and wonder if she will be able to imagine what I mean.

The cow is still grazing in the field inside a wooden fence with a wide gate. I go to the fence and lean upon it and stare at her, confounded that she is so completely unaware of me. I could be a bird, maybe even a vulture waiting to make a meal of her. And to think, she made all that fuss before over one harmless girl, and now she doesn't care a wit. I am just noticing how short and brown the grass is wherever she has been, when I sense movement behind me and turn to find the boy coming this way from the barn. He is not smiling, but neither does he look as peevish as he did on our first meeting.

"Does Signora Ricci have nothing for you to do?" he asks, opening the gate.

It swings out, but he closes it behind himself and doesn't invite me in.

"I am here to rest," I tell him.

"You seem well enough."

"Enough for what?"

"For ordinary chores."

"And is that what you are doing as you waltz around your cow?"

I can tell he is offended by the way his eyes grow darker still and his mouth turns down. "I do nothing of the kind. I've come to groom her."

He has a flat, oval brush fastened to one hand that he begins to pass over the sagging sides of the beast in much the way I've seen a carriage driver do when currying a horse right in the Riva.

"You take good care of her," I say to appease him.

"The Riccis gave her to me. I will have a barnyard full of animals one day."

"Will you have a bull?"

"Yes. Undoubtedly a bull if there are to be calves."

"And sheep like that little black one in the barn?"

"You were spying on me."

"I came to find you, but not to spy."

"Yes, I will have sheep. And chickens."

"I don't see any chickens."

"They're over in the henhouse. Would you like to feed them?"

"Is it hard work?"

"You *are* a lazy girl!"

"That's not true at all. I work very hard at the Ospedale. We all work hard. We practice our instruments for hours every day. And we have lessons in language and history and solfeggio. It is a different life from yours, but no less difficult."

"In Venice."

"Yes. Have you never been there?"

"I have never been outside this village. Everything I want or need is here."

How blind he is.

"You cannot know that," I say, "when you have no knowledge of any other place."

"What did you know of the country until a few days ago?" he counters.

He is right, of course, but I am determined not to let him know this.

"It was not so strange to me. I had seen pictures."

"Pictures. With so little logic, you will not win arguments with me."

I am confounded by that remark, for it makes me realize that he is better schooled than I had supposed. He does, in fact, speak in a way that is different from that of other peasants I have encountered. It is very like the speech of my fellow students at the Ospedale.

"Do you attend some school, then?" I ask.

"My mother was raised in Florence, a city of great beauty with many works of art."

"I have seen pictures of Firenze, too. I know about the works of art."

"Do you want me to answer your question, or would you rather continue to tell me all that you know?"

What do I say to that? I am determined not to apologize.

After a period of silence between us, he goes on.

"She brought many books with her when she came here to live with my father. Everything I know I have learned from those books. And from her. She was my teacher and school."

"What of your father?"

"He is a simple man. He has vineyards, and he works in them himself. My mother loved him very much."

He is speaking about his mother as if in the past. I want to know the reason for this but am afraid to ask.

"I have a mother," I say. "She is both learned and beautiful."

"Orphans do not have mothers."

"Most orphans don't. I am different."

"Well, if it is true, which I doubt, you are very fortunate. I, myself, am no longer so."

I have been led to ask why. It cannot be avoided.

"She is dead," he answers.

He does not say "has gone to her heavenly reward" or "is with the angels" or "has passed into a better place," as most people do. He does not try to soften the awful word at all.

"How did she . . . die?" I ask.

"Something inside of her. Some terrible canker that grew within her breast."

His eyes are not wet at all, but mine are. His seem beyond tears, beyond any hope of surcease for his pain.

"I am so sorry," I say, and when he looks over at me, something in his piercing glance tells me that he, indeed, feels my compassion in the same way that I feel his great and unimaginable loss.

Chapter Thirty-five

Anetta

THE DUKE IN QUESTION is coming to tea today, and I am to be seated near Prioress, where, I'm told, he may wish to converse with me. I am also told that I should keep my answers short and not say anything to offend. What things he might take offense at I can only guess. Perhaps such categories as odor of breath, length of beard, stains on waistcoat, quantity and quality of belches should be avoided. Silvia claims he is sure to be portly and pig-eyed. I expect nothing and will be disappointed by nothing. It is simply a tedious routine we older girls must endure from time to time. I had not known that my turn would come so soon, and it behooves me to remember that no one is forced into any arrangement. Sometimes, however, there is firm encouragement in one direction or another. It will profit me to keep my wits about me, something for which I would be better prepared if only Rosalba were here to counsel me. This day I pray my angel guardian will find a way to substitute Rosalba's reason for my own.

Father Vivaldi is not at tea today, either, a fact that further disappoints me as he would have been placed near enough to be a source of lively conversation. Only Signora Mandano, Prioress, Maestro Scarpari, and the few girls already spoken for will be at table. Maestro Gasparini has been unwell for quite a long time. Some weeks he only makes an appearance at the concerts and leaves Father Vivaldi to handle all the rehearsals, a rather more pleasant arrangement as far as I'm concerned.

Cook has provided a honey cake and a *panna cotta* with peaches from the two trees in the yard. There are some filled *cannoli* and other sweetmeats, much more than at an ordinary tea, which makes me think that I am either highly regarded or that any bargain for my hand will be most difficult. I am so detached from the outcome that my only thought at present is how to manage to get my fair share of treats. It is most discomfiting, however, to be paraded in with Prioress, after the duke has been positioned at the table so that he can view me distinctly and undisturbed. His first remarks are so frank and rude, I almost giggle.

"I had not thought that she would be so large," he says, his eyes traveling from toe to top and back until they rest upon my bosom. It is not clear if he refers to my entire form or to my breasts, which my fichu, even with its extra rushing, does not hide so very well.

I have been told to curtsy to him, which only makes the situation worse. It is an awkward curtsy to be sure, and gives him opportunity again to closely view my chest. When I, at length, sit down across from him, he turns to Prioress and does not look at me at all. While he is so engaged, I take the chance to look at him. He's neither small nor large but somewhere in between. His nose is a trifle handsome, but his eyes have no distinction except that one is brown and one is blue. I'm pleased to see there is no beard at all and no paunch resting on the table edge. His ill-fitting wig conceals, no doubt, secrets of his head and hair that I'd rather not consider yet.

When Prioress turns to me, I must collect myself.

"Anetta can play many instruments, though it is on the viola d'amore that she excels, as you have heard."

"It was a moving piece. She played it well."

"And she has many other talents that her artistry upon the viola would not suggest. She is, in fact, the only one beside the *commun* girls allowed full access to the nursery. She knows just how to soothe and care for babes of any age."

Though not the ogling, smoking kind! I think.

His eyes go to my bosom once again, and I begin to understand his fascination there. He wants not only mate but mother, and I have been described to him as nurturing.

"Does she know how to entertain?" he asks of Prioress, still not addressing me.

"Oh, yes. Our girls are schooled in all the social forms. She can instruct a cook, prepare and pour a pot of tea or coffee, arrange a comely table."

"Sir," I interrupt, and he is most disconcerted. He looks from Prioress to me and back, but she does not seem disturbed and does not indicate a will to intervene.

"I have some questions of my own," I say.

To my left, Signora Mandano gives me a nudge between the ribs and clears her throat in a way that sounds as if a table leg has scraped the floor, but I ignore her.

"How many children do you have? When did you lose your wife?"

His face grows violet around the eyes, rose red down to his chin. He turns to Prioress. "That information is quite private. I gave it to Signora in the strictest confidence."

But Prioress surprises even me.

"Anetta will need to know the whole of it at some time. Where our girls' futures are concerned, we don't believe in keeping anything a secret."

"I am a recent widower, it's true," he says at last, now looking at his plate and delving between his teeth with a goose-feathered pick. "My former wife was decorous to a fault and left all conversation up to me." With this last pronouncement he does look up and meet my gaze, expecting, I suppose, that I will look away. Instead, I lock my eyes upon him.

"I had not thought this young woman would be so bold," he says, to Prioress again. "Her playing was controlled and accomplished to be sure, but she herself seems quite unbridled."

As in a very large *wild horse* perhaps?

"Yes," she replies, "our Anetta can be outspoken"—another nudge from Signora—"but ladylike, you can be sure, in all other ways."

"Hmmpf," he utters, unconvinced. He has not addressed both my questions, however, and I should like to know the answers. As would Rosalba, I am certain.

"The number of your children, sir?" I ask. And while I have his ear, "How many of them boys, how many girls? And, oh, yes, their ages from the youngest to the eldest."

He claps one hand upon his heart, his cheeks balloon, and his unmatched eyes begin to pop a bit. I wonder if there's something stuck within his throat. But there is not a coughing fit to follow, and when Prioress expresses her concern, he waves his handkerchief before his face, blows his nose, and acts as if such an extreme reaction must be the normal one to questions asked he doesn't wish to hear.

"More tea?" asks Signora Mandano when his silence is unbroken, her voice grown small and tight. She fills his cup and he consumes another honey cake before rising from his chair and bidding Prioress and everyone but me good day. As he walks away, I notice that his hips are wider than his shoulders, another reason to rejoice that he is leaving.

Prioress rises, too, to see him to the door, casting a sour look at me upon her way. Signora Mandano waits to deliver her short tirade until they both are out of earshot.

"Ungrateful girl! What were you thinking? We finally manage to find a mouse to take the cheese and you snatch it back. By Our Lord's own wounds, I can't imagine what got into you today."

I do appreciate their efforts and know they want only good things for my future, but this man was impossible. Without the strength to tell them so myself, my prayers, if that is what they be, were obviously listened to.

And so I answer her.

"Signora. It must have been Rosalba."

Rosalba

WE HAVE BEEN PERFORMING in the Piazza San Marco and other nearby *campi* for many weeks, and still there has been no instrument procured for me. Every time Pasquale mentions it (for I have given up and am still conflicted about the playing of the oboe here in Venice; it confounds me how I miss it so) Salvatore or Lydia says that with one more mouth to feed, there's not even enough money in the coffers for our daily needs. I have no way of knowing if this is true. What amount is expended upon me, however, must be minimal, for I have little appetite and small need of anything but sleep. Lydia has only recently begun to sew another dress for me, as mine is getting tight on top and in the waist. It is of rough material (I had hoped for taffeta in summer) and looks very like the loose mantuas of women on the street who are with child. This, of itself, makes me think that Lydia has sensed my secret. I made Pasquale swear to keep the knowledge to himself, and I am certain he would not betray me.

Pasquale's argument for the instrument is that we're taking in more ducats since I've joined them, not less. For my part, I have lost interest in the simple kinds of tunes they play and am sick at heart when I recall the intricate melodies and challenging inventions I had grown accustomed to playing at the Pietà. Even singing the gay bawdy songs has lost its first appeal. I must pretend enthusiasm, however, for Salvatore is ever vigilant for anything that will give proof of my unworthiness. He chides me constantly for all the naps I take, for sleep is lately at my doorstep at all hours of the day. My only hope is that I quickly learn to push a broom around and doze all at one time.

One late Saturday, we have begun a performance at the Campo San Anzolo, and it is time for me to step forward and sing my songs. I have grown accustomed to having the audience so close, and launch into my limited repertory with the same "lusty" voice I have not been able to change. Though I still blush at the lyrics of a few of these ditties, the audience seems delighted and eagerly joins in at places familiar to them.

It is when I come to the end of the second song and am about to begin a third, that I see him, Father Vivaldi, at the very edges of the crowd. With his eyes upon me, it is all I can do to continue, and when I finish singing the embarrassing words, I do not stay to bow, as I've repeatedly been instructed to do, but back away into the shadows. The little band of instruments begins to play again, and I hope that I can hide somehow within its loud sound and the dark shadow of the nave of San Anzolo, cast across the *campo* by the moon.

Imagining, without reason, that I am less likely to be seen while my eyes are downcast, I am soon gazing at the square toes and pinchbeck buckles of Father Vivaldi's best boots. He extends one hand to lift my chin, causing me to look directly into his kind gray eyes.

"I have been searching for you for weeks," he says in a rush of words. "My brother, Guido, had told of seeing you about the neighborhood with this little band. At first I could not believe him. I am still shocked and appalled."

What can I reply? I simply continue to look at him, my eyes feasting on the sight of a face so dear and familiar to me.

"Why did you run away?" he asks. "What made you seek a life like this upon the streets? A *signorina* of your talent and spirit! And one already a *maestra*. I find it very hard to believe."

The words come slowly from me. I have to push each one into the air. What, after all, can I tell him? That I was a foolish and capricious girl with grand romantic fantasies? That I did not appreciate the kindness and care of the Ospedale? That I have set things in motion that cannot now be changed?

"I am told I can never go back."

He takes my hands in his. He holds them out between us.

"*Cara mia,*" he says at last. "You have been given the correct information. That is, sadly, I'm told, the rule. The rule of the board. Apparently, it has long been so, and they do not listen to composers or violinists or those who repair instruments."

My words catch upon the sob that rises in my throat. "So I have no choice. These people," I say, glancing over at them, "have taken me in. They have allowed me to perform in their group."

"*Allowed!* What is this word, *allowed*? Do they realize how privileged they are to have a talented musician trained at the world-renowned Pietà in their troupe? Do they have any idea at all of who you are?"

"I am just one more orphan. That is what they know. And they know that I sing rather well. Or rather badly, according to Lydia."

"And where is your instrument? How can you live this long without your instrument?"

When he says this, I realize how very difficult it has

been, how playing the oboe had been second nature to me. Without it, these months now, I am functioning without a necessary appendage. Why had I bridled so under the gentle constraints that Father used in helping me to perfect my playing? Why had I not seen the great value of all that was right under my spoiled and fickle nose?

"Here," says Father, reaching into the pocket of his waistcoat and handing me a small piece of paper on which he has written an address.

"What is this?" I ask.

"The name of a friend in Vienna who may be able to book you as a oboist in other cities, to help you build a career away from the Ospedale. With Signore Gasparini ill so often, and with me having to fill his shoes more and more, I need you badly to teach the young ones. How ironic that it can never be."

There are no pockets in this strange new mantua, so I stick the note under my capelet in between my breasts.

He tips his hat in a courtly way as if I'm a person of importance. He takes my hand and kisses it with true affection. Another sob almost chokes me, and tears begin to flood my cheeks, even before he turns to go. He waves his hat as his lithe body backs away into the night.

"Take care, Rosalba. Take very good care."

"Who was that man?" asks Salvatore as soon as Father has left.

When I tell him, he is openmouthed and quickly disparaging.

"You expect me to believe that the composer Vivaldi, a man whose operas are becoming world renowned, that he would seek you out and kiss your hand?"

Even as his *flauto* was being blown by his lovely lips, he had been spying on me.

"Don't tell me," says Lydia as she begins to pack her violin, "that you're given to exaggeration. At the very least, I thought you'd be a truthful girl."

"He was my teacher," I say. "At the Ospedale. He was my best teacher."

"You see," says Pasquale. "She is well thought of. She needs to have an oboe of her own."

"Did he tell you that you cannot sing in Venice?" asks Lydia.

"No. He said nothing of my singing."

"Perhaps he feels, as I do, that it's too robustious."

"The patrons like it," says Pasquale.

"Patrons!" exclaims Lydia. "Listen to him. You have your own grand delusions. I'd barely call the motley baggage that gawks at us an *audience,* let alone *patrons.*"

Going back to the apartment, Pasquale walks with me, a little behind the others. "There was more money in the basket tonight than on any other," he says. "There is simply no reason except spite that Salvatore refuses to procure an oboe for you. Tonight I will insist."

"Don't do it, Pasquale," I tell him. "I'm out of

practice. I'm tired all the time. I'm used to a good instrument. I don't want to play some beaten-up old thing."

"You deserve the finest instrument in the world, it is true. When I make my fortune, I will buy one for you."

"Just how do you intend to make your fortune?"

"With you to inspire me, I will think of a way."

He means very well, and he does truly care for me. This has been apparent from the first. But he is sometimes totally impractical—one reason, I suspect, that the purse strings are securely tied to Lydia and only wheedled away by Salvatore.

When I hear him refer to a future that includes me, I want to dissuade him, but his words are never ordered into a direct question to which I can give a direct answer. That is, they have not been until today, when he says, "And you must not worry about the future. The child you carry will have both father and mother. Can I not be entrusted to take care of both of you?"

"Pasquale," I say, "you are perhaps the only reason I did survive my ordeal, but I do not expect or want you to feel indebted or responsible for me."

"Rosalba. How can you fail to understand? I do not feel indebted to you in any way. I am, however, in love with you, and I would wish to be in your love as well. May I not hope for that?"

Dear and good Pasquale. My savior. My defender. How is it that I do not love you? And what can I say that will not cause you much hurt?

"Good friend," I begin, and can see from his face that he does not appreciate my choice of salutation, "you have been nothing but kindness itself to me since that first awful night. No one could have been more compassionate or caring. You have helped me understand and bear the information of my present predicament. I should love you for all of this, and in a way, I do. But it is not in the way that you would like or that you perhaps deserve."

"Is it Salvatore, then?"

"No. Not Salvatore. How could it be Salvatore! Not anyone. I am not ready yet to attach myself to any man." *Nor may I ever be.*

His look of instant dejection turns to one of so much hope that I try to think of other ways to discourage him gently, but am too weary by half.

"When you are ready," he says softly, while tenderly lifting the hair from my neck that had been caught under the cape. "When you need me, I will be there."

Chapter Thirty-seven

Luisa

On the day that Signora comes for Catina, I fear that she will want me to return with her as well. It is a long trip, and I cannot believe that Signora Mandano will wish to make it twice. Knowing of my worry, Signora Ricci keeps delivering assurances that I am eating well again, sleeping soundly, and benefiting in many other ways.

Signora Mandano sighs languorously after viewing the verdant sloping vineyards and filling her lungs with country air.

"I could use a *villeggiatura* myself one day," she says. "Perhaps when I return for you, Luisa, I will stay a few days."

"It would give us great pleasure," says Signora Ricci. I let out a breath of relief at the thought that she is planning to return and that I will be staying.

Signora Mandano hands me a letter from Anetta, and I go to put it under my feather bed so that I may read it when I'm alone. Catina is folding the last of her things into her valise as I enter the room.

I am sad to see Catina making herself ready for the journey back. She is so accepting of each turn of events, never complaining or wishing that things could be otherwise, as most children would, that it makes me sadder still. If she would but fly into a tantrum, it might be easier to let her go. Always selfless, her only concern is for me and that I profit from this vacation and am returned to better health.

"Think of it, Luisa. Because of this lovely little trip, I have seen much more of the world than I ever expected. I do thank you for watching out for me and for the beautiful day in the apple orchard."

She hugs Signora Ricci with arms that seem even thinner than when we started out, and plants a kiss upon my cheek that feels like the brush of a bird's wing.

"Things will be all right again. You'll see," she says to me in her confident way, as if I were the one being taken back to Venice. Then, like a pronouncement from a messenger from heaven, she adds, "You mustn't be so much afraid."

She is right to have noticed my fear. Although I never speak of it, it is always with me. I am afraid for Catina and her fragile hold on life. I am afraid that I will never sing again. She seems aware of both these things without a word from me. What I have also not shared with Catina or Signora Ricci is that it is no longer this pastoral place alone that draws me to it, but the beautiful boy — known to me now as Alessandro — for he has become — how can I explain it — both destination and twin to my very soul. Each day I rise joyfully with the expectation of seeing him again, and all my hours are spent in pleasant companionship with him. We laugh at things together; we exclaim at the same sights and sounds; I help him with simple tasks; on some afternoons we rest against each other in the clean straw of the little barn. Even the apple of his eye, Evangelina, has become so used to me that she will let me milk her with almost no complaint.

Sometimes Alessandro says my name and I his, and we look at each other in amazement. What angels planned for us to meet? How did God create one person to be so absolutely perfect for another?

"Like Eve, you were taken from my rib," he jokes. But it seems so nearly true, I am quite ready to accept his reasoning.

"What if we had never met?" I say to him one day

as we are resting, his arm serving as pillow for my head. He is so near that I feel the warmth of him from head to foot, and without any warning a song comes to my lips and escapes in pure tones I'd never thought to find within myself again.

Surprised, I sit straight up, and he turns upon his side, resting on an elbow.

"What was that?" he exclaims, laughing. "Where did it come from?"

"When I was small, my mother used to say it came from heaven. Since my illness, I think it has been waiting in some anteroom for quite a time."

"I have not heard such singing in my life. It is as if an angel warbled in my ear. Go on. Go on. Please do not stop."

And so I sing a little sonatina I remember. It flows as fluidly from me as if a little brook has bubbled up. The trills, the *rallentandi,* the high notes—they are all there within my grasp just as before. What saint has intervened and brought my voice to life again I cannot guess.

Afterward, Alessandro puts one hand up to my cheek and touches it as if I'm made of something that will break. In just moments he has lost his caution, however, and pulls me to him in a way he has not done before. We are so close at first, I cannot breathe. But then he strokes me with such gentleness, it seems most natural to remove clothing that would serve to separate us. And when he shows me how well our bodies fit together and how we can delight in each other in this way, it is but proof of how our souls have been already joined.

Heading to the farmhouse for the evening meal, I am so filled with joyfulness that I must remind myself I must not sing. For Signora Ricci would indeed tell someone at the Ospedale, and my days here would be shortened. The thought of leaving Alessandro so soon is something that I cannot bear. When, at length, such a thing must happen, perhaps I will have learned to be braver. And though Catina cautioned me to fear less, she could not have known that I would substitute my greatest fear with one that would transcend the other two.

Supper with the Riccis is quiet without Catina. Signore has little to say on any occasion, and Signora is busy filling our plates and recounting the high points of her own day. I listen as best I can to problems with the workers, the plight of a runaway goat, and how surprised Signora has been by the small crop of potatoes. The minestrone is heavy with vegetables of every sort under a dusting of cheese, and the polenta is much lighter and more flavorful than Cook's. There is a delicious mixture of what Signora calls *frutti di mare*, with every manner of fresh food from the sea. A compote of newly picked peaches ends the meal, which has filled me so completely that I feel ready for sleep. It isn't until I am making preparations for bed, however, that I recall Anetta's letter and take it from beneath the feather bed and over to the small oil lamp, which is my only light.

Anetta's hand is large and bold, like herself, and seeing it inscribed across the pages, I can easily conjure her countenance, which, I realize with some surprise, I've genuinely missed. The letter is a great deal longer than my own was and, gratefully, filled with much news. It is only right that Father Vivaldi has at last written a concerto for her instrument. How strange to think of Beatrice ever leaving the protection of the Pietà. Stranger still to imagine Anetta being courted by a duke. I cannot think that she will take his attentions seriously. In the remote possibility that she does, I hope it will be years before the gentleman comes to collect her. For she and I do share a bond now, that neither of us has sought. It seems we are the only two people on this earth who are concerned for Rosalba, and the two most helpless to do a thing about it.

Chapter Thirty-eight

Rosalba

SINCE I CANNOT COOK OR SEW or do any of the things
they seem to expect of me, I have been assigned the job
of emptying the slops. In truth, Pasquale helps me with
this odious job from time to time, but claims he cannot
do it overmuch or it will seem that I am idle. To think
that at the Ospedale, I found it almost more than I could
bear to dispose of my own waste. This family's gargan-
tuan appetites and penchant for onions, garlic, and all
manner of beans makes the task especially foul. And the
constant feeling of late that I am about to spill the turbulent and minuscule contents of my own stomach is no

assist to me. There is no garderobe, so I must stack the chamber pots within the tiny hallway until their contents can be dumped into a pail and carried down the stairs.

Pasquale does commiserate with me as best he can and spends much time procuring songs for me to sing and learning their accompaniment in order to ensure that I may stay here. It is unimaginable that I have traded the sweet confines of the Pietà for this! It is a punishment severe enough to make me realize how great is my guilt. Pasquale claims I can't be faulted for a foolish heart or someone else's evil deed, but I've not told him of my countless schemes to free myself from all the duties that seemed so unpleasant then but that I know now were for my utmost good. Because of my inability to hold almost any food within my stomach for very long, I have not blossomed yet into the portly likes of women with child whom I see daily on the streets. It is a blessing to have someone else to share my secret with, however. Left all alone with it, I do not know what I would do.

It has become my habit to nap each afternoon upon the bed I share with Lydia at night. At such times I can claim the whole of it, as she is off to market or deep in conversation with those who also use our well and *campo*.

Afterward, learning the songs is pleasant enough as is listening to Pasquale upon the lute. He has a talent for the instrument, but I can't help thinking that if he'd had instruction, his fingering would be the more precise. While Salvatore is off somewhere, as is usual, romancing harlots or engaged in games of chance, Pasquale talks with me of things he couldn't otherwise.

At first when he describes his dreams of how he'll care for me and this new soul I carry, I argue that it can't be so, that I will manage on my own. He always continues, however, as if there is nothing I can say to discourage him, and I soon learn to hold my tongue and listen, for the picture that he paints is very comforting—a man, a wife, a tiny babe, a little house along one of the small canals. Sometimes he adds a boat, our own domesticated goat, a caged canary for the child. He owns a music shop, and we entertain our friends at sprightly musicals. I play my oboe in the drawing rooms of noblemen.

But when not caught up in his fantasies, the brutal facts of my existence accost my thoughts, and I see no real opportunity for any other life than what we know. A child raised in this same squalor, no matter how well loved, can never have the possibilities and guidance that I took for granted. If there is barely enough money to feed and clothe me, how would there be enough for my *bambina*'s needs as well? I do sense the baby is a girl, perhaps because I am so used to them and would not have the faintest notion how to raise a boy. This is my second secret and one I do not feel the need to share with anyone except Anetta or Luisa, if ever I am given such a chance. Their reaction to my sudden disappearance and the fact that I have not returned can barely be imagined. Can they even guess what has become of me? My greatest sorrow is that I have caused them pain and cannot share my life with them again. At such moments I am like a dry well that has no tributaries feeding it, no aquifer from which to draw the waters of my life.

"Child," says Lydia as she bustles in with her basket of day-old vegetables and fruit. Her selection is always peculiar and consists of whatever was overripe but not yet rotting. I am reminded of the burgeoning fruit bowl at the Pietà that sat upon the sideboard in the refectory and that we were allowed to pick from at any hour of the day.

"Child," she says again. I have relinquished my name to her long ago, but she chooses not to use it. "Surely you can wash these snap beans and collard greens. Surely you know how to do that!"

I take them from her basket and into the room that serves as kitchen. They are so wilted as to be unappetizing and have a sad little smell that turns my stomach even further around. Sprinkling them with water does not revive them in the slightest. Why not let them die in peace? But Lydia makes a fire in the woodstove, puts them in a pot, and boils them to death, covering their remains with one of her thick unidentifiable sauces.

When I eat only the bread, which, too, is stale but at least edible, she calls down curses upon the Ospedale for producing anyone so finicky. Tonight Pasquale has procured some milk for me—from cow or goat, it matters not. I lap it like a hungry cat, and it sits well with me.

"No, thanks," says Salvatore, as if he had been offered some. "I don't know why you spend your precious share on something that a grown man's stomach will regurgitate." He looks at Lydia, and she smiles complicitly. "Or a grown woman's for that matter."

But Lydia is acting coy tonight. She pats Pasquale's hand.

"You children will enjoy it, I am sure."

She stresses the word *children*, and I am once again quite certain that she knows about the child. I am determined not to grasp at these stray hints, however. For the longer that Salvatore is uninformed of my predicament, the safer I will be. Glancing over at him now, I wonder that I ever found him handsome. His chiseled features are quite unpleasant to me; his constant surly attitude has colored all my earlier impressions of him.

I am exhausted tonight as we trudge the distance to Campo Santo Stefano, where Salvatore thinks we may attract a fresh audience. And there are some new faces, but ultimately no new money. Salvatore blames my listless singing. Lydia thinks I have improved some under her tutelage. Pasquale chuckles at both of them, and tells me my performance was *bellissima*. In his eyes or ears, it is always *bellissima*.

All evening I have been feeling less queasy, and when I tell Pasquale, he says that perhaps the worst has passed. Not knowing that it can be otherwise, I had expected to be ill like this until the birth itself. Where he discovers such oddments of information is a mystery, but I am grateful for it and pray to all the saints that it is true.

Chapter Thirty-nine

Anetta

IN MIDDAY, RIGHT AFTER the noon meal, there is a great bustle in the front entry, a shuffling of objects along the floor, and the familiar clucking noises of Signora Mandano when she is trying to calm herself. I run down the stairway so quickly that my cap flies off and my hair floats free.

"Goodness," says Signora when she sees me. "How unkempt you always appear, Anetta, as though you were more accustomed to wearing breeches."

I could mention how disheveled she and Catina appear as well, but hold my tongue in my eagerness for news of Luisa.

"Have you a letter for me?" I ask before anything else.

"Settle down a bit, my dear," says Signora, unfastening her bonnet and sighing as if to shed all the weary miles she has just traversed. She even removes her cloak and pats her hair before answering me.

"No, Anetta. There is no letter this time, though I did deliver yours. I can tell you that Luisa is well, and that the color has returned to her face a bit. Signora Ricci described her appetite as lately robust, something it has never been in all her years at the Pietà."

"Did she send no words for me at all?"

This time it is Catina who answers in her authoritative little voice, which always surprises.

"She was on her way to collect the milk as I recall, just as we were leaving. I'm certain that she wishes you well."

"And misses me?"

"Oh, yes. I'm certain that she misses you."

"And will be home soon?"

"No," Signora interjects. "She will be away at least another month or more. If only Catina could have benefited from the country in the way that dear Luisa has. She's quite a different child."

I look closely at Catina as she, too, removes her traveling cloak, and am struck by how spindly her little body beneath it appears, how thin her arms have become, how the cavities between her neck bones are so deep they look like large blue bruises. When she begins to cough, her small skeleton begins to shake so violently that I want to clasp her tightly enough to make the tremors stop.

"She should not speak at all," says Signora, hustling her off to the infirmary. "It always starts a coughing fit like this."

"I'm so sorry," I say.

"Oh, you couldn't have known," says Signora when Catina has rounded the corner and is on her way upstairs. "She's so much worse than when she left here. It got so bad on our journey back that I almost expected the breezes along the canal to take her final breath with them."

"Is there nothing to be done?"

"We'll try the usual remedies and some that have worked well with the Red Priest. His presence always cheers her.

"And," she adds, "we'll pray for her."

And do you pray for Rosalba? Does anyone else beside Luisa and me pray for her?

It is some consolation, of course, that Luisa is well, but how I would have loved news of her again in her own hand. How I had looked forward to sending a letter back, to tell her what has transpired since last I wrote.

—∾—

Dearest Luisa, I would have said.

> *The days are truly much longer in the absence of your sweet presence and of Rosalba's. Though they are filled with the usual activities, the minutes seem to crawl in a most peculiar way. I look at the clock from time to time throughout the day to get my bearings, and am astonished to find the hands advancing in so slow a fashion as to seem to creep across its face. When I perceive it should be afternoon, it is merely the middle of the morning; when it appears that evening light should start to settle in the drawing room, it isn't even halfway to our suppertime.*
>
> *Father has made great progress on* Moyses Deus Pharaonis. *There is even a part for me, a small one in my range. But the part for you is large and wonderful. So operatic that I know you will be pleased, as will your mother.*

And I would tell her, too, how Maestro Gasparini will soon leave his post and how it is taken for granted that Father Vivaldi will assume it, a situation that the strings, especially, will welcome. *As you will, too, I'm certain,* I would say. *His operas are becoming known and sung throughout all of Europe. Just think of it, Luisa, your opportunity to see the world and have renown now rests with our own dear teacher. Could we ever have conceived of such a thing?*

After I place Signora's additional parcels at her door, I go into the nursery, for there is still time between Latin and string ensemble in which to play with Concerta. She claps her hands whenever she sees me, and her smile is always one of purest happiness. Today, she crawls to me, pulling a tiny soldier with her as she goes. I sit upon a chair so she will try to stand, and I let her struggle till her golden head is even with my knee, whereupon her eyes search my face for my approval. At first I don't express it, but wait until she squeals, and then I catch her up and lift her high into the air and tell her what a good thing she has done, how proud I am of her. Upon her feet again, she tries to hum a simple little tune, and soon is opening her tiny mouth and letting out the nearest sound to something like a song I've ever heard from her before.

"She's singing!" I exclaim to Sofia and the wet nurses sitting somber-faced along the wall, one with a *bambina* on each breast.

"Those stumbling little noises," says Sofia. "If that's a song, I'll eat my best cap, lappets and all."

"As well you may need to, for song it is, I swear upon my . . . my . . . friends."

"Who are not here to testify and cannot hear what you hear."

"But would if they were."

Oh, Luisa. Don't you see? It's happening the way I'd hoped and prayed. Concerta will be just like you. She'll be a privilegiata *like both of us and charm her audiences. Father will someday write grand oratorios especially for her, too.*

"And have you told your fine friends about the wealthy Duke of Viani, a pillar of the republic, a man with a fine wide forehead and grand nose?"

"The beak was his only good feature, Sofia."

"Have you told them how you sent him away like some commoner, how you spoke up to him as if you were the duchess and he the orphan, how you squandered your best opportunity for a life outside these walls?"

"How do you know it was my best opportunity, and why do I need a life outside these walls?"

"Believe me, you will not want to stay here forever, as I have done. I was a *commun* girl once. Nursing was the only occupation besides lace-making that was offered me, and that only because I did not swoon at bloodletting and wasn't squeamish at the sight of open sores. I was not pampered nor put on show and taught the finer things like you. I never had a chance to have a family of my own."

"Or someone else's. He wanted me to tend the many babes he'd fathered by another woman, who was so worn out she'd finally died."

"Women die for many reasons that have nothing to do with the number of babes that they have borne."

"And he did not wish for me to have a tongue within my head. At least not one to be of use in speaking."

"And what else? What other frivolous reasons can you give for sending him away?"

"His calves bulged in their tight hose, and, like an elephant, his legs did not taper as they should at the ankle."

"Frivolous indeed! Did no one tell you of his high position? Of his great wealth?"

"It would not matter to me if they had."

Concerta pulls at my skirt, and a glance at the clock tells me I must run all the way to Father's workshop if I'm to retrieve my instrument in time for the rehearsal of next Sunday's concert.

"I have to go, now," I tell Sofia while leaning down to kiss Concerta. I pull her little arms from where they reach around my neck, and she begins to cry.

"Go, then," says Sofia, lifting her up.

"If I see the duke," I tell her, "I will send him and all his children to you."

"You'll understand one day," she says. "You will. You'll see. But it will be too late."

Chapter Forty

Luisa

I AM AWAKE at first cock's crow, knowing full well that
Alessandro will not rise until the milking time for
Evangelina. The wagons with the vineyard workers will
soon be going past this window, some of the pickers half
asleep and leaning against one another, some convers-
ing so loudly it will sound as if I'm once again upon the
Riva. The sky appears to lift itself with the sun, which
burns pink streaks into the vast blue space that seems
painted across an infinite ceiling. I lie upon my feather
bed, hands behind my head and eyes upon the scene,

until it feels as if I travel with my gaze onto the slopes and pastures. Soon voices in the kitchen will tell me that Signor Ricci and some of the workers are taking their breakfast. I will wait until their words fade and there is silence in the house again before I dress and make my way to the privy.

This morning I am slipping in and out of sleep when the word *Alessandro* surprises me. I do not know at first if it has come to me in a dream or has been spoken in the other room. But then I hear it once again, and it is clearly from the tongue of Signor Ricci. Rousing myself, I creep upon the cold tiles to the door and press my ear against it. It is minutes before I hear the name again and can distinguish any of the words that follow. This time it is Signora Ricci's voice, and it is clearer than her husband's.

"They are both so young," she is saying. "I find it hard to believe there is any danger."

Danger?

"I'm telling you what Felipe saw," replies her husband. "The two together in the little barn. It did not look so innocent."

I am so startled by this word, *innocent,* that the ones that follow are all the more distinct.

"But a chaperone? A chaperone out in the country? I've never heard of such a thing."

"Then keep her here. With you. Let her be of use."

"I am not paid so she can do our chores."

"If things get out of hand, you'll not be paid at all. We returned the one child with her malady increased. We must return the other in the same state, at least, as when she came."

"Alessandro," I whisper to myself. "What can be dangerous about Alessandro? He is the most gentle person I have ever known."

I hear the scraping of the chair legs against the floor, a clatter of plates one upon another. More muted voices. A door squeaking open and then slamming shut.

What am I to do with this new information? How am I to comport myself now that the sweet idyll of my days here has been poisoned by another's thoughts? Does Alessandro think of me with the same joy with which I think of him? Is he, at this very moment, waiting for me in the barn?

When I first step into the kitchen, Signora is busy putting something in the small oven built into the bricks around the fire. She jumps back on seeing me, bids me *buon giorno*, takes a plate and starts to fill it with what she had prepared much earlier. There are cheeses and warm breads, a bowl of fruit from trees that touch the house. She pours a special tea from rose hips that I've grown to like. This time she fills a large cup for herself and sits across from me.

"So," she says at last, circling the cup with her hands to warm them, "how have you been amusing yourself without Catina?"

"Oh," I say, "it has not been hard. I roam about. Sometimes I help the boy who owns the cow."

"Alessandro?"

"Yes." I do not say his name, suddenly afraid he can be taken from me if it should escape my lips.

"How did you meet?"

"Catina and I. We watched him milk one day." The half-truth comes so easily.

"And now that Catina is gone?"

"He is good company. I stay out of his way."

"As well you should. He's here to work, you see. You're here to breathe the fresh air and get well. You must not distract him from his duties. It's how he earns enough to keep the cow."

I had not thought of that, that he has duties for which he is paid.

"I only try to help."

"Well then, you can help me. Today I bake the bread for the entire week. The kneading is the hardest part. A pair of extra hands will be a boon."

"I . . . I never baked before."

"It isn't hard," she says, and hands me a rough apron I must double at the waist to fit around me.

"With the two of us working," she continues, "we may be finished by the afternoon."

It is in fact the longest morning of my life, and doesn't really end at noon, as she had promised. My hands ache from the constant kneading and squeezing and pounding of the vast amounts of dough. My forearms feel as if they have been pummeled. In truth, it was not hard to learn, but it was harder to endure than any practice sessions back-to-back, and so much less enjoyable.

"There," says Signora Ricci at last, filling a basin in which to wash the flour from my hands and the dough from underneath my fingernails. The loaves are stacked up neatly by the hearth. She's managed somehow to prepare a hearty soup of vegetables in oxtail broth, and I collapse before it like an animal before its only meal in weeks. Afterward, she lets me take my ease out in the sun, where I fall fast asleep still sitting on a chair made from a tree with all its bark.

I do not know the hour that I waken to a shower of dry leaves upon my head. Confused at such a happening in this growing season, I squint into the sunlight with one hand above my eyes. There, a dark shape in silhouette, stands Alessandro, smiling at me with great mischief in his face.

Before my wits have awakened with me, Signora is outside the cottage door and greeting Alessandro with much affection, her plump arms encircling him as if he is her errant child.

"I came to find what happened to your boarder here," says Alessandro, "and to bring the milk," he adds, handing a pail of it to Signora.

"Luisa helped me with the bread," she says, as if it had been my idea. "I'll make a baker of her yet before she has to leave."

Leave. Why is she even using that word? I have been here such a short time. I cannot leave. I can never leave Alessandro.

"While I had thought to turn her into a milkmaid," says Alessandro.

"And I have decided," I say, finally collecting myself, "to remain a musician. Wait here."

I fetch my mandolin and sit back down again upon the scratchy chair and play for these two new people in my life, but I do not sing. I must be careful not to sing, for then Signora will believe that I am cured.

With great concentration I direct my thoughts to Alessandro, the only recent witness of my gift returning. *Don't tell,* I beg of him in silence. *Please. You must not tell.*

Chapter Forty-one

Anetta

ANOTHER LETTER FROM LUISA has arrived at last. It is so near the end of summer that I thought she would be home by now. In her absence, I am eager for a letter nonetheless and save it for a time when I am in the nursery, alone with all the little babes. It is their time to nap, and I can sit and rock and read without disturbance.

Dear Anetta,

Your story of the duke who came to claim you made me laugh. But then I thought of how you'll need to search again and make a match before too long. I hope next time that he is handsome and a match to you in kindness as well as all your other good and comely virtues.

There is a young man here who seems so much a twin to me in thought and understanding that I cannot imagine my future with anyone but him. Alessandro is his name, and he is beautiful in every way and well schooled for a boy who's lived his life outside the city. For reasons that are not quite clear to me, there is some effort being made to keep the two of us apart, but it will do no good.

It is to him I owe the resurrection of my sing-ing voice, which, as you know, has been in hiding all these months.

You are the only one to whom I have conveyed this news or told of Alessandro. But I needed to tell someone whom I trust, for I know that you will not divulge it. If Prioress should find out that my voice has been returned to me, I would be sent back to the Ospedale just as quickly as they could arrange it. Your generous soul I'm certain will delight in my great happiness and be joyful knowing of the cause of it.

These past few weeks I've been consumed by
Alessandro, but I have not forgotten our Rosalba and
her plight. Has there been any news of her? Please tell
me, too, of how Catina fares when next you write. It
was with so much sadness that I watched her leave.
    Your friend,
    Luisa

No *Dearest friend* again. But no matter. There are
other things about this missive that do not cheer me in
the least. It seems a country boy has claimed her heart.
What future can there be for her in that? And at the very
point that her glorious voice has been returned to her.
Also she has sworn me to keep secret something I would
sooner shout to one and all. Was not such a cure the
reason for her *villeggiatura*? Shouldn't she return to us
at once? Should not Father Vivaldi be the first to know?
But it will be just as she wishes. For a while. I will in fact
destroy the letter, tear it into little bits, to keep it from
the prying eyes of Silvia.

I am lost in this troubling conundrum when Father
stops me on my way to a sectional in chapel. My head is
down, and he must reach out and put an arm across my
path, an action that indeed arrests my woolgathering.

"We'll try again," he says most earnestly.

"What do you mean?"

"I've composed a new concerto for your wily

instrument. We'll make another stab at landing you a paramour."

"Signore." I laugh. "Is there no end to this? Must I go angling for a fish I do not wish to catch?"

"I have my orders, child. If it were up to me, I'd much prefer to keep you here, brandishing your bow, singing your harmonies, and spoiling the *bambine*."

He hands me pages that have not yet seen the copyist. His mysterious markings still adorn the margins. The many ornaments denote another aspect of his style that anyone would recognize.

"We won't debut this for another month or more. So take your time."

"Time is what I do not have right now," I tell him, but in truth, I am quite pleased that he has written something just for me again, and I make promises within myself to learn it well and cause him to be proud of both the work and me.

He climbs the stairs into the loft that is my destination as well, where there's a sectional for altos with Maestro Scarpari.

"Children," Father says when he arrives there out of breath. He claps his hands and gasps for air a moment. "You must bear with me this afternoon. Maestro has been called away."

Anna Maria goes at once to the continuo, ready to accompany our efforts, while Father wields his small baton and taps the music stand. It is his own composition that we sing, a short cantata with some places that are difficult where melody and harmony cross and sound most dissonant. The contralto solo opens this new work and is sung legato by Brigitta, but at the *tutti,* Father jumps about and shouts, *"Agitato, Signorine! Molto agitato!"* He makes us try the passage many times before he moves ahead to the next section, which is marked *dolcissimo* but which he urges us to sing *ancora espressivo.* At the *marcato,* he asks for *un poco allegretto,* which is not marked within the score. We please him, however, at the passage marked *sforzando* and are beginning to feel in synchrony with him and with the music when he suddenly becomes the true violinist, directing us to "sing with longer bows," while rising on his toes and gesturing into the air. "That's right, Signorine," he calls out to us. "Much longer bows."

He asks me later if I've had any new letter from Luisa, and I tell him yes. But when he also asks about her voice, I say as little as I can and feign no knowledge of it. I very much regret deluding him. Is someone truly sworn who does not wish to be and has not herself agreed to it? Whom can I ask who will not make me give the truth away?

It's not until I'm passing by the kitchen that I see an opportunity. Catina sits upon a stool and watches Cook. The child's so thin, it looks as if she'll slip right off her perch into the pot of soup. Her face is ashen and her tiny body stooped. Her raspy breathing colors all her speech.

It doesn't stop her constant questioning, however, which seems to drive poor Cook a little mad.

"I told you, dear," she tells Catina, "the water has to boil before you put the pasta in."

"It takes so long," Catina says. "Isn't there a better way?"

"Just watch me, and you'll learn how it is done."

On seeing me, Cook takes her chance.

"Anetta," she says, "Catina here is getting tired. Take her out into the air a bit. Go help her find some marjoram and thyme to dress the fowls for supper."

"I don't know one herb from the next," I tell her, but she winks at me and gives silent permission to return with anything at all.

"Just go," she says.

We start out for the little patch in back that is abloom with leafy things that must be herbs and gated by a squat white fence — to keep the rats away, is my guess. It's well beyond the lines for drying clothes and up against a higher fence along the street.

At first Catina seems quite happy to be outside in the air, but at a grassy place beneath the trees she drops to her knees.

"I'm very tired now, Anetta. Will you pick the herbs?"

She curls up on her side and plucks at dandelions. I sit beside her and stretch out my legs.

"What about Cook?" she asks.

"I'll get the herbs she wants. I'll do it in a while."

For quite some time we stay this way and do not talk. I think she may, in fact, be falling off to sleep when I decide to whisper, "Today I had another letter from Luisa."

She looks up from her prone position, squashing all the dandelion pieces in her hand. "I'm glad that she could stay in that nice place. It was so beautiful."

"She says there is a boy there. Alessandro. What of him?"

"I saw him once. He keeps a cow."

"And did Luisa sing to him when playing on her mandolin?"

"I never heard Luisa sing at all the while that I was there. She played sometimes, but did not sing. Did not Luisa tell you that?"

She turns upon her back and looks up at the sky. I pick the petals from a daisy in the grass.

"The things Luisa tells me in her letters, the things that she instructs me not to tell a soul. What do you think? Am I obliged to keep her confidence?"

"Why are you asking me?"

"You have a way of speaking frankly," I say, laughing. "As if you are an oracle."

"I make the others angry when I'm wrong."

"But sometimes you are right."

"Sometimes."

"And so. What do you think?"

"I think you do not have to keep a secret if you did not ask to have it given to you."

"Truly?"

"And if that secret, being kept, will harm the one who trusts you with it." She pauses to suck a clover stem. "That's what I think."

"Thank you," I say, for I am stunned at just how wise she appears, this delicate young girl who seems to lately hover between earth and heaven.

It is an answer I did not expect and one that I must contemplate awhile. I have no question as to what is best for my dear friend. But if I act upon the truth of it, I stand to lose entirely the very love I seek.

Chapter Forty-two

Luisa

EACH DAY SIGNORA RICCI invents new tasks for me to
do around the cottage. When I am finally free to run
into the fields, it is so late sometimes that Alessandro has
already left for home. I have picked apricots and plums
until my fingers blister, fed chickens in the morning and
the night, stretched bed linens upon the line, and even
helped to beat the rugs. I dare not remind her that I'm
here to recuperate for fear she'll simply make me stay
inside with naught to do, for it is clear they mean to keep
me far away from Alessandro at all costs. The why of it

is not so clear, and the wanting has been made the more intense. Just to be able to catch sight of him returning from his work is boon enough to send my spirits flying through the trees.

Today it has been raining, and I have some idle time in which to dream and think about the letter to Anetta that I sent with Davio a week or more ago. In it I bared my soul and told my friend of Alessandro and the secret that we keep about my voice. I also made her swear to closet all I say within her heart and not divulge a particle of it to anyone. Because she loves me as she does, I'm certain she will do as I request. The part about my learning to conjoin with him was better left unsaid. I would have been hard put to make her understand my pleasure and my joy in it, nor did I wish to share this knowledge.

At noon there is a knock upon the door, and I am wild with hope of seeing the one who fills my thoughts at every hour of the day. I run into the kitchen just as Signora takes the milk pail from his hands. He stands dripping at the entry, and Signora fusses with a mop about his feet while he looks down with great discomfort. It gives me time to look at him while unobserved, and when at last his eyes are raised and meet my own, his smile is like a streak of sun across a cloudy sky.

"Buon giorno," I say for lack of something I can wish him that is more sublime. *Buon mondo? Buona vita?*

He returns my greeting, and we both stay feasting on each other's faces until Signora chortles to herself, then takes my chin, turns my face to hers, and asks, "What say you to inviting Alessandro here to midday meal?"

"Oh, yes," I answer, and press my hands together like a little girl, while Signora takes his wet outdoor attire, hat and boots and jacket, and sets them by the fire to dry. She fills large bowls with a fragrant stew of sausage, beans, and lentils, and sets an entire loaf of bread between us, from which we break large chunks to dip in oil. It is an unexpected celebration, and being such, we appreciate it all the more.

He asks about the way in which I've spent my days since last we saw each other. I tell him about Signora's many relatives — the brothers, sisters, cousins, aunts, and uncles — who come to visit and to pick the grapes. There are so many, I've not yet learned to know one from the other or who it is that sits at table with us. The Red Priest is the only other person that I know from such a large brood, members of which are rarely seen about the Ospedale. I question Alessandro about his lamb, if she has grown a winter coat, and ask after Evangelina.

"I think she looks for you," he says. "I see her lift her head at any stranger's step upon the straw."

"I was just learning how to milk her properly."

"Perhaps you'll come and try again."

"I think not," says Signora, sitting down across from us. "Luisa has so many other things to do."

After the meal, we sit before the little fireplace awhile and listen to the rain upon the roof of thatch.

Signora sorts the peas and snaps the beans and boils an oxtail for another pot of soup. I pick up my mandolin and play some tunes that have no words to them, fearful I might forget myself and sing to ones that do. For a time, it seems as if we're sealed into a warm and changeless place. There is no Ospedale in this place, no Venice, no vineyards, and only a faint apparition of Signora Ricci far off in the corner of the room or fast asleep behind a cupboard.

"You must have other duties," Signora says at last, becoming very real again, addressing Alessandro and breaking the golden spell. "Doesn't your father need your help today? Surely there are indoor duties, bottles to be filled and stored, labels to be inscribed. A vintner's life does not end when rain begins to fall."

"Yes," he tells her. "I thank you for this lovely meal, this lovely time." He turns to me and takes my hand to lift me from my chair.

Just then the Riccis' wagon comes rattling along the road and pulls into the yard behind the house. Davio makes the usual clamor while taking off the horses' harnesses, wiping the animals down, and leading them to the trough. The commotion does not capture my attention, and I do not even question where the wagon's been.

When Signora goes to call the wagon driver in to lunch, I pull Alessandro toward me, and he puts his other arm around my waist.

"When can we meet again?" he whispers in my ear.

"I'll try to find a way," I tell him. "Signora watches me the whole day long."

"What did you tell her?"

"I didn't tell her anything. Someone saw you and me together once when we were in the barn. They think I need a chaperone."

"This is too hard," he says, pulling me closer to him. "I need to see you more than this."

When Signora rushes into the room, we spring apart, but she has noticed how we held each other. Instead of her reproach, however, I am astonished when she starts to speak in such staccato exclamations I must piece the words together for myself.

"Catina. That dear girl. That child. The *bambina* with a curse upon her head. The one I couldn't do a thing to cure no matter how I tried. Who knows? Perhaps it was the evil eye when she was very young."

"What are you trying to say?" I ask in an attempt to stop her staggered exclamations, which have begun to frighten me.

She puts both hands up to her head and moans and strikes her breast before she answers me.

"Davio. He has brought back news from the Pietà." She hugs me to her tightly till I almost cannot breathe. "The little girl." She smiles somewhat even as her eyes crease up and tears begin to flow. "Your little traveling companion. Catina. Yes, Catina. The one who was so wise."

Signor Ricci comes inside the room, which swims now with confusion and distress.

"The little one," he tells me kindly, "she has been taken up to heaven."

His eyes roll toward the ceiling. Then he adds, "Signora Mandano says she'll come for you in a day or two so you can say your last good-byes to your young friend. She says it's time that you return."

Catina. Dead. I'd known that it was possible. I knew that she was frail. But frail enough to die? There was such a timelessness about her.

"I'm so sorry," Alessandro says. He did not know her at all, but seems so stricken that I sense it is because I'm being sent back soon. My own grief is so deep that I almost cannot separate the two painful feelings it includes — grief for loss of one I love and fear that I will lose another when I have to leave this place. There is some little hope within the last, while none at all for seeing sweet Catina once again.

"She's with the angels," says Signora, dabbing at her eyes with both her bare hands and then an apron hem.

I cannot think of her in some strange heaven high above the clouds. In my mind's eye I see Catina that first day here, her sleeping form upon the blanket in the orchard, the peaceful smile upon her lips, the bright mantle of white apple blossoms that covered her. As softly as a prayer upon the wind, the flowers drift and drift and swirl.

e∞ Chapter Forty-three ∞e

Rosalba

THE OTHERS THINK I have retired early. It is a Monday and the day on which we rest, for at the start of any week there are few about the streets with time to listen to our little troupe. There is a soft rain, enough to clear and freshen the hot air of afternoon and to make the cobble-stones glisten and polish the church spires. The usual beggars are not in their usual places; the gondoliers are under cover of their gondolas. No one will notice as I walk alone, my cloak covering all, my bush of curly hair tied back beneath my hood, and nothing exposed that would distinguish man from woman, royalty from renegade. I even wear Pasquale's boots.

For all the miles from the house in which I stay, I have walked as quickly as my condition will allow. My steps begin to slow only when I reach the Riva degli Schiavoni. They quicken as I pass near the Bridge of Sighs and over the Rio del Vin, and do not slow again until I cross over the Rio del Greci and am right in front of the school and chapel and so close to the Ospedale that I can hear sounds from inside — the dinner bell, random scales, instruments being tuned, shrieks of laughter, the great stew of noise I used to hate. Many windows are wide open, heavy wooden shutters pushed back against the stucco walls. Girls pass back and forth behind them, never pausing long enough for me to see just who they are. Is that Anetta, the one much larger than the two others she is with? Is that Luisa, her mouth open wide and sliding into notes that I could never reach? That one who just dashed across the room, was that the churly Silvia, and is her tongue still sharp? I wonder who has taken my place in their chamber. Do they, does anyone, ever think of me?

There are pools of light that mingle right below the building, and I'm careful to keep out of them and to the shadows and to make no noise. Weeping can be very silent, I have learned.

Everything looks so well ordered and happy inside, so full of life. Such a good life! Why did I not know it?

The door on the Calle della Pietà opens and two girls run across to the chapel, chattering together as they go. Their watteaus, shining bright blue when in the open doorway, turn black enough to be invisible when the door shuts behind them. How well I remember wearing those everyday costumes; how drab they appeared to me then; how often I managed to lose my cap. My waist was small, my body not swollen with child, my hunger always appeased. And music. The glorious music of Father Vivaldi sounding always in my ears. It was my heartbeat.

Later in the week, Pasquale purchases an oboe for me with his own ducats, and he presents it to me, as if it were a stuffed goose on a platter, while the others are at market.

"See?" he points out. "There is a barely visible seam where it has been repaired. It does not, my friend assures me, affect the tone."

"Who is this friend?" I ask, not really caring to know, but anxious to say something—anything—to hide my disappointment. It is a very old instrument and has not been well cared for.

"He is a pawnbroker, but an honest fellow, and he

let me know of this fine instrument the moment it was popped into the shop."

"Popped?"

"Pawned."

I have no wish to blow upon this gift, but Pasquale's kindness must be rewarded. And so I lift it to my lips with no great expectations. It falls so short of what I've been accustomed to, however, as to make the tears, which seem to live right near the surface of my eyes, begin to flow again.

"You are not used to it as yet," says Pasquale. "It will take time to make it seem your own."

My own. Where is my own oboe? How could I have left it behind? It was so like another arm, I thought it always would be there, and until now I did not appreciate its many virtues — the polished and stained boxwood, the square silver keys and perfect swallowtail great key, the soft veiled tone.

"I have no music," I tell him.

"I will buy some scores. We'll find something you like to play."

I am confounded at his urgency. He seems so anxious that I can't help asking why.

"Salvatore has noticed your . . . predicament at last. He says we cannot have you standing up to sing — not for your sake, but because he will not be made a laughingstock. He says that you must sit with Mother at the back and play an instrument."

"He says all that, does he? And what did you say back to him?"

"I said that I would talk with you. That I would find you something you can play upon."

"Or . . . ?"

"What do you mean?"

"Or what will Salvatore do? How will he punish you or me, for that is what your words imply."

"Salvatore can make it very hard for you. And for me. You think that he has been unkind before, but you have only felt a little of his rage. Since I was a small boy, I've thought of him as a caged tiger who needs regularly to be appeased."

I have known this for some time, for now that Salvatore is so used to having me around and does not notice me at all, he storms through the narrow house from floor to floor whenever he is crossed.

"What kind of life is that for you or me? Did you never stand up for yourself? Did Lydia never try to protect you?"

"I learned early that it was best to be agreeable. It is not so very hard. They do not buck me in the things that matter to me most."

"Like what, Pasquale? What matters to you that they don't oppose?"

He hesitates and rubs his stubbly chin, on which he has been trying for some time to grow a beard.

"You," he says in his same quiet way. "You matter to

me most of all, above all else. They know I mean to care for you, to raise your child. They have not dared to buck me there."

"And you think that by my acting just like you, by always doing what they say, it will go well with both of us?"

I put the oboe down. It is as offensive to me as someone else's worn-out glove and a symbol now of what will be expected. It is a threat, and with such a trap, there is but little place to stand above and not fall in.

"I'll find a better one," Pasquale says, retrieving it. "I'll see what has been popped today and make a trade."

"Bring me a piccolo," I tell him. It is an instrument I've seldom played and therefore one that I may definitely toot upon while still in Venice. Or so I reason.

Poor, doting, kind Pasquale. He is much cheered by this. And for my part, it buys me time before I need to come to a decision, the thought of which is pressing like a large and leaden fist upon my soul.

"No more tears," says Pasquale, taking my hands in his. "You see, isn't it much easier to be agreeable?"

Easier and so deceptive, for I do not mean to be agreeable for long.

"Here," I say, placing his hand upon my belly where the baby thumps quite lustily. Pasquale's eyes smile down at me with such clear happiness, I almost start to think that we are indeed a little family.

—⁓—

It is many weeks before I slip away again to walk the Riva and to view the Ospedale in the dark. I wait to leave until Lydia is so sound asleep I know she will not stir again till morning. Her heavy snores accompany my footsteps down the stairs.

The streets are washed again by rain. It has stopped falling and is being held in clouds so dark they fade into the blackness of the sky and mask the stars. The lagoon is sleeping, only one or two gondolas plying purple waters under a curious moon that Father Vivaldi used to call "the old moon in the young moon's arms." There is that pervading sense at midnight of the turning of the spheres that used to keep me wide awake with longing.

This time there is only a faint glow from the few candles left to burn throughout the night. It creeps around the edges of the shuttered windows and turns the ones left open into softly shining shapes. A boat is coming to the pier as I approach, and I quickly duck behind a pillar of the chapel. There are two passengers alighting, a woman and a younger female, judging from their stance and walk. The gondolier carries their cases to the door of the Pietà, leaving both the travelers to grapple with the unlit door. When the *signora* manages to put a key into the lock, the *signorina* pushes and the sticky hinges grant a slender opening through which the ladies pass into the hallway and drag their baggage after them. The candlelight inside illumines both their faces long enough for me to know exactly who they are, but I'm confounded as to why they are arriving at the Ospedale at this hour. Luisa's face is streaked with tears; Signora's is set, determined, much more tired than the face that I remember.

Chapter Forty-four

Anetta

THERE WAS SOME COMMOTION in the night, but that is always so in this building of many rooms, filled with girls of all ages. Not a night goes by that someone doesn't waken from a dream or have a stomachache or need to use the chamber pot. I've learned to sleep through all the nightmares and the terrors, and I barely stir when Prioress does her heavy pacing down the halls, even sometimes in the early hours before dawn.

Come morning I don't find it strange at first that someone's sleeping in Luisa's bed, never imagining that she'd be sent back to the Ospedale in the dark. I just assume that one of the other girls has climbed into the wrong cot. But then I see these tresses on the pillow, as black and shiny as a shoe, and that pale skin, so marble white with that blue tinge at the temple from tiny veins right near the surface. My heart begins to leap within my chest, just as if I'd been surprised by someone jumping out at me.

How I wish to wake her and gather her into my arms, but she's so still, so sound asleep, and would never allow such an embrace from me. Did she allow such overtures, I wonder, from the boy Alessandro? It makes me feverish to think of it.

Brigitta has tiptoed around her, but Silvia bumbles through the door, dropping her books and then her music, the pages fanning out into the hallway.

"The duchess has returned, I see, " she says while scrambling for them. "I wonder what she'll do this time to gain attention. I'm told the squawky little bird has lost her song at last."

"You don't know that for certain," I tell her. "No one knows that for certain."

"We'll soon find out," she says, and scurries after her newfound friend, Brigitta, who has recently been settled in Rosalba's space.

In my excitement, I dress as quietly as possible, but cannot wait to find Signora and have her explain this riddle. Does she, does anyone but me, know about Luisa's voice returning or of the farm boy? How did they cause her to leave Alessandro? Has she returned to us to stay?

In the refectory I catch up to Signora, who looks drawn and tired in the extreme. Tangles of her hair, which is usually gathered into neat rolls, escape a pleated cap. She gazes at her bowl of millet as if she is a fortune-teller reading tea leaves in a cup, and barely stirs when I sit next to her.

"Signora," I address her, "why did you bring Luisa back? It gave me such a start to see her there upon her cot when I arose this morning. You must have traveled half the night."

"We did, indeed, for Prioress insisted that she be here for Catina's funeral. You may not know that it was Father Vivaldi who requested such a ceremony. He had a special bond to this unfortunate child and has written a new *Agnus Dei* that he plans to have Luisa sing."

"If she is able."

"Of course, if she is able. We do not know that yet."

"Have you asked her?"

"She was so overcome with grief on the entire trip, I didn't think that I should speak of it. I'll wait until she's rested. Until she's had something to eat."

"That's probably best."

"You are usually such a sensible girl, Anetta," she says, changing the subject so that I am put off guard. "I hope you will not ruin any opportunity for marriage that comes your way again."

"You are not married," I make so bold as to observe.

"No. Such an alliance is not for everyone."

"Then why need I comply?"

She slowly chews the porridge in her mouth and swallows it before she answers me.

"Our prioress believes it best for you. She knows about such things. You should defer to her good judgment."

And not consider my own discernment, which has served me rather well these sixteen years.

There is no point in telling her just now why Prioress may be in error. And so I finish my repast and take my leave, hoping to have some minutes to see Luisa and consult with her before the first ensemble of the day.

Retracing my steps back to the bedchamber, I think how when we learned, days ago now, about Catina, it was no great surprise to those who had been with her near the end. It was still so very sorrowful, however, even knowing how her little body had been wracked with every breathing crisis and seeing her released from all of that. At the last, Sofia says it was as if she'd stepped into another, a more peaceful, room. I think myself, she was not meant to stay on earth for long.

And I do understand Father's fond attachment to her, which began because they shared the same affliction. But above that, there are always certain souls here who have a special attraction for each other and between whom there is deep friendship, even love. Concerta's happiness has been my great concern right from the start; my love for Luisa, though not truly reciprocated, is a constant, and she will always be most dear to me.

When I enter our room, it is in a slow and quiet manner, but Luisa is already dressing and rubbing sleep from her eyes. She does smile heartily on seeing me, which makes me think I may have indeed been missed. The smile fades quickly, however, and her wan appearance matches a desultory attitude and displays itself in listlessness, as if she carries unseen burdens on her spare shoulders.

"I did not tell about your voice," I blurt out after some pleasantries have passed between us. No need for her to know that I would have, given enough time, or how Catina counseled me. But then I shock myself by adding, "Except for Catina. I did at length reveal the glorious news to her. I simply could not help myself."

To my surprise, Luisa says, "I'm glad she knew before she died. She worried when my voice did not return as if it were her own." And then she says, "The summer's coming to an end. They would have sent for me no matter. They would have torn me from the arms of Alessandro."

I sense my own eyes opening wide. "Is that what happened?"

"I feel as if it did. I was all packed and set to leave in such a short time and never had a proper chance to say good-bye."

"Will you not see him once again?"

"Somehow I will. Somehow—I don't know when—I'll manage to go back to him. You'll see."

"I'm not the one who separated you. I never told a single soul about that."

"I know, Anetta. It isn't you I have a quarrel with. You are a loyal soul and would not betray my trust. And Signora Ricci didn't tell, I'm certain. She was so anxious that I leave before we were found out."

I wince within, thinking of the great temptation that lingers still to reveal and try to end her little love affair once and for all. More than once it has occurred to me that if I but told the whole of what I know to Silvia, she'd slither off with it to Prioress, and then it would be Silvia who takes the blame.

"But have you told Signora or Prioress that your singing voice has been returned to you?"

"Alessandro has been taken from me. Rosalba is still missing. Catina is dead. What is there to sing about?"

"You should talk with Father Vivaldi," I tell her. "You should do it right away."

The funeral for Catina the next morning is better attended than one would think for someone so often ill, for many of the older girls did not know her very well. Sofia is here and Signora Mandano, Geltruda, Brigitta, and Anna Maria, as are all of the *iniziate*, each little downcast face soggy with tears. The Mass is celebrated on one of the side altars, in front of which Catina lies within a plain pine box, a spray of flowers from the kitchen garden on the lid. I think of the marble caskets Father talked about once that enclose the remains of royal children. He saw them in some famous basilica, and on top of each of these was a marble effigy of a child in peaceful sleep surrounded by many sculpted angels and by garlands made of stone. Will Catina's reward be different from the one that they receive? Will their heavens ever meet and will they play together?

I look for Luisa immediately on entering the chapel, thinking to find her in the choir loft. But she is neither there nor in the church below. When a few of the younger girls sing the entrance hymn and the later Offertory, it is clear she must be indisposed and doesn't mean to come. At the *Alleluia,* however, I cannot help but listen for her voice among the rest, but, alas, it is not there.

Right before Communion, I am so deeply wrapped in prayer for Catina's precious soul that the first notes of the *Agnus Dei,* though not fortissimo, enter my consciousness like a thunderclap and spark my instant recognition of the perfect voice, Luisa's own, that I carry in my mind. They are so pure, so rich in tone, so otherworldly, as to make me certain I will soon be tasting the true bread from heaven.

Chapter Forty-five

Rosalba

SALVATORE WILL NOT LET ME play or sing from now until the child is born. He says I am too large and that I look ridiculous. Pasquale says his brother is afraid his whores and paramours will think the baby is his own, the very thought of which disgusts me. Most nights I go out with the family until they find a spot in which to settle, and then I sit upon a bench or rock or anything that will not break under my bulk. Sometimes I stay alone within the little house, but it was blistery hot in midsummer and presently is as cold as the outdoors and creaky, and there are no locks. The rats within the walls are most rambunctious. Sometimes they scurry out and run across the floor.

And so tonight I troop behind the family once again. Even Pasquale walks ahead of me. There is no spring in my step. My belly's heavy, my feet are leaden, and my breath is short. It feels as if the babe has slipped much lower just since yesterday. An old cape of Pasquale's covers most of me, but I feel like a barge in the lagoon that plows the waters more slowly than a boat adrift. I wonder how I'll manage with a child in tow.

All summer we performed while it was light, but lately the dark falls earlier. I welcome it, the way it drops just like a mantle in whose folds I like to hide.

And I really do not mind that I can't play their tunes with them. I have grown weary of the ones they know and am too well aware of their mistakes. Pasquale tries to improvise at times but doesn't do it very well.

Tonight they've chosen to perform in the little *campo* near the Ospedale, a way in back of it, in fact, where Father Vivaldi and his brothers live. I tell Lydia this, but she remarks, *"Non c'è problema,"* and flicks her chin as if to say, *Don't bother me.*

I pray that he will not see me in my present state, that he will notice I'm not playing with the group and pay no mind to them. Perhaps he's staying late in his repair shop, which I can picture in my mind—the tools neatly arranged upon his worn wooden bench, a variety of instruments lined up in the order of their having been delivered to him—or is rehearsing for the concert on Sunday or composing something in that little private room beside the choir loft. It matters not. I only pray that I'm not observed by him. And so, as they set up while it is light, I lean against the wall along the alleyway and listen to them as they tune their instruments and start to play the tunes I've grown to hate. I'm appeased some when I see that they do not draw as large a crowd as when I sang with them. From time to time, I hear a few people in the crowd ask about the lovely girl. Pasquale always says, "She'll be back soon"; Salvatore only grunts. Lydia flirts and asks if she will do.

My back aches so that, as the shadows start to form, I ferret out a place to sit beside the well, which does not catch the light from windows on the little square. My knees pulled up, I could well be a mound of mud in all this darkness, a large stone, a wagon cushion, a bag of refuse, something of no account. What I would really like to be is lithe again or so small as to be invisible.

It seems that I have dozed a little, for next I know, the crowd is thinning and Pasquale's playing his last solo. Lydia is packing up her violin and shaking out her stiffened shoulders. I am standing to stretch as best I can, still in the dark, when there's a hand upon my arm and another body very close to mine. I am too terrified to scream and barely hear the whispered voice that tells me not to be afraid. "It's only me, Rosalba. Don't you know me?"

I look as closely as I can with eyes that are accustomed to the dark and notice first a faint red crested pate, quite wigless, and then the kindly face of Father underneath. He seems to wear a nightshirt with his trousers as if he snuck out of his chamber in the dark. The pressure of his hand upon my arm increases, and with the other hand he holds a package out to me that's wrapped and tied and long.

"Take this," he says. "Conceal it underneath your cloak."

When it is placed into my hands, I know exactly what it is.

"My oboe," I exclaim so quietly I hope he hears me. "How I have missed it."

"Not in Venice," he reminds me. "You must never play it here."

"I know that, Father."

"I heard you on the piccolo one time. It will not make your fortune."

I cannot help but laugh at his assessment, for it is so apt.

"And so I thought I'd bring you your true instrument."

"You cannot know what you have done," I tell him. "How can I thank you?"

"Be well, my dear," he says, and then he turns and, in just moments, he is gone.

Walking back, I hold the oboe up against my body, with its length along the inside of one arm. The baby kicks against it once or twice as if she does not wish to share this space.

"You must be tired," says Pasquale, slowing his pace to mine. "Perhaps next time you shouldn't come with us."

My back aches more than ever and my stomach hardens in an odd way every little while. Soon these episodes are painful, but I refuse to drop to my knees in the street.

"It isn't far," says Pasquale when he sees me stumble. "You'd better let me carry you."

I look at just how slight he is and smile at the mere thought of him supporting all this girth. "You couldn't do it," I exclaim.

"Well, then, Salvatore. We'll ask Salvatore."

"I'd rather die," I say, and mean it. But just the thought of being held in that man's arms gives me the strength to shuffle on. By the time we cross some bridges and come up to the street on which we live, my feet can barely move apart, and a strange wail escapes my lips, causing Lydia to run back down the stairs she has already climbed. She arrives just as a sudden gush of fluid travels down my legs and forms a puddle at my feet. I bend as best I can to look, but cannot see the color of it. It smells of water from the ocean and of something primal as the flotsam of the sea.

Chapter Forty-six

Luisa

I SWORE THAT IF SIGNORA made me leave Alessandro and the countryside, I would never sing again. But what else could I offer sweet Catina whose short life was so marred and whose soul was so very old? And how else can I live but as the person I was meant to be? When Father showed me the new *Agnus Dei,* I could tell without bringing forth one note that it was very beautiful. Singing it, I decided, would be my gift to her, but, as it happened, no less gift to myself, for once again the music of my mentor and my friend, within the chapel where I first performed it, invigorated all my sensibilities.

Afterward, Father Vivaldi spoke to me again about his oratorio, the one on which he has been working for so long, the one that has a major part for me. I had anticipated this, but I had not anticipated what would follow our discussion. With hindsight, I am very sure he planned it, but at first it seemed to be an odd and unexpected mix of circumstances.

It is when coming back from the sad duty of sending prayers aloft for dear Catina, already basking in her heavenly reward, that Prioress takes me aside. I am impatient to resume my studies as a means to mask my longings and to quiet my great need for Alessandro, and do not wish to be forestalled.

"Your mother," she begins, "is here to see you."

My hand goes to my throat. It has been over a year's time since I have heard from her at all. By now I was quite sure she had abandoned me. Remembering the times I called for her in my delirium, and the long wait of all those days and nights without a word, I find it hard to believe she is really here within these walls.

But Prioress assures me. "She was in chapel, too. She heard you sing."

"Why?" I ask immediately. "She did not know Catina."

"But Father sent word to her that you might sing the *Agnus Dei*. He was sure she'd want to be there to hear your voice restored."

If I had only known, if I'd been told, what would I have done differently? For a certain I would have spent more time on the score. I would have concentrated on those places that I knew I could improve upon.

"Why are you so flustered, Luisa?" Prioress asks. "Your mother had most complimentary things to say. She was quite overcome."

I can't imagine this. My mother overcome. Her strong composure was the shell that I could never penetrate. Knowing I soon may have the very approbation that I've prayed for in the past paralyzes both my thought and movement. I cannot speak.

"She's in the parlor, the one that has the grille. She's waiting for you."

The parlor with the grille. It means that others may look out at us. Someone like Silvia could try to see how I comport myself.

"Can you not put her in the back parlor, which is more private?"

"I suppose I can," says Prioress. "If that is what you want. But do come to her quickly. She came by gondola, I'm told, and wishes to return as soon as possible."

I straighten out my apron, remove my cap, and pinch my cheeks to put more color in them. I try some phrases in a low voice to myself. *How are you, Mother? What a pleasure to see you.* But such proper expressions quickly turn to *Why didn't you come when I needed you? Why come back at all? Why have you really come today?* I stop myself when tears begin to spill.

When enough time has passed that she must now be in the other room, I hold my breath and proceed slowly down the narrow hallway. It is a short distance, truly, too short for me to sort my turbulent feelings. The door is closed. I leave my hand upon the knob for such a long time, its coldness turns to warmth. When I finally twist it, Mother is standing by the window, looking out, as decorously dressed as I remember, this time in a traveling suit with open overskirt revealing a fine petticoat, the closed bodice pinned and laced at the front and sides. Her frontage when she comes to meet me is not quite as high as I recall, or else I have grown enough in height to make it seem so.

"Luisa," she says, quite tenderly for one who for such a time so willingly absented herself. And then she gathers me into her arms the way she always has before, and I am clinging to her as I used to and feeling somewhat dizzy from her lovely scent. But this time I do not beg to go along with her or call her *Mother.* This time I don't say a word.

"Your *Agnus Dei* was magnificent," she says. "You performed it splendidly."

"Thank you," I respond.

"Your voice, it has continued to improve even through this long time that you could not sing at all."

She knew of that! She knew and did not succor me in any way.

"And such a voice!" she continues. "Maestro Scarpari tells me yours is far and away the best voice he has ever trained. And Father Vivaldi extols its operatic qualities, so apparent in your solo. Our dreams are coming true."

"Our dreams?"

"Has he not told you of his recent triumph? Of the magnificent opera *Ottone in Villa* and now this major oratorio he has planned? I'm told he's written a large part in it especially for you."

"You're told by whom?"

"My friends on the Board of Governors," she says with no hesitation. "But I have it now from the Red Priest himself, who has beseeched me to intervene in any way I can. That was, of course, before you sang his little *Agnus Dei* and proved that your voice has been restored."

"I see."

"I wonder if you do. It means the things we planned together, you and I, they're coming true."

"I was a child of four when sent here, if you recall."

"Of course I recall."

"And do you remember how I kicked and screamed and yelled my little lungs out, certain even after you had left that you'd hear me and return?"

She pats a roll of hair, tucks a stray lock, and looks away. She sighs.

"You're fifteen now, Luisa. Surely you're old enough to understand the reason for my actions then. What could a mother with no attachment and no patron do with such a child? What future could I have given you if left to my own devices? Do you not think it was hard for me to leave you here?"

"You orphaned me, Mother. You saw to it that I had a life the same as any child who'd ever been upon the wheel. The others laughed whenever I would claim to have a parent, something none of them had ever known. They'd taunt me further whenever I would say that you would come for me."

"And so I have. I will. Though not until you've had a chance to study opera more in depth and to sing the oratorio that's been planned. After such a grand production, the name of Luisa della Pietà will be upon the lips of everyone in Europe and beyond."

Remembering the glory of the moment when I'd sung that day for Alessandro, I tell her that I do not care for adulation or renown. And I do not wish to change my name.

"You must," she says. "You owe this to me. It is your destiny. And mine."

Later, at the noon meal, when Anetta asks if I found my mother well, I think back to the times Anetta used to watch our short reunions, all the questions she would ask, the way she pined to have a mother, too.

Then she says, "I am so glad your voice is back, Luisa, because we all have missed it so." And I see how very different, how sincere and true, her love for me is. In some ways she's cared for me the way a real mother would. She does this for Concerta, too.

"My mother thinks I have a future in singing opera," I say lightheartedly, so as not to seem to boast.

"To be doomed to squawk forever on a stage?" says Silvia. "Better to be given to a hunchbacked, beak-nosed duke."

"Whom you yourself will surely snare," says Anetta, "leaving her no alternative but to turn into a diva of renown." But then she turns to me and says, "If that is what you truly want."

What I truly want. I want Alessandro. I want the idyll of this summer past. I want to sing again just for the joy of it.

Chapter Forty-seven

Anetta

THE NEW CONCERTO is so difficult that I have needed to spend many evenings in the choir loft alone, perfecting passages that trouble me. It has been some time since I've worried so about a solo or felt so unprepared for the degree of difficulty this intricate new work presents. Sometimes I find it hard to sustain the necessary energy throughout the passages of vigorous rhythm. It is difficult, as well, to maintain the freshness Father insists upon. The first movement is as agitated as any of his other concerti and has a curious aspect of urgency, while the second is typically languorous, a place where I may lose myself in the pleasure of the bowing, the calm and precise fingering, the sweet harmonious clamoring of string to string. I am surprised by the introduction of a refrain and then the repetition of it in a different key, something I have never heard before. It has the strange effect of invigorating the music further, and in practice sessions such as this, I do not have to be concerned that if I play with all the passion the music draws from me, I will attract another odious nobleman.

Tonight there's just the light from my one candle, but I'm well acquainted with the shadows here and inured to all the noises, the heaves and moanings of this beautiful old structure. The tiny votive light above the main altar, a small pinprick of fire in the sacristy, assures me once again that my dear Lord is present there and watches over me.

I lose all track of time when here alone and have no notion of how long I've been trying to perfect one section, then another. I hear the heavy doors creak open once, and think it may be Prioress about her evening prayers or the custodian. There is another creak much later in the night when I am almost ready to depart. It is the heavy turning sound I've heard before that sounds so like a drawbridge being lifted for a boat to pass. I recognize at once the noise I heard that night when someone left Concerta on the wheel.

Breathless with hope, I place my viola upon the chair, take up my candle, and hurry down the several tiers of winding stairs so quickly that my little light can scarcely keep up with my feet. The church is as empty as I felt it was, no sign at all of who had pried the large doors open earlier. I rush right past them to the wheel, which does indeed contain a swaddled form. I unwrap the outer flannel at once to see exactly what's inside.

This child is not so newly born as to be soiled with afterbirth. It is a girl, still in her swaddling bands, but with a flannel petticoat, linen shirt, and sturdy muslin overmantle. The cap has knotted fringes and silk braid and is quite finely sewn, as if there was much care expended in the making. The tiny hands are curled up tightly, the face as fair as any I have seen upon a newborn babe. Her eyes are shut in sleep, but she has what I've heard referred to as a rosebud mouth, which purses in and out as if to suck.

Sometimes there is a note with children who are left. When finding none, I gently lift the child and search within her garments, where I discover something so surprising that it makes me weep. My touch is quizzical at first at what I seem to feel, that is held tightly by the bands. When I loosen them and bring the object out into the candlelight, I nearly swoon. It is Rosalba's pigeon mask for Carnival, the feathers just as sleek and shining as the day she fashioned it, the eyeholes that had framed her flashing eyes as empty as the hole within my heart where she herself is lodged.

I clutch this baby to me as if she is my very own, as I will strive to treat her henceforth. Part of me rejoices that Rosalba, for a certain now, is still alive and still in Venice. But it is tragic that she's given up this child and still continues to be hidden from us. As tragic as the fact that I do not know of any way to find her. I'm comforted to think she heard my playing in the loft, and knowing that the music must be coming from my bow so late at night, she left this precious little girl into my care, for that is surely what she did intend. *Madre di Dio*, what a gift she's given me. And what a great and wonderful responsibility.

Even knowing it must be too late, I put down the babe and run into the Calle to call and call Rosalba's name into the night. I call so loudly that she must hear me from wherever she has fled so swiftly. I call so she will know for certain that her precious child has been discovered by her loyal friend

Back in the chapel, I lift the small sleeping form, hold it closely to me, and go with all speed to the nursery, where I wake Sofia to receive the child. When she expresses her surprise at the great care with which this one is dressed, I say only that it demonstrates the love her mother had for her. And when I hesitate to put the baby in her arms, she says, "Oh, not again, Anetta! Not another orphan you would make your own. You'd think you were a *commun* girl with time to spend on such domestic things. Signora tells me how she thinks we should discourage you from being here too often with the babies. She says you need the time upon your instrument and that you'll soon be old enough to have a family of your own. And yet you choose to form a bond with any castoff such as this."

"Concerta is not *any* castoff," I tell her. *Nor,* I say to myself, *is this dear little girl, dearer to me than you can ever know.* When Rosalba comes back for her, my closest friend will find that her trust in me was not in vain.

"And what shall we call this one?" asks Sofia.

"Rosa," I tell her, knowing it, for a certain. "Rosa is her name."

There is only one other person I can tell the truth of this astonishing event: she whose voice has now come back to life and whose bright future seems assured. She's been back here just one scant week, but the *maestri* have been encouraging her in every way, providing private voice lessons and making sure she is not stressed so she may learn the taxing music she is capable of singing. I see her now only at string ensemble or solfeggio, when she's not otherwise engaged. Somehow I must find a private time with her when this momentous secret can be shared.

And so I plot to meet her when I know that she'll be moving from one room into another in the school. (Always before, I knew her schedule, and it was very like my own.

But now I've had to sleuth and scheme to find out all the places she is in attendance throughout the day.)

During the time that I have chosen, she has stayed behind to speak with a new teacher named Maestro Scarlatti, and it takes so long for her to come into the hallway, that I'm ready to give up my plan. Just as I turn to scurry to the class where I belong, however, she does emerge and seems surprised to see me there.

"What are you doing here, Anetta? I never know where you'll show up."

"I only have a moment as, I'm sure, do you. It was important that I find you."

"Can't it wait?"

"You will not think so when I tell you what I know. You will be glad you tarried for a little while."

"Well, say it then," she says, annoyed, the old Luisa traveling into her eyes. I cannot bear for that side of her to reappear.

"It is about Rosalba," I blurt out. "She is in Venice. She is nearby."

"How do you know?" She wants to be assured at once. "Where did you come by this new information?"

I have to pause to organize the words I want to say. It is a hard truth that I must pass on, and Luisa may not find it joyful in the least.

"I was practicing within the church last night, the way I often do."

"Yes. What of that? It is your usual way."

"A new baby was delivered to us on the wheel while I was there. She is a beautiful child, with something upon her person that I recognized at once."

"You do create a mystery, Anetta. Please. Continue on."

"It was a mask. Rosalba's own blue-feathered mask. The one she made for Carnival."

Luisa looks quite beset, but she doesn't make a sound. I wonder if she understands the whole of what I've said. Slowly, her hands go up and rest against each cheek, her eyes grow round.

"Rosalba's child?" she asks. "It cannot be."

"If you were but to look at her, you'd know."

"The infant's here?"

"Within the nursery."

She grabs me at the waist and dances once around, then stops and says, "We cannot tell a soul."

"There is no one who needs to know," I assure her.

"But knowing this ourselves, we must endeavor to take care of this small child, Rosalba's child, as if she were our very own."

"It need not be your obligation."

"What do you mean?"

"Just that wherever your career may take you, I will be here."

"How can you assure me of that?"

I had not meant to tell anyone, but perhaps what I

reveal now to her alone will be another bond that she and I may share.

"I have been planning," I say at length, "to stay and teach within the Ospedale."

"What of those persistent dukes Signora keeps unearthing? What of a family of your own? Please be quite sure of what you want before you take the final steps to seal your future here."

To think she worries for me is a gift I did not think to merit.

"I am," I say. "I am quite sure."

Sure that things can never be exactly as I might want them. Sure that a life with any duke at all, no matter how presentable or kind, would not be possible for me. Certain that my love is best expended on the children who are most in need of it and who will always give it back to me a thousandfold.

When Luisa still seems concerned, I take her shoulders and look purposefully into those conflicted eyes framed by the sweet face I love above all others. The temptation is so strong to kiss her full upon her blushing lips that I must bite my own and remind myself why I am here and how I wish with all my heart to set her mind at ease. If she should now recoil from me, it would spoil everything.

"And I can promise you," I begin firmly.

"I need no promises," she counters.

"You will want this one, I assure you."

She smiles. "All right. What is it that you promise me?"

"I promise you, I swear upon Our Savior's Holy Cross, that on the very day Rosalba comes to claim her child, I will be here and waiting."

Chapter Forty-eight

Luisa

W HEN EVERYONE DISCOVERED that I could sing again, it was as if I were a sailing ship immediately told to change its course and ply new waters, deeper and more dangerous than any I have known before. The short time of sweet languor in the countryside became at once a distant memory and Alessandro placed so out of reach, I must fight hard to keep his touch, his beautiful face, alive within my thoughts.

Whatever influence Mother has, she has used all of it, and I am tutored in so many ways that it is quite dizzying. Diction, expressive singing, German, concert decorum—

anything that I may need to aid my mother's operatic aspirations for me. If Father Vivaldi, too, were not so insistent, I, perhaps, would balk, but it does please him so to hear me sing his melodies, and I am joyous beyond belief to have the best part of myself returned to me.

I'd missed the comradeship I had known within the Pietà, but lately I've once again been set apart as if I'm one of Father's private students. Mother has been here so frequently to check upon my progress that she might go unnoticed if it were not for her bright swishing silk mantuas and stylish taffetas. Our little conferences, so longed for in the past, are becoming tedious, and I can't help questioning the course we've embarked upon. She will not hear of this, and I'm forced to bottle up the things I feel.

"You must forget your little tryst," she says one day, so unexpectedly I stare at her in great dismay. How had she learned of it? What does she really know?

"I see that look emerge within your eyes, that dreamy languid look that takes you far from me. And I know about the object of your fond affections. Signora told me."

"She did not know a thing. She could not."

"And was there much to know?"

"How could there be with Signora Ricci turned watchdog overnight?"

She grows suspiciously into a confidant, and seems about to comfort me.

"These young attachments. They can seem quite

strong. But you are still a child, my dear, and only play at love."

"It was not play. It was all good and true!"

"I'm certain that it seemed so at the time."

"It *was* so. It was the worthiest, realest thing I've ever known."

"You will recover from this love, though it appears at times, to you, that you will die of it."

"I want no such recovery."

"You will recover whether you should want to or not. Make no mistake. I have not used my wiles and kept some odious alliances just to see you throw your present opportunities into the wind."

"Your many love affairs?" I thrust at her.

"If that is what you wish to call them. There is nothing I have ever done in my life without your future in my mind."

If I believe her, what a burden! If I do not, I am still encumbered with the talent God has given me and with the many chances for its use that He has placed along my path.

When Anetta tells me of Rosalba's child, it is hard to comprehend. Harder still that we may never know her reason for abandoning the babe, how the infant was conceived, or even see our friend again. The little that I know of what can pass from man to woman makes me realize that such a circumstance was almost mine. I can only make a supposition as to how it would have changed my life. This knowledge doesn't lessen my longing for Alessandro. It does give pause when I consider running from a destiny that has appeared on my horizon like a great benevolent sun eager to warm me in its wide rays.

There is no one that I dare tell my quandary to. No one who can conspire to lift even a little of this heaviness from my soul. Unless . . . I make an effort to divulge the puzzle to Anetta, for effort it would be. And can she understand the love I feel for this fine boy, knowing how she has never seemed inclined to take a man into her bed?

When at last I do seek her out, she is so eager for my confidence that I feel just a little of the same revulsion she once sparked with too much toadying. And when we sit upon the garden bench in privacy, she is so pleased that I wonder if her happy mood will make her indisposed to understand the pain of my conflicted state.

Her mood does change, however, when I tell her of my deep love for Alessandro. I am, in fact, confounded when she seems as downcast as if he were her rival, which of course he cannot be, for love of friend and love of woman for a man are not the same. When I explain this to her, she listens to the whole of what I have to say without an interruption. She's quiet still when I conjecture who it could have been that told Signora of my strong attachment.

"Perhaps it was the more disapproving of the two, Signor Ricci, and not his wife at all," I say. "He was the one, if truth be told, who conjured the odious pact to keep me from my lover. Or it could have been the farm-hand who first noticed us together. If it were he, how bold he was to speak up to Signora in that way."

Anetta sighs most heavily. She chews her bottom lip and twists her fingers.

"What do you think?" I ask. "Who do you think betrayed us to Signora?"

No longer as clear-eyed as before, she looks at me when it is obvious I'm through divulging my discordant feelings and speculations, and takes my hand in hers.

"You have a gift, Luisa, that is much greater than you know. I think you realized a little of this at a time when others chided you for boasting. Do you remember how I never faulted you for that, believing always that you had the right?"

"I do indeed recall it. You and Rosalba. You were the only two who came to my defense."

"How the others envied you, and do so still."

"I do not pay them any mind."

"Because you know at last the truth of what I say." She whisks away a leaf that's fallen on her apron.

"But what of Alessandro?" I ask.

"I think—though of course I do not know—that you are much too young to make an assignation. And from what you tell me of the boy, he is not ready yet to take a wife."

"All that is true. I see the sense of it. But how do I forget the feelings for him that I harbor?"

"I think . . . " she begins again. "I cannot tell this for certain, for, as you say, the kind of love you speak of is unknown to me. But still, I do believe that love, once rooted in the human heart, will stay there, for as long as you should choose to keep it."

Though she has not said so many words, the ones she speaks have made me feel as if a little of the weight upon my sensibilities and mind is lifted.

Quite suddenly, however, an expression appears upon her face that makes me think she's harboring some private grief; her countenance becomes excessively disquieted as though she suddenly despairs. I am alarmed to hear great sobs escape her throat and see her bosom heave as if in pain.

"What is it, dear Anetta? What afflicts you in this way?"

Her words come slowly, and she does not glance at me at all. In fact, she looks away so I can't see into her eyes.

"It is this," she states after such a while that I thought she'd been struck mute.

When I reach up with my free hand and turn her face to mine, she clears her throat and looks down at her lap. She starts again.

"It is this. I am your betrayer, Luisa. I am the one who told Signora Mandano of your love for Alessandro."

I pull my hand away from hers. I ask her to repeat what she has said, for I cannot conceive that it is true.

"Why?" is all I manage after she has thus obliged me.

"Because, heaven help me," she sobs out, her voice grown loud and turbulent as if a storm is welling in her chest, "I *do* know the love you speak about, the love of man for woman, woman for a man. By some strange twist of God's design, my love for you is of a strength unmatched by any liaison that one can name."

She stops to catch a breath.

"And I possess the envy of a lover, too. It is that which caused me to betray your trust. That and the conviction deep within my soul that you are destined for most wondrous things, that there's a world in waiting for the voice that has meant everything to me."

Stricken at first to my own silence, the only words I finally thread together do not address this awful knowledge I have gained of something she has borne alone for all these years.

"But what of trust? Both things I swore you to keep secret you have told to someone."

"I did it for your better good. I swear. For your career."

For my career! I am not sure now how I feel about the glittering prospects close at hand at last. I am not certain any longer what to feel or think or even wish for. Does having a career mean giving up the other things in life I cherish? Will my voice become the mistress of my life and dictate all of my pursuits? Does a career justify the betrayal by my friend, the cold and calculating actions of my mother, the forced separation from the one I love?

Something more than anger infects me till I almost

cannot breathe or voice these questions or move. Could I lash out, it would be to flail at all the objects of this rage that now present themselves to my imagination. Anetta, being so close by, would surely bear the brunt. I did not ever ask for her protection nor seek her great devotion. I merely counted on her trust.

But as I sit and simmer here, attempting to assuage my temper, one thing occurs to me—that if Anetta could retain for years a love so unrequited as her own for me, should not a love reciprocated fully such as mine for Alessandro last no matter what the difficulties? I am so cheered by this last thought that I turn back to Anetta, who sits forlornly next to me and has not raised her eyes or changed her bent position.

"Anetta," I say. "Friend—for friend you will continue to be because we share too much." My anger unappeased as yet, I'm amazed at my forbearance and at what I'm able, after these first few words, to add. "And I begin to see the reasoning behind your disregard for my confidences and how neither offense was for self-gain."

"That is exactly what I prayed you would understand."

She tilts her face up till her eyes are resting on me once again.

"I'm sorry you have suffered for my sake," I tell her then. "I never knew before how painful such a love, even if returned, can be when the object of it is so far removed . . . in one way or another."

"It is not so very bad," she replies, "now that you've assured me that I keep your friendship, it is truly not as bad as some might think. In some ways, I have grown quite accustomed to it."

I am both comforted for her and shocked to hear it, for that's precisely what I will not ever do.

"You made a promise to me not so long ago."

"About Rosalba's child?"

"And I, in turn, will make a promise, too."

"You said yourself that there is no need of promises."

"Well, I will make it nonetheless. It is a promise to myself."

She laughs and says with great good nature, "I should have guessed."

I rise from the bench and stand above her, taller than her by a head this once. I put my hand upon my breast as if to swear.

"I will visit this voice of mine upon the world," I tell her, "just as you and Father Vivaldi and Mother and all the others have convinced me that I should."

For fear it would inflame the envy I have quieted, I do not tell the rest of it—how I will never become accustomed to my loss of Alessandro, how I will bring my love for him into every opera house I travel to, will gather it into whatever bed I sleep upon, how I'll hold it close for all the many years we cannot be together until I put it back again into his open heart.

335

Chapter Forty-nine

Rosalba

I WOULD HAVE called her Rosa.

It is her birthday, and I think of how she must be talking now and running down the halls when given a chance, and will soon be playing tricks, as I used to. I wonder if she has my heavy hair, my black eyes. I wonder if Anetta has spoiled her and if she and Concerta are like true sisters. I wonder if she is musical. But she must be, for I willed her that gift with my whole being while she was still a part of me.

Winter in Vienna is quite different from winter in Venice. I have experienced three winters here and am no longer surprised at the deep snowdrifts by my door and the difficulty in getting about the streets. I employ a carriage on the stormy days, always thinking back to that first frigid time when I arrived here with nothing but my oboe, the worn clothes upon my back, and the address that the Red Priest had given me one awful day when I was singing in the streets.

This is a musical city, much like Venice in that, but very different from it in other ways, as it lacks the waterways and gondolas. The wide cobbled streets have a beauty of their own. The man whom Father sent me to booked me at once when hearing of my training at the Pietà, and it wasn't long before I was playing solo parts, some of them the same as I had played at the Ospedale, for Antonio Vivaldi's work is known and highly favored here. I have also had occasion to play work of Maestri Corelli, Bach, and Geminiani, and another Venetian named Tomaso Albinoni. Soon I was able to afford a nice apartment and a mantua maker, who draws upon French fashion and favors exotic silks. A *modiste* attends upon me often as well. She brings me petticoats and caps and ribbons and such, and curls my unruly hair with hot irons. Someday I may even have my own *maîtresse couturière*.

I favor rather solemn fabrics generally, preferring not to draw attention with anything except my music. I do, at long last, own a lavishly embroidered black velvet cloak with a lining of red satin, something I saw Luisa's mother wear once and longed for inordinately. My occasions to don such a cloak are not infrequent, as I am escorted to the theater or a ball from time to time by any of a number of distinguished gentlemen. (Often we travel in a carriage as elegant as any gondola, with ornamented wheels, brocaded silk interiors, and windows made of glass.) One suitor in particular has taken my eye, but has not turned me lovesick, I am pleased to say. I gaze on all of them with a more level scrutiny that Anetta would indeed approve of.

It has been mentioned in the newspapers when, on occasion, Father Vivaldi has come here on his way to visit his publisher, Estienne Roger, in Holland, or to mount another opera in Vienna, but we have not met. I like to think that he has sometimes been in the audience when I have performed, and I imagine the places in my solos with which he would have found fault, where he would have instructed me to make some small improvements, the sections he would have complimented.

When his first oratorio, *Moyses Deus Pharaonis*, was performed at the Pietà, I chanced upon the program notes that one of my musician friends had procured. But when I looked for Luisa Benedetto's name within it, I was surprised to find that Anastasia had sung the part of Sapens Primur that had been written for Luisa. The part of Moyses had been sung by Barbara; that of Aaron, by Candida. Even Silvia and Michelina had been chosen for small parts.

I've lately heard that Father has been named *maestro di concerti,* as well he should be, since he has truly filled that role ever since Maestro Gasparini resigned a few years past. He also plans, I'm told, another large oratorio, this time to stir up patriotism for the Venetian war against the Turks in Corfu. It will be called *Juditha Triumphans.* On hearing this, I thought how, if she is not ill again or has no more contact with the Ospedale, it might be possible for Luisa to be featured at long last in this grand production. I'm even told that four or five arias have basso continuo and full string accompaniment that includes the viola d'amore.

"Five more minutes, Signorina della Pietà," Gregor, the stage manager, calls through my dressing-room door. I have been closeted here between performances that feature my playing of an oboe concerto by Albinoni. Staying true to the habits of the Ospedale, I never rehearse right before a concert or at an intermission, but try to keep my mind and body as unfettered as Father Vivaldi always cautioned us to do. What better way than to reminisce about my friends there and to call up that magic time.

There is recent talk of a new young singer at the opera house with an astounding voice who they say was trained at the Pietà. Perhaps one day soon I'll be a member of the orchestra when she performs. Perhaps I'll look up from the pit during a section when my instrument is idle, and it will be Luisa standing there upon the stage, and I'll hear her full, resplendent voice resounding from the rafters and shimmering through the glass chandeliers. Perhaps I'll meet her afterward in the wings and we will hold each other and cry a little, and she will tell me of my Rosa, and I will tell her of my life singing on the streets of Venice and how I wanted Rosa to have something more than that. We'll talk about Anetta and our many lovely days, the three of us together at the Ospedale, when we and all the other girls so privileged, sang and played for supper and for sustenance and, if we had only known it, for our very lives.

In this book, I chose to concentrate on six pivotal years
when Antonio Vivaldi worked as a violin teacher and
ultimately *maestro di concerti* at the Ospedale della Pietà.
These were the years before Vivaldi's fame as a musician
began to grow and make his life more public. I framed
my novel in this time period in order to provide a clear
window into the life of the orphanage and Vivaldi's
role there. I focused on three fictional members of the
privilegiate del coro, which included only those girls chosen to play and sing in the concerts of the Pietà, concerts
that were to become renowned throughout Europe. It is
assumed that these more privileged students were picked
for the *coro* because of talent and musical ability. They
were also given privileges such as the ability to earn spend-
ing money as *maestre,* the right to pass judgment on their
own tutors (which could affect a teacher's income), and
even the opportunity to sing operatic parts occasionally
in professional productions outside the Ospedale. The
main characters of my story grow in disparate directions
as they come of age within the highly evolved social service system of the Republic of Venice under the doge.
Minor characters often possess the same names as students

who were at the Ospedale during the years covered by my book, and I sometimes identify them by the instruments they actually played, but they are fictitious in all other ways.

The work of eighteenth-century composer Antonio Vivaldi is played frequently today, but his folios had actually been forgotten for two hundred years, only to be discovered in 1926 in an Italian monastery. And although scholars have been able to document many of the performances of his work that occurred during his own lifetime, the details of that life are somewhat sketchy. We do know that he lived, well into adulthood, with his parents and siblings. The *campo*, or small square, their apartment looked upon still holds the church where Vivaldi was baptized and is very close to the Ospedale della Pietà.

To find out as much as I could about the Ospedale, Vivaldi, and eighteenth-century Italy, my reading material included books and websites about the composer, his contemporaries, his music, and the political history and social service system of that day. I also traveled to Venice, where I discovered the Hotel Metropole on the site where the Pietà once was. Situated on the Riva degli Schiavoni, the Pietà faced the lagoon between the Grand Canal and the San Marco Canal—very near Saint Mark's Square and the Palace of the Doge. Because of its location, the orphanage must have provided a view of the very center of Venetian life, which was in stark contrast to life within it. Ca' Rezzonico, which houses the Museum of Eighteenth-Century Venice, was an excellent source for a sense of those times.

The chapel that I refer to in the text was reconstructed in 1745, and the Santa Maria della Pietà still exists today as a church building designed primarily for musical performances. For the purposes of my story, the interior of the original chapel, the school, and the Ospedale itself are imagined. Some reports state that the main building was occupied by as many as a thousand students at a time. The present hotel structure, which is said to correspond to that of the Ospedale, is so small, however, that perhaps this number is an exaggeration. Saint Mark's Square is much as it was in Vivaldi's time, as is Saint Mark's Church itself and the Palace of the Doge. In fact, most of Venice appears to be very much the way it was in that Baroque world in which I thoroughly immersed myself.

To care for the illegitimate and abandoned children in Venice at that time, four *ospedali* for both girls and boys were established as part of an advanced social service system that provided some surprising opportunities for these orphaned children. The foundling wheel itself was an innovation from the Middle Ages, and it is interesting to note that it's being replicated today in hospitals such as Rome's Casilino Polyclinic, where something closer to an incubator-type drawer has recently been introduced.

Although some boys were apparently educated until their teens at the Ospedale della Pietà, it was principally considered a school for young women. Girls in the *figli di commun,* whose musical education was not so intense, learned skills such as lace-making, dressmaking, and nursing. Those in the *figli di coro,* however, could become *maestre* before or after they left the Ospedale or paid performers if they chose not to marry, but they couldn't perform anywhere within the La Serenissima, the Republic of Venice. From what I could discern, although Italy was a Catholic country and the orphans were somewhat cloistered, the *ospedali* were not convents. The students were free to follow a religious vocation later if they so desired, but only in a convent outside Venice. It was a time and place when music was considered a necessary part of a superior education offered even to foundlings, a concept very much in conflict with our present educational system in the United States, where the arts are often considered an appendage or even expendable.

For four years I was a day student in an all-girls boarding school, so the issues, concerns, and problems that come up in a highly charged, predominantly female atmosphere are very familiar to me. Also, as a singer with Cantemus, a chamber chorus north of Boston, I have sought in this narrative to combine my musical knowledge with my writing and storytelling skills.

Ultimately, within these pages, I've been able to indulge my great interest in the music of the Baroque and to live for a while in a period that spawned many innovative musical talents and continues to excite my imagination.

ACKNOWLEDGMENTS

Grateful thanks are due to the members of my writing group—Ellen Wittlinger, Nancy Werlin, and Anita Riggio—who listened to this book chapter by chapter and gave sage advice and unflagging support. I'm also indebted to my husband, Wally, for entering into my search for Vivaldi and the orphans with gusto; to Betsy Lebel and Lenice Strohmier for their careful attention to the first draft; to Chris Brodien Jones, Laurie Jacobs, Donna McArdle, and Patricia Bridgman for advice and encouragement; and to Ed Monnelly for useful information. I was also inspired by the talented members of the chamber chorus Cantemus, and by our conductor, Dr. Gary Wood, whose teaching abilities and musical knowledge infused my interpretation of Vivaldi. I have a deep appreciation as well for the informed eye of my editor, Hilary Van Dusen, and the guidance of my agent, Lauren Abramo.